IN THE HIDEOUT
OF THE GANNON GANG . . .

Cole Gannon, the leader of the gang, took out a watch with a dried-up, withered object tied to its stem by a leather thong.

"Four thirty," he said. "I think it's time for a drink."

"Funny watch fob you have there, Mr. Gannon," said young Nate Cook, who'd just ingratiated himself with the Gannon gang by rescuing one of their number from a raging lynch mob.

"Ear of a little bastard who sassed me once," said Cole, starting to pour the whiskey.

"That's what I figured," Nate said. "It's mine." He pushed the hair away on the right side of his head.

Cole Gannon put down the bottle and stared at him.

"You cut it off just after killing my father, and just before you and your brother raped my mother. I'm Nathan Cook."

There was a split second of astonishment. It never crossed the minds of the five outlaws that this stripling could match one of them, let alone survive all five.

Then, everyone reached for his gun, as the sound of a lone .41 caliber revolver racketed in the room . . .

The Making of America Series

THE
BOUNTY
HUNTERS

Lee Davis Willoughby

A DELL / JAMES A. BRYANS BOOK

Published by
Dell Publishing Co., Inc.
1 Dag Hammarskjold Plaza
New York, New York 10017

Dell ® TM 681510, Dell Publishing Co., Inc.

ISBN: 0-440-00746-1

Printed in the United States of America

First printing—February 1984

CHAPTER I

Little Doe was nursing the twins when she sensed, rather than heard, the approach of horsemen. Laying the babies on the bed, where Ash immediately began to cry but James merely gurgled, she buttoned her gingham dress over her bosom and went to peer out the front window of the one-room sod hut. It was a bright, sunlit day and she could see for miles over the arid wastes of the Texas high plains. No one was in sight to the west.

She circled the hut, looking out the other three windows, still seeing no one but still sensing horsemen out there somewhere. They must be to the north, she thought, because rising ground in that direction restricted visibility to about two miles, while in the other three directions she could see to the horizon.

She wished Ashley was there, but her husband was driving the ranch's first marketable steers to Fort Worth to sell to the army, and would be gone for weeks. Then she was glad he wasn't, for if it was the Comanche approaching, they would leave Ashley dead and scalped, whereas she at least had a chance.

5

At the top of the rise to the north there appeared a dozen horsemen. At that distance she couldn't make out whether they were Indians or cavalry. The horses stood in an unmoving line.

Then a mounted figure appeared in the center of the line, and even at that distance she could make out the feathered war headdress of a Comanche chief.

Little Doe ran to the center of the cabin, gripped a loop of rope and pulled open the trap door leading to the vegetable cellar. Ash was still howling and James now began to whimper. She started to pick them up, then paused to run look out the north window again. The horsemen were descending the slope at a walk, and behind the front rank came another and another and another. She estimated fifty in the war party.

If they continued at a walk, it would be half an hour before they arrived. Quickly she unbuttoned her dress, ran to pick up a baby in either arm and let their mouths find the nipples. Returning to the window, she stood there watching as they suckled.

It had never seemed to Little Doe that the babies took long, probably because she enjoyed feeding them. Today they were agonizingly slow. The Indians continued to approach at a measured tread that was somehow more ominous than a war-whooping charge. She resolved to stop nursing when they came within two-hundred yards. Just short of that both twins turned loose and Ash burped.

Little Doe ran to lay James on the bed, burped Ash again, lay him down to burp James, then picked Ash up and carried both babies down the earthen stairs into the cellar.

Enough light came through the trap door from above for her to see. After a quick glance around, she settled on the pile of sacked potatoes against the south wall. Laying the babies on the dirt floor, she went over to lift one of the rearmost sacks atop the forward sacks. The sacks were three deep, three high and three lengthwise. When she finished rearranging them, they were still three lengthwise, but only two deep, with four high in the front row and five high in the rear.

She picked up James, lay him behind te sacks in the trench she had formed close to the rear end of the cellar, then picked up Ash and lay him in the forward part. Both babies cooed and kicked their feet.

Then, after running upstairs, she closed the trap door and ran over to the north window. One hundred feet away mounted Indians sat motionless on their ponies, gazing at the hut. She circled the room, looked out all the windows. The hut was completely surrounded.

The east window looked out to the rear of the hut. There the war-bonneted chief sat his horse. When she saw it was Fighting Wolf, she sank to her knees.

The chief issued orders. Four braves dismounted; two went into the barn, another looked into the storage shed and the fourth opened the door to the outhouse. All returned and remounted. Fighting Wolf rode his horse around to the front of the hut.

Little Doe stepped outside, pulled closed the door and leaned against it. The chief dismounted and came close.

"How did you find me?" Little Doe asked in Shoshonean.

"The horse trader left a trail," Fighting Wolf said in English. "Not a clear one. It has taken twelve moons."

Still in Shoshonean Little Doe said, "Why do you speak to me in the white man's tongue, my father?"

"Because you became a white woman when you ran off with the horse trader. I am no longer your father. Tell the horse trader to come out."

"He is not here," she said, again in Shoshonean.

"Step aside, white woman."

"He left ten days since for Forth Worth, driving the herd to market."

"Step aside."

"You crossed our range, my father. Did you see anything but cows and calves? Did you see steers? They are on their way to Fort Worth."

Fighting Wolf drew a knife from his belt. "Step aside."

Little Doe turned, opened the door and went inside. Fighting Wolf followed, holding the knife in his hand. He glanced around, his gaze taking in the scant furnishings and the incongruous bookcase full of books against one wall, then settling on the loop of rope. He went over to lift the trap door. Whn he descended the steps, his knife held ready, Little Doe followed.

The chief looked around. "I told you he was not here," Little Doe said, still speaking in Shoshonean.

A cooing sound came from behind the stacked potato sacks. When the chief looked that way, Little Doe said, this time in English, "The cat. She has been missing. I did not know I had locked her down here."

Sheathing his knife, Fighting Wolf went over to look behind the potato sacks. The light was dim there, and he had to bend low and peer. Reaching down, he picked up Ash.

"Please, my father," Little Doe said, again in Shoshonean. "The child has done you no harm."

Ignoring her, Fighting Wolf brushed by and climbed the steps with Little Doe hurrying after him. As he opened the door and carried the baby outside, she ran after him to clutch at his elbow; he backhanded her and knocked her to the ground. Mounting his horse, the baby cradled in his left arm, he looked down at her. Slowly she climbed to her feet. Ash cooed and gripped the necklace of bones around Fighting Wolf's neck.

The chief said, "My former daughter is white, but my grandson shall be a brave."

He kneed his horse around and rode off. The warriors followed. Little Doe did something unseemly for the daughter of a chief. She sank to her knees and cried.

She was seventeen. The year was 1856.

It was four-hundred-fifty miles from Fort Worth to Ashley McKay's ranch, and in between there were only a dozen ranches and three trading posts. At each stop he heard harrowing tales of Comanche raids on isolated settlers as well as encouraging rumors that a regiment of U.S. Cavalry was close on the Comanche's trail.

At Abel Adams' trading post, one hundred miles from home, he found the bearded Adams behind the bar and the barroom packed with drunken soldiers. "What are they celebrating?" he asked Abel.

"They caught up with Fighting Wolf and wiped out the whole camp. Just miles from here, at the Prairie Dog Town Fork."

"Jesus," McKay said.

The trader raised his voice. "Hey, Buck, come tell Mr. McKay what a complete job you did."

Lurching to his feet from a nearby table, a burly sergeant made his unsteady way to the bar. Leaning one hand against it, he peered drunken at McKay.

Abel Adams said, "Ash McKay, from up on the high plains, Buck. Sergeant Buck Masters, Ash."

The sergeant threw a sloppy left-handed salute. "You want to know about the massacre?"

"Massacre?"

"They been massacring whites, so we massacred them.

The Colonel said don't leave a single goddamned redskin alive, squaws and kids included. You know what we left? Not a single goddamned redskin alive—not a brave, not a squaw, not a kid."

McKay looked sick.

"You know what I done?" the sergeant said. "I went in this tepee, and there was this squaw with a baby no more'n six weeks old. I shot the squaw and then the baby. It was orders."

He began to cry.

"When was this?" McKay asked Abel as the sergeant reeled away.

"Dawn this morning. They just left 'em there to rot in the sun."

A lean, handsome, bearded man of about thirty drove the lone Conestoga. An attractive woman of twenty, in a white dress and white sunbonnet, sat beside him.

"I hope California isn't this bleak, Ephraim," she said.

"You read what Philip wrote. It is the Garden of Eden. We will be within walking distance of the Pacific."

"Your brother was trying to convince you to come. What will we do if they don't need a doctor?"

"Since they have none, they must need one."

"Will we ever see Boston again?—What is that funny cloud ahead?"

He peered upward in the direction she was looking. "That's not a cloud, dear, it's a flock of buzzards."

Five miles closer to the cloud of soaring birds the stench hit them. "What is that?" she asked.

"Death," her husband said.

"How do you know?"

"Shouldn't a doctor know death when he smells it?"

As they continued on, the stench became overpowering.

They neared what seemed to have been an encampment, but was now a razed area of collapsed tepees and dead Indian ponies and sprawled bodies. A huge flock of buzzards rose into the air and flapped away.

"Please go no nearer, Ephraim," the woman said.

"There may be someone still alive, Abigail."

"No, there couldn't be. Please go around."

He continued on to the center of the desecrated camp. Holding a handkerchief to her nose, Abigail gazed up fearfully at the hundreds of circling buzzards. Climbing down from the wagon, Ephraim explored the battlefield in ever widening circles. The dead were all Indian braves, squaws, children and infants, and he guessed there were one hundred fifty bodies.

There were no survivors among the bodies in the open. He began dragging the collapsed tepees aside. There were thirty, and he found nothing but dead beneath the first twenty-nine. As he stopped to grip an edge of the sewed animal skin of the thirtieth, he heard a baby cry. He dragged the collapsed tepee from a warrior lying on his back with an infant in his arms. The baby was not nude, as Indian babies usually were, but wore the swaddling clothes of a white child.

The warrior was perhaps fifty; he had a bullet wound in his chest and his eyes were glazed, but he was still alive. Ephraim knelt, lifted the crying baby from his arms, lay it aside and said, "I am a doctor. I will try to help you."

"You cannot," the Indian said in a bare whisper. "Return the child to his mother."

"Who is that?"

"Little Doe," the Indian said, and died.

The sky was overcast and there was a cold wind presaging snow when Ashley McKay dismounted in front of the barn. Little Doe came running from the hut to throw her arms about him.

After kissing her, he said, "I have some bad news."

"It can't be worse than mine."

"Your father is dead, honey."

She looked up at him, and he was surprised to see more relief than grief in her eyes. "How?"

"The cavalry raided his camp at Prairie Dog Town Fork, about a hundred miles from here. It was a massacre. They killed everyone—warriors, squaws, children, even babies. There were no survivors at all."

Little Doe fainted.

CHAPTER II

The spacious adobe house was situated centrally in the village of San Buenaventura, yet was isolated enough for privacy because the few homes in the village were widely scattered. It was an ideal house for a physician as there was a central hallway leading from front to rear, the forward section of which could be used as a waiting room without disturbing the privacy of the living section. Sliding doors on either side of the hall just inside the front door led respectively to the parlor on the right and the treatment room on the left. Also on the left side of the house was a surgery and, at the very rear, Dr. Ephraim Cook's private office.

One whole wall of the office was lined with books, and there were two desks. In addition to the doctor's desk there was a school desk by the window. Nathan Cook sat at it, doing his sums. He was a handsome, well-built boy with dark, smooth skin and coal-black hair.

"I'm finished," he said to his father, who sat at his own desk, reading a medical book. He carried the paper over to the other desk and waited while the doctor checked it.

"Excellent," Dr. Cook said. "Not a single error. What was this week's reading assignment?"

"You have me reading Immanuel Kant's *Critique of Pure Reason*, sir."

"Oh, yes. Have you finished it?"

"No, sir; about half."

"It is pretty heavy reading. What have you gotten from it so far?"

The boy said, "He addresses the problem of the nature and limits of human knowledge. He refutes Hume's claims that generalizations are unjustified because our experiences are limited. Kant says the mind organizes experiences into definite patterns, and therefore all things capable of being experienced are arranged in these patterns, even though we may not yet have experienced some of them. At least I think that's what he's getting at."

"A fine synopsis, son, although a little over-simplified. I'll give you another week to wind it up."

Abigail Cook opened the door from the hallway and said, "A patient, Ephraim."

The doctor rose and took the other door through the surgery and treatment room. Abigail said, "Supper in an hour, Nate."

"Yes, ma'am."

As his mother closed the door, Nate reseated himself at his desk and opened the *Critique of Pure Reason*. In an hour he should be able to plow through two more chapters of the German philosopher's dense prose.

He became so absorbed that he was unaware of the passage of time until the door from the hall opened again and his mother said, "Supper, Nate."

When supper was over and the three of them were sitting at the dining room table while Nate's parents had coffee, Dr. Cook said, "What is today?"

"Thursday," Nate said.

"I meant the date."

"October fifteenth, sir."

The doctor's face assumed a thoughtful expression. "October fifteenth. Seems to me something important was supposed to happen today, but I can't for the life of me remember what."

His wife said, "I forgot we had dessert," and left the table to go into the kitchen.

She was gone several minutes. When she returned, she was carrying a cake with white frosting and twelve burning candles. She set it before Nate.

Grinning, Nate said, "I knew you didn't forget. I smelled the cake baking."

He made his wish, blew out the candles, then was allowed to cut and distribute the cake. Afterward he received his presents: a fishing pole from his father and a fancy hand-sewn cowboy shirt from his mother.

"It's my best birthday ever," he said. "I wish I knew for sure it really was my birthday."

"Do you doubt your physician father's skill at estimating a baby's age?" Dr. Cook asked. "You were exactly six weeks old when we found you."

"Couldn't I have been one day less, or six weeks and one day?"

"Six weeks to the minute."

"In the mirror I don't look Indian," Nate said. "But I must be if my mother's name was Little Doe."

"You don't look un-Indian, dear," his mother said. "You could be half. Or she could have been your adoptive mother, like me. You could have been kidnaped by the Indians from one of the families they massacred. You were in swaddling clothes, which Indians don't use."

"Anyway, I'm glad you found me instead of somebody

dumb. I would probably have grown up to be an illiterate cowboy instead of a famous scholar.''

"One of the qualities I have always admired about our son is his modesty," Dr. Cook said to his wife.

In the middle of the night Nate was awakened by pounding on the front door. He heard his parents' bedroom door open and moments later heard voices in the entry hall. Shortly after that he heard his father say in the room next door, "Get up and dress, Abigail. I have a wounded man and need your help."

Nate heard some movement, then heard both parents leave their room. Slipping from bed, he peered into the hallway. Light came from the treatment room. In his nightshirt he tiptoed along the hall and looked in. The room was empty, but he could hear voices and some groans from the surgery. Its door was open, too, and light came from it. The grandfather clock in the treatment room said 1:20.

Backtracking to the door from the hall into the surgery, Nate cracked it open and peeked in. The coal-oil lamp suspended over the surgery table was burning, and a burly man stripped to the waist was lying on it. In addition to his parents, two other men were in the room, one standing at the foot of the table and the other at its head. Both wore holstered six-guns and one also had a bowie knife in a sheath. The one at the foot of the table, long and lean, with pale blue eyes and a vaquero mustache, was the one with the bowie knife. The other was shorter and heavier-set and pockmarked, but had the same pale blue eyes and some facial resemblance to the taller man. Both looked in their thirties.

Nate's father, in shirtsleeves with the sleeves rolled up, stood on the opposite side of the table, facing the door and probing a wound in the prone man's shoulder with forceps.

Nate's mother, in a house dress, stood across from the doctor with her back to Nate; she was handing her husband cloths to absorb blood. The man on the table emitted a constant moaning.

"Be easy on him, Doc," the man wearing the bowie knife said.

Ignoring him, the surgeon continued to probe. Moments later he held up a blood-coated slug, set it on a small stand next to him and rinsed his hands in a basin on the same stand.

As he dried his hands on a towel, Dr. Cook said, "Whiskey, Abigail."

His wife uncorked a nearly full quart of whiskey sitting on a table beside her, which contained surgical tools and supplies, and poured a dollop into the wound. The wounded man let out a yell of pain.

"Stop being such a baby, Willie," the long, lean man said.

The doctor said, "Batting," and Nate's mother handed him some cotton batting from the supply table. After arranging it over the wound, the doctor said, "Bandage."

He wrapped the shoulder tightly with the strip of bandage his wife handed him, tied the ends and said, "That should hold you. How do you feel?"

"Weak," the man on the table said.

"You've lost a lot of blood. It would be wise if you stayed here tonight. There is a cot in the treatment room."

"Can't, Doc," the lean man with the vaquero mustache said. "We have to ride."

"Then he should lie here at least an hour. He couldn't possibly ride in his condition."

"Hell, how do we kill time for an hour?" the pock-marked man said.

The other man reached over to lift the whiskey bottle

from the surgical supply table, uncorked it and took a long pull.

"That's for medicinal purposes," Nate's father said.

"I felt sick." Passing behind the doctor, he carried the bottle around to the pockmarked man at the opposite end of the table. "You feel sick, Jube?"

"Yeah, I think I got the vapors."

He also took a long pull.

Nate's father said, "When he's up to riding, you gentlemen may leave. The fee is four dollars, if you plan to pay it. You may leave it on the table. Come, Abigail, let's go back to bed."

Taking his wife's hand, he started for the door to the treatment room, but was halted by the lean man placing a hand against his chest. "You ain't going nowhere, Doc, or the pretty lady neither."

Dr. Cook said, "You certainly know how to show gratitude."

The man on the table said in a weak voice, "Leave them alone, Cole. They did us a favor."

"Not us; just you, Willie. If we have to hang around here a whole hour, waiting for you, we got to have some fun."

He held out his hand for the bottle. Jube gave it to him; he took a swig and handed it back.

"Think you could hold one down, Willie?" the pockmarked Jube asked.

"I wouldn't advise it," Dr. Cook said. "In his weakened condition it could knock him out."

"Doc says you can't have none, Willie. Sorry." Jube took another snort and handed the bottle back to Cole, who also drank.

With the two men blocking the doorway, Nate's parents had to stand there and watch them kill the bottle. When it was empty, the slender Cole, who had the last drink, set it on the stand containing the wash basin and said, "Now what do we do?"

"This is a mighty pretty lady," Jube said.

"Yeah, we can use that cot Doc mentioned."

Cole gripped Abigail's arm and started to drag her toward the treatment room. Nate's father grabbed him around the neck and threw him against the far wall.

It happened so fast, Nate hardly knew it was happening until it was all over. When Cole bounced from the wall like a rubber ball, the heavy blade of his bowie knife was glittering, and Nate's father fell to the floor with blood gushing from his throat, his head nearly severed.

Nate's mother screamed; Nate kicked open the door and charged into the room to slam his left fist into the killer's stomach so hard that the man gasped and backed into the same wall he had just bounced from.

"Why, you little son-of-a-bitch," he said, and the knife flickered again.

Nate felt a stinging sensation on his left cheek, but it didn't keep him from flying in with both fists swinging. Cole grabbed him by the hair, shoved him against the surgery table and stuck a knee in the boy's stomach to pin him there. Nate kept flailing away, but he was now too close to his target to land effective blows.

Cole snarled, "You little bastard, I'll learn you to respect your elders."

The man transferred his grip from Nate's hair to his right ear and pulled it straight out from his head. The knife flashed again and Cole stepped back. Nate gaped in horror, and again his mother screamed, as Cole held up the bloody ear and laughed.

"Look, Jube, I got me a fancy watch fob," he said, then tucked it into his pocket and sheathed his knife.

Abigail started to run to Nate, but Cole grabbed her arm and, when she tried to shake him off, slapped her face. When that shocked her into ceasing her struggle, he dragged her toward the treatment room.

The wounded man struggled to a seated position and said, "Cole, you crazy bastard."

Cole halted long enough to let his pale blue eyes glitter. "Like me to collect a fob from you too, Willie?"

Willie lay down again and Cole continued to drag Abigail toward the door.

"I have to bandage my son," she yelled.

As he pulled her through the door, she shouted, "Press batting tight to both cuts, Nate. Just hold it there until I can fix you."

The pockmarked Jube followed Cole and the struggling woman into the treatment room. Nate grabbed two handfuls of batting, pressed one to where his ear had been and the other to his cheek. Then he just stood there, in physical shock, gazing dully at the doorway into the other room from an angle where he couldn't see into it, but couldn't help but hear his mother weeping and the heavy breathing of the rutting males.

By the time Abigail's ordeal was over, the hour of rest ordered by Dr. Cook for the wounded man was up. Willie's two companions helped him outdoors, and Nate heard horses pound away.

Still pressing the batting to his wounds, Nate went into the treatment room to find his mother spread-eagled on the cot, naked and barely conscious, and her shredded clothing was strewn across the floor.

"Mama," he said, and began to sob.

That roused her. Pushing herself off the cot, she staggered and nearly fell, then steadied herself, gripped his arm and propelled him into the surgery.

"Get on the table," she said.

Still naked, with her dead husband lying at her feet, she bandaged him as she had so many times watched her husband bandage patients. Then she got another bottle of whiskey from a cupboard, mixed some in a tumbler with water and made Nate drink it. He hated the taste and it made him dizzy. He was almost staggering when she led him back to bed.

After tucking him in, she went to her own room and dressed. Then she went to the barn and hitched up the buggy.

Sheriff Philip Cook lived beyond the mission, nearly a mile away. It was 3:30 a.m. when Abigail pounded on his door.

Her husband's younger brother answered in his nightshirt, holding a lighted candle. When he saw who it was, he stepped aside, went into the parlor and lighted a lamp. Abigail followed, sank onto the sofa and burst into tears.

Philip looked at her in alarm. "Has something happened to Eph or Nate?"

"Both. Ephraim is dead and Nate lost an ear."

So far Abigail had held up magnificently under the strain. Now she began to weep hysterically. Philip's pregnant wife Martha, wearing a nightgown, appeared in the doorway, ran over to sit next to her and put an arm about her shoulders. She gave her husband an inquiring look.

"Eph and Nate have been in some kind of accident. She says Eph is dead and Nate lost an ear. I'm going to get dressed. Sit with her until I come back; then you can dress. I want you to come with us."

He was back in no more than four minutes, fully dressed, including his gun belt. Martha had gotten nothing from Abigail meantime, because she was still hysterical. Martha was holding her in her arms and giving her comforting pats.

Philip said to his wife, "Run get dressed and I'll stay with her."

When Martha got up, Philip sat down and cradled his sister-in-law in his arms. She buried her head on his shoulder and continued to sob. After a time the sobs subsided. She sat up and wiped her eyes with a handkerchief.

"It was three men," she said. "One was wounded, and they came to Ephraim for help. After he bandaged the wounded man, the two others got drunk. One of them killed Ephraim and cut off poor little Nate's ear; then both of them raped me."

"My God! Who were they?"

"They called the wounded man Willie. The other two were named Jube and Cole. Those two looked like brothers."

"They are. The Gannon brothers and Willie Dobbs. The stage from Fillmore to Santa Paula was robbed by three masked men today, and the guard wounded one. Where's Nate?"

"In bed. After I bandaged him, I knocked him out with whiskey."

Martha came back in wearing a shawl over a house dress, and Philip stood up. He was taller and leaner than his older brother had been, and he wore a pointed black mustache. He always reminded Abigail of pictures she had seen of Wild Bill Hickcock.

He said, "Did you come horseback or in the buggy, Abby?"

"The buggy."

Philip said to Martha, "Pack something to stay all night and ride back with her. I'll be along after I raise a posse."

Abigail had to repeat the story to Martha during the

drive home. She had left a lamp burning on a small table in the hall. When they entered the house, Martha glanced apprehensively into the still lighted treatment room, then across the hall into the dark parlor.

"He's in the surgery," Abigail said, picking up the lamp and leading the way along the hall, past the closed door to the surgery and into the kitchen.

Martha immediately started a fire in the stove to make coffee. Abigail left the lamp on the table, lighted a candle and went to check on Nate. The boy was sound asleep.

Philip arrived as Martha was pouring coffee. Abigail let him in, said, "In the surgery," and returned to the kitchen.

Moments later Philip came into the kitchen, his face pale with rage and grief. "I have to ride with the posse," he said to Abigail. "I stopped by Lyman Ingalls and got him out of bed. He'll be over to take care of Eph."

"Thank you," Abigail said.

Lyman Ingalls was the undertaker.

The day after the funeral Abigail and Nate had a family conference.

"Your Uncle Philip thinks the two of us should stay right here," Abigail said. "He thinks I could continue your father's practice at a lesser degree. There's no doctor nearer than Santa Barbara to take his place, and Phil thinks I could bill myself as a midwife and nurse. I helped your father for so many years, I know how to deliver babies, treat injuries, set broken bones, and even treat some minor illnesses. What do you think?"

"Is Uncle Phil going after those men again, or is everybody just going to let it drop?"

"Nate, you weren't even listening."

"Well, is he?"

"The posse lost them in the mountains. If your Uncle

Philip gets word that they've been seen, he'll go after them with another posse. Do you want to discuss the matter at hand?''

"I heard you," he said. "I don't care what you do."

"Nate!"

"I didn't mean that sassy, ma'am. I guess what I mean is I don't care what we do."

Abigail looked at his poor bandaged ear and his poor bandaged cheek and gathered him into her arms. "We have to go on living, honey. Please don't let me down."

He gave her a gentle kiss on the cheek. "I won't, Mama. I won't ever let anyone hurt you again."

He didn't sound like a child. It was a flat promise, delivered in a strangely adult tone.

CHAPTER III

A sign on the front door read: MRS. ABIGAIL COOK—MIDWIFE AND NURSE—ENTER. Father Hernandez went in, looked into the treatment room and the parlor, saw both were empty and rang the little bell on the hall table.

When there was no response, he called, "Abby!"

There was still no response. He was turning to leave when five rapid shots sounded from behind the house. Sighing, the elderly priest took out a heavy gold watch. As usual, it was exactly 3:00 p.m.

He walked along the hallway to the back door and outside.

Young Nathan Cook was reloading a long-barreled Colt percussion revolver. The ground beyond a rail fence twenty yards from him was littered with shattered glass from broken bottles. This side of the fence, off to one side, was a wooden case half filled with empty whiskey bottles.

"Afternoon, Nate," the priest said to the boy's back.

Nate glanced around, looked guilty and holstered the heavy gun. "Afternoon, Father. If you're looking for Mom, she's out to the Morales ranch, delivering a baby."

"It was only a social call. Still in training to become the best shot in the West, I see."

"Just getting in a little practice, father."

The old priest studied the boy with mild astonishment. He seemed six inches taller than the last time he had seen him, which was an indication of how often he came to mass. Father Hernandez tried to figure his age. The Cooks had arrived in San Buenaventura the year of the big earthquake in Los Angeles and the terrible brush fire here that had come close to destroying the mission. That had been early 1857, and Nate had been an infant, as the priest recalled having to postpone his baptism because the mission had to be evacuated while volunteer firemen battled the blaze on the hill behind it. It was now 1871, which made him fourteen, probably close to fifteen. Although still gawky from too rapid growth, he was the size of a man, nearly six feet, broad-shouldered, and leanly muscled from his part-time job as the blacksmith's assistant and from year-round swimming in the surf.

He had grown into a handsome lad, the priest thought, with dark, sharply defined, even features. Father Hernandez knew that his right ear was missing, but thick black hair, parted in the middle and falling to the jaw line on either side, concealed that deformity. The thin, white, slightly puckered scar on his left cheek rather added to his handsomeness. It reminded Father Hernandez, who had been born in Spain and had once traveled widely in Europe, of the duelling scars university students in Prussia deliberately courted as emblems of manhood. It gave the boy a dashing, piratical look.

The priest said, "Would your father have approved your spending so much time practicing a killing art, son, when he devoted his life to healing?"

"I don't do it all the time, Father."

"You do it every afternoon. We can hear you clear at the mission, and everyone knows it is you by the timing. Sister Agnes always says, 'Ah, it is three p.m.,' and tells the bell-ringer to ring the bell for three o'clock mass."

"I will vary my timing, Father."

"No, that would confuse Sister Agnes. Better you should stop altogether and come to three o'clock mass. Your appearance would serve the good sister as well, and think of the money you would save on ammunition."

Nate grinned. "How save? You would only expect me to drop it in the collection basket."

"That would get you to heaven quicker than spending it to shatter bottles, my son."

"I'll think it over, Father."

"Do. I will expect to see you at mass."

That was unlikely, Nate thought. His attitude toward religion was inherited from his father. Dr. Ephraim Cook used to distress Nate's mother by calling himself a nominal Catholic, which he defined as one who approved of everyone else attending mass regularly.

When the priest left, Nate decided not to set any more bottles on fence posts that day. He went inside, cleaned and oiled his gun, and hung the gun belt in his closet. Then he wandered downtown.

He thought over what Father Hernandez had said. Lots of boys engaged in target practice. It was probably his consistency that drew attention. His mother was always harping at him to spend less time and money on practice, too. But it was his own time and his own money, earned from his job at the blacksmith shop. He wondered if his obsession was beginning to show, if anyone suspected why he had to keep practicing. Father Hernandez's joke about him training to become the best shot in the West had been right on target. That was Nate's goal.

At the sheriff's office his Uncle Phil was working at his desk. Glancing up, he said, "Hi, Nate," and went back to work.

"Hi, Uncle Phil," Nate said, heading straight for the "Wanted" posters on the wall.

The posters for Cole and Jubal Gannon and William Dobbs were still there, respectively offering $4000, $3000 and $1000 rewards, dead or alive, and two new ones had been added. There were $500 rewards for Joseph (Little Joe) Hensen and Manuel (Manny) Villanova, identified as members of the Gannon Brothers Gang. Little Joe was described as about nineteen, five-feet-eight to five-feet-ten, one hundred fifty to one hundred sixty pounds, with blond hair, a narrow face and blue eyes. Villanova was described as about thirty, five-feet-ten to five-feet-eleven, one hundred seventy to one hundred eighty pounds, olive-skinned, with black hair and a mustache. There were no pictures of either.

Going over to the desk, Nate said, "The Gannon gang has two new members, Uncle Phil?"

"Not new," the sheriff said without looking up. "Just newly identified. The gang's been operating with five members for some time. A teller recognized Little Joe and Villanova when they all robbed a bank in northern California last week. Seems the two of them once held him up before they joined the Gannons."

"Still think their hideout is in the mountains north of here, Uncle Phil?"

The sheriff gave up finishing his report and looked up at his nephew. "They probably have hideouts all over the state. At least they're hitting banks and stagecoaches all over the state."

Nate said, "You and Aunt Martha and little Phil are coming to supper Sunday, aren't you?"

"We wouldn't miss your birthday, kid."

"Could you come a little early, Uncle Phil, and give me a lesson out back?"

"Your mother doesn't like that, Nate."

"She's changed her mind. She says if I insist on learning, I may as well learn right, and she would rather have you show me."

The sheriff said, "Your biggest problem is that old cap-and-baller that belonged to your father. What you need is one of these."

He drew his short-barreled Navy .41, ejected the cartridges onto his desk and handed it to Nate.

Hefting the gun, the boy said, "Better balance and a lot lighter than my blunderbuss."

He spun the gun by its trigger guard in a sort of reverse border-roll and handed it back butt first.

"You're sure getting fancy," his uncle said. "How'd you like a job as deputy?"

"Love it."

The sheriff chuckled. "Your mother would skin me alive. She still wants you to go to college and become a university professor."

Nate said, "I may do that after I finish some other things I have to do."

When Nate got home, he found his mother at the stove in the kitchen, cooking dinner.

"The baby came?" he said.

"Yes, a boy. Mother and child are both doing fine."

Nate cut a slice of bread, buttered it and poured himself a glass of cider.

"You'll ruin your dinner," Abigail said. "No, you won't. You won't even dent your appetite. I swear you'll eat us out of house and home."

"I'm a growing boy." He seated himself at the table. "Father Hernandez called."

"What did he want?"

"He said just a social call."

Abigail peered at him over her shoulder. "He probably wanted to talk to me about you and that gun."

"He won't have to now. He talked to me about it."

"You hardly read anymore; you're so busy breaking bottles."

"Mom, I've read every book on Dad's shelves and every other one in town I could borrow."

"You could read them again. There are only two practical uses for a gun, Nate. You can become an outlaw, which I'm sure you have no desire to be, or a lawman. Your Uncle Philip is a fine man and I love him dearly, but I want more for you than a small-town job like his."

"I know, Mom. I'm still planning to go to Oakland."

He referred to the new University of California, opened two years previously.

"You haven't even written."

"Mom, they won't take you until you're sixteen."

He got up to cut and butter another slice of bread.

On Sunday Nate's Uncle Philip and Aunt Martha and Nate's two-year-old cousin, little Philip, arrived at four o'clock. Nate immediately went to get his gun belt.

When he carried it into the parlor, his mother said, "Nate, you're not going to do that now?"

"That's why Uncle Phil came early, Mom."

Uncle Philip said, "Let's have the presents first."

"We generally have those after the cake, sir."

"Let's have at least one now, anyway." He handed Nate a flat, oblong package. "Happy fifteenth birthday."

By the weight Nate knew what it was before he opened it. Ripping off the paper, he lifted the lid of the box and took out a .41 caliber Navy Colt in a hand-tooled leather holster.

"Gee, thanks," he said after a long pause, so excited he almost forgot to say it.

His mother said, "You shouldn't have, Philip. It's far too expensive a gift."

Nate knew her real objection wasn't the expense.

He removed the worn holster of the percussion pistol from the gun belt and affixed the new holster. Strapping the belt about his waist, he picked up the new gun, which he had laid aside while he changed holsters, checked to make sure it was empty, then spun it by the trigger guard and slapped it into the holster.

The sheriff stood up and said, "Let's go try it out."

"Can I come, Papa?" little Phil asked.

Pulling the two-year-old onto her lap, Martha said, "I don't want you out there with shooting going on, honey."

Out in back Nate lined up five bottles on fence posts. When he returned to where his uncle stood, Philip said, "You wear that belt too high."

Nate had it strapped around his waist right over his pants belt. He said, "I always wear it that way. It feels better."

"You won't be able to get it out as fast as you would if you wore it like mine," the sheriff said, slapping his low-slung holster. "The butt should be where your hand hangs naturally."

"Yes, sir, but I like it as it is."

Shrugging, his uncle said, "Stand to my right and watch exactly what I do in slow motion."

"Yes, sir." Nate went around to his right side.

Facing the fence, the sheriff gripped the butt of his pistol, slowly drew it from the holster and slowly swung the muzzle forward, talking throughout the operation. "You pull straight up, cocking it as you draw and slipping your finger into the trigger guard. You start to squeeze the trigger as you swing up the muzzle, and finish squeezing it just as you center on the target. Don't jerk; squeeze. Your gun should be waist-high when you fire. Point it just like you'd point your finger.''

"Yes, sir.''

Uncocking the gun, he returned it to its holster. "Now watch it in fast motion.''

His hand swooped to the gun butt; the gun seemed to jump from its holster, the muzzle swung horizontal and he fired. One of the bottles shattered.

Holstering the gun, he said, "Now you try it.'' He pushed six cartridges from the loops in his gun belt and handed them to Nate. "You don't need an empty chamber to rest the hammer on, like you do with a cap-and-baller. You can load all six.''

Nate loaded the gun, hefted it, spun it by the trigger guard, hefted it again, gave it the fancy spin he had in the house and slapped it into its holster. The sheriff moved around to his right.

"Go ahead.''

The sheriff didn't even see the gun come out of its holster. There were four shots so closely spaced that they sounded like one long explosion, and four bottles shattered.

"Why, you young scalawag,'' Nate's uncle said. "You didn't want instruction; you just wanted to show off. I can't teach you anything.''

CHAPTER IV

During the next year Nate grew another inch, to six feet, which was to be his permanent height, and continued to fill out. He still had some filling out to do, but he already weighed one hundred seventy-five pounds, and it was all bone and hard flesh.

The day after his sixteenth birthday his mother said, "You promised to try to get into the university when you reached sixteen, Nate."

"School is already in session, Mom. I'll have to wait until next September."

She said, "Maybe you can't start until then, but you can register any time. We will go up to Oakland Monday."

"We?"

"I want to make sure you get registered."

Nate said, "College costs a lot of money. Can we afford it?"

"It's nearly a year until next September, Nate. I'm hoping you can save a little money. Maybe Mr. Flores will let you work full-time at the blacksmith shop."

"I'll ask," he said.

The Central Pacific Railroad was building a line south
from San Francisco which eventually would go through
San Buenaventura, but so far it extended only to the San
Joaquin Valley. Nate and his mother had to take the packet
boat from nearby Port Hueneme to San Francisco and ferry
across the bay to Oakland.

At the university Nate discovered he had to take entrance examinations. Not only did he pass them with ease,
but also the registrar told him and Abigail he had made the
highest score in the school's three-year existence. His
enrollment for September of 1873 was accepted.

He discovered he would be going to school in Berkeley
instead of Oakland, which was only a temporary location.
The new town of Berkeley, to be the university's permanent
site, was being built on part of the enormous Peralto
Ranch, and neither the town nor the university would be
finished until the fall of 1873. Nate would be in the first
freshman class at Berkeley.

It developed that blacksmith Tomaso Flores couldn't use
a full-time helper. The only other job in the area available
to a sixteen-year-old was punching cows for thirty dollars
a month, and since Mr. Flores paid him $7.50 a week for
his part-time help, there was no point in switching jobs.
His target practice went neglected as he began to save
nearly every penny he earned.

On a Saturday early in June Nate left the blacksmith
shop at noon and, as usual, stopped at the sheriff's office
before going home for lunch. He had hardly greeted his
uncle when Ned Lucas, the twenty-year-old dispatch rider,
galloped up, ran in waving a sheet of paper and yelled,
"The Gannon brothers are coming!"

As he threw the paper in front of the sheriff, Nate
rounded the desk to read over his uncle's shoulder. It was
a penciled note from Sheriff Morgan Wayne of Santa

Barbara, reporting that the Gannon Brothers Gang had robbed the Santa Barbara bank at nine o'clock that morning, had killed a teller and a customer, and that four of them were heading south. The fifth, Little Joe Hensen, had been captured and jailed.

The sheriff gave the messenger a disgusted look. "If they were headed here, they would have arrived before you, Ned. They're holed up in the mountains."

Nevertheless, he rose from his desk and went out to raise a posse to head north in search of the bank robbers.

Nate returned to the blacksmith shop to tell Mr. Flores he might not be in Monday, and possibly not all next week.

"That's all right, son," the blacksmith said. "But if you don't come in, you don't get paid."

His mother had lunch ready when Nate got home. As he wolfed his sandwich, she said, "Please don't eat so fast, Nate."

"Yes, ma'am," he said without slowing.

They finished together because Abigail was having only a slice of bread and butter. "May I be excused?" he asked.

"All right, but what's your hurry?"

"I have to go to Santa Barbara."

"Santa Barbara!" she said, coming to her feet.

Starting for the door, he said, "Only for a few days. I want to look for something better-paying than the blacksmith shop."

She ran after him to grab his arm. "Where will you stay?"

"They have a hotel. A bed costs only fifty cents."

"You'll probably bring home bedbugs. Can't you look around here?"

"I've looked, Mom."

"All right," she said. "You're sixteen, so I guess I can't order you around anymore."

Putting his arms around her, he said, "Sure you can, but I really want to go."

She leaned against his chest and cried as though he were going to the moon. Santa Barbara was twenty-eight miles.

Five miles from Santa Barbara Nate met the sheriff's posse coming back and reined in his loping horse. The posse, traveling at a walk, also stopped.

"Where you going in such a hurry?" Nate's uncle asked.

"Santa Barbara."

His uncle took in his black trousers and black shirt and black, flat-topped sombrero, the gun worn high on his right side and the blanket roll behind his saddle. "Planning to stay a while?"

"Just to see if I can find something better than the blacksmith shop."

"Let me guess," the sheriff said. "You think maybe the Gannon brothers will try to bust Little Joe out of jail, and you'll be on hand to avenge your father."

"No, sir, that never occurred to me."

"It occurred to Santa Barbara's sheriff. He has riflemen on roofs all around the courthouse."

"I didn't have that in mind at all, Uncle Phil. Honest."

"Well, stay out of trouble."

He motioned to the posse and they rode on. Nate heeled his horse to a lope again.

He rode into Santa Barbara in late afternoon to find Anacapa Street in front of the courthouse packed. "What's going on?" he asked a boy of about ten in the crowd.

"There's a delegation trying to talk Sheriff Wayne into turning over Little Joe Hensen to them for a rope party."

From horseback Nate could see over the heads of the

crowd. A burly, black-browed man wearing a star and carrying a shotgun under his arm was standing on the courthouse steps facing a group of half a dozen men at the foot of the steps. Nate was too far away to hear what was being said.

"Who's Little Joe Hensen and what did he do?" Nate asked the boy.

The youngster looked up at him in surprise. "He's one of the Gannon Brothers Gang. They robbed the bank this morning and killed Tom Hadley and the widow Ramirez. Where you been, mister?"

"Just got in town. How'd they capture Little Joe?"

"Shot his horse from under him. The rest got away."

"Little Joe hurt?"

"Naw, just his horse."

"Where's the jail?" Nate asked.

"Round back of the courthouse."

Nate skirted the edge of the crowd to the rear of the courthouse. The building was completely circled by at least three hundred men and boys, plus a few women. Those in back were hurling taunts and threats at the single barred jail window. Some people were right under the window, but they couldn't see into it because it was too high from the ground.

Dismounting, Nate tied his horse to a palm. The approximately seventy-five people back here were widely enough spaced so that he didn't have to elbow his way to the front. He zigzagged through the crowd until he was ten feet from the window.

Three thick iron rods barred the window. The rear wall of the courthouse was adobe, and the bars were set right into the hardened clay. By the depth of the window Nate estimated the wall as two feet thick, and the bars probably extended both up and down into the adobe for a couple of feet.

Still, they were only set in dried clay, he thought.

The shouts at the unseen prisoner were too loud for the questions Nate wanted answered to be heard by anyone there. Retreating to the edge of the crowd, he picked a well-dressed man who looked like a merchant.

"Why doesn't the sheriff have a guard back here?" he asked.

The man looked at him, took in his youth and smiled. "Front's where he needs guards. See that door over there?" He pointed to the rear door of the courthouse.

"Yes, sir."

"Solid steel and barred from inside. You couldn't get through it with dynamite."

Nate looked around in all directions. The riflemen his Uncle Philip had mentioned must all be around front and on the two sides, he thought, because, except for a couple of houses some distance away, there were no roofs back here to conceal snipers. Then he spotted men wearing pistols at either corner of the building, leaning against the wall and trying to look unobtrusive. The sheriff hadn't left the rear completely uncovered after all.

"Where's the livery stable?" Nate asked the well-dressed man.

"Two blocks that way and left," the man said, again pointing.

Remounting, Nate rode to the livery stable. A middle-aged black man was in charge of it.

"Want to rent a horse, but don't want to take it now," Nate said. "How late you open?"

"I sleep here, boss. You kin come any time"

"Let's see what you got."

He picked a sturdily built horse that looked as though it had a lot of strength in its shoulders and still could be fast.

"I'll need a saddle and a blanket," he said to the black man.

"Yessuh, everything'll be ready when you come by."

"I want to leave my horse until I pick up the other. Rub him down and water him easy and feed him."

"Yessuh."

"I'll pay you now, so I won't have to bother later."

"Yessuh. Twenty dollars deposit on the rented horse, against a dollar a day. You get back what ain't used. Yours will be a dollar."

Nate had brought fifty dollars with him. He handed over twenty-one, then had an afterthought. Studying the rope looped over his saddle horn, he said, "Have any rope thicker than my riata?"

"Got all kinds of rope, suh. This way."

The black man led him to a shed behind the stable, where, among other items such as bits and bridles and stirrups and saddles, there were a half-dozen large spools of rope of varying sizes suspended on a long axle so that they could be turned. Nate had him cut fifty feet of tough one-inch rope. It was five cents a foot, and Nate gave him another $2.50.

Coiling the rope, he told the hostler to hang it on the saddle horn of the rented horse.

It was now 6:30 p.m. He found a cafe, had supper, then toured the area surrounding the courthouse until he found the nearest saloon to it. Called the Lucky Tiger, it was about a block from the courthouse.

It was the first saloon he had ever been in. Although it was only about eight o'clock, the place was jammed. There was none of the loud talk and laughter that he had heard coming from saloons at home when he passed them, though. There was only a low drone of conversation with an ominous overtone of anger.

There were a half-dozen gaudily dressed and painted women in the place, but no one seemed to be paying any attention to them.

He halted near the crowded bar to listen, just in time to hear a man say, "Poor woman never knew what hit her. I hear the son-of-a-bitch blasted her just because she didn't move fast enough to suit him."

"He'll never see a judge," the man's companion said. "Comes about midnight the good citizens of this town'll descend on the courthouse like a swarm of locusts, and Morgan Wayne better put down that shotgun and step aside if he knows what's good for him."

Everyone was talking about the bank robbery and the prisoner. Nate repeatedly heard the word *rope*. From what was said he gathered that Cole Gannon had killed the teller and Little Joe Hensen had shot the woman customer.

A man lurched away from the bar, leaving a vacant spot, and one of the two barkeeps startled Nate by saying, "What'll it be, sonny?"

Nate hadn't expected to order anything, but thus confronted, he felt obligated to order to justify his presence. Moving into the vacancy, he said, "Got any sarsaparilla?"

"One sarsaparilla coming up," the barkeep said, placing a glass before Nate, then bringing a bottle from beneath the bar and pouring a frothy liquid.

As Nate gave him a dime, a huge drunken cowboy of about eighteen, standing to his right, turned to focus his gaze on him. He was about six-feet-six and must have weighed two hundred twenty pounds.

"We got us a sarsaparilla drinker," he said. "Your mama know you're out, little boy?"

"Sure. Your keeper know you're out of your cage?"

Not caring for further conversation with a drunk, Nate picked up his glass with his left hand and started for the far end of the bar. He had taken only two steps when he was spun around, roughly, so that he spilt a little of his sarsaparilla, and then the drunken giant was gripping his shirtfront as he drew Nate to tiptoes.

"Listen, pipsqueak—" he started to say.

That was as far as he got before Nate brought up a knee. Releasing his grip, the big cowboy bent over and groaned.

Careful not to spill any more of his drink, Nate laid a right on his jaw that made a noise like a dropped watermelon. The cowboy hit the floor on his back and slid several feet before coming to rest open-eyed, slack-jawed and unconscious.

That brought momentary silence at the bar. As everyone turned to look down at the sleeping giant, the barkeep who had waited on Nate said, "Get him out of here, Charlie."

A large man at the bar stooped to grip the unconscious cowboy under the arms, dragged him to the bat-winged door and pitched him into the street. Conversation at the bar resumed.

Nate continued to the end of the bar, where a place for him instantly appeared. A pretty, but somewhat faded woman in a sequinned dress came over and said, "For a kid you sure got dynamite in them dukes."

Not knowing what else to say, Nate said, "Yes, ma'am."

The woman squeezed in next to him. "I'm Kitty."

"How do you do, ma'am. I'm—" He paused, aware that everyone around was listening, and it suddenly occurred to him that he didn't want to leave any clues to his identity in Santa Barbara. "I'm Jack Coe."

"You're sure cute, Jack. Want to buy me a drink?"

"Sure, ma'am."

The woman signaled the nearer barkeep, who set a shot

glass before her and poured whiskey. "Twenty-five cents," he said to Nate.

Nate fumbled a quarter from his pocket and laid it on the bar.

Kitty raised her glass, said, "Here's to you, honey," and took a sip.

Raising his sarsaparilla, Nate said, "Here's to you, too, ma'am," and also sipped.

"Will you stop calling me ma'am?" she said. "You make me feel like your mother."

One of the men at the bar said, "You're old enough to be, Kitty," and the other nearby men laughed.

"Let's move to a table," Kitty said. "The company in this neighborhood stinks."

She led the way to the only vacant table in the house, one for two against the wall. As they sat across from each other, she said, "At least for a minute we made them forget that poor guy they're gonna lynch."

"You think they'll lynch him?"

"They'll try, soon as they're liquored up enough. Morgan Wayne's a pretty tough cookie, but he won't want to kill half a dozen or more upright citizens to save the skin of a murderin' rat. They'll probably succeed. Wanta go upstairs, kid?"

He looked at her blankly. "Upstairs?"

"You know—upstairs."

He got it then, realizing she was a prostitute. He blushed deeply.

"My gawd," she said. "You thought I *was* your mother. How old are you, kid?"

"Sixteen, ma'am."

This time she didn't correct him. "Jesus, I thought you were at least eighteen. What the hell you doing in a saloon?"

That put a defensive look on his face. "I'm only drinking sarsaparilla."

"That all it is?" she said, looking at it. "I thought it was beer."

"No, ma'am, just sarsparilla. You want me to go away so you can—I mean—"

When he floundered to a halt, she said, "So I can ply my trade? Nobody's interested tonight, kid. Their only lust is blood lust. Let's sit here and I'll talk to you like a mother. What *are* you doing in a saloon?"

"I just came in to hear what they were saying about Little Joe."

"Why, you know him?"

"Only by reputation. I heard someone say he was the one who killed that woman."

"That's what's gonna get him lynched. She was a nice old lady, they say; never harmed no one and did a lot of charity work. The teller Cole Gannon shot was well-liked, too. Hardly more'n a kid, maybe twenty."

Nate said, "I heard a man say he thought a mob would form about midnight. If they are going to do it, why would they wait so long?"

"Got to get their courage up, kid. They couldn't face Sheriff Wayne without their bellies full of booze. Do we have to talk about this?"

"What would you like to talk about, ma'am?"

"You. Are you from around here?"

Nate visualized her being questioned by the sheriff. "San Jose," he said.

"How come you're so far from home?"

He had improvised an answer before the question was asked. "I'm here with my parents, visiting an aunt."

They sat talking until nearly eleven o'clock, and Nate found himself liking her more and more. While she was uneducated, there was nothing crude about her, and beneath her surface hardness he discovered surprising warmth. Besides, she obviously liked him, and it was flattering to have an older woman show interest in him.

Once she went to the bar to get another whiskey and another sarsparilla, and she paid for them herself. Then, as he was preparing to go get a third drink for her, but none for himself, a man came over and whispered in her ear.

Rising to her feet, she said, "Don't go away, kid. Be back in twenty minutes."

She went off with the man.

Nate went over to listen to more conversation at the bar. It struck him as uglier than before, and more purposeful than the vague threats he had heard when he first came in. Now he heard discussions of actual plans to break out the prisoner. None he overheard were very sensible, ranging from fanciful ruses to lure the sheriff out of town to plots of dynamiting the steel back door of the courthouse, but he got the impression that all the schemes were advanced seriously, even though colored by too much booze.

It looked to him as though the crowd could explode into a mob at any minute. He regretted having to leave without telling Kitty goodbye, but it was time.

CHAPTER V

Nate left the horses tied in an alley a block from the courthouse and continued on foot. He could hear the angry shouting of a mob gathered on Anacapa Street in front of the courthouse as he tied up the horses, and could see the rioters from a block away the moment he emerged from the alley onto Anacapa Street. Although it was a dark, overcast night, with visibility limited to about fifty feet, a dozen flaming torches illuminated their faces.

As he drew near, he saw that there were at least two hundred men in the crowd and that Sheriff Morgan Wayne, backed against the courthouse door, was holding a shotgun with its twin muzzles elevated above the heads of the crowd.

Nate slipped along the right side of the building to the rear corner and peeked around it. Apparently, general knowledge of the barred steel door in back had discouraged any would-be lynchers from trying to get at the prisoner from that direction, because they were all around front. The two guards were still on duty back there, though, and the one posted at this corner was facing Nate from six feet away.

He stopped reaching for his gun and turned rigid when he saw Nate's Navy .41 pointed at him.

Nate crooked his finger and the man came closer. Nate spun him around, slapped the .41 into its holster and landed a rabbit punch behind the guard's right ear. The man fell like an axed tree.

Quickly, but quietly, Nate walked toward the other side of the building, past the barred cell window, past the steel rear door. The second guard stood with his back to Nate, as he was watching the corner. His first and only indication that anyone was behind him was a blow that felt like a rocket exploding behind his right ear.

Nate took off for the horses at a dead run; he was back astride his horse and leading the other in less than two minutes. Reining in next to the barred window, he said, "Little Joe."

From the darkness a wary voice said, "What?"

"I've come to get you out of there."

"Who are you?"

"Never mind. If you want to escape that lynch mob out front, get over here. Are you dressed?"

"Yes." A pale face appeared in the window.

"You standing on something?" Nate asked.

"No, the floor's higher than the ground. There's a basement under it."

Nate passed one end of the heavy rope he had bought inside to the right of the right-hand bar, reached inside past the left-hand bar to grip it and pulled it through until there was an equal length of rope on either side. Pushing the portion of the rope inside up to the top of the window, he said, "Hold this in place there."

The prisoner's hands gripped the rope in either upper corner of the window and held it there. Taking the end of the rope coming from the left upper side of the window,

Nate threaded it past the right-hand bar, around the middle bar outside again, and drew it taught. He repeated the process in reverse with the other end of the rope. The rope now ran behind all three bars at the top of the window, formed an X across the outside of the bars, and ran behind the bars at the lower end of the window, where they crossed at the center bar so that both ends came outside with the center bar between them.

"Keep holding that up there," Nate said as he tied one end of the rope to his saddle horn and the other end to the saddle horn of the rented horse.

He pulled out his clasp knife, opened it and held it in his right hand as he gathered both sets of reins in his left. Reining his horse around with its rump to the window, he pulled the other horse alongside of it, then drove his right heel into his horse's flank and simultaneously kicked the other horse with his left toe and yelled, "Haayaugh!"

The horses bolted. When the rope tightened, it didn't even slow them. There was a rending sound as a whole section of adobe above the window and another section below popped outward. The clasp knife flashed twice to cut the rope free from both saddle horns; Nate snapped it closed and dropped it back in his pocket at the same time he reined in the horses.

Little Joe was squatting in the window as the two horses wheeled by. He made a flying leap into the saddle and both horses pounded away to the south.

There was no immediate pursuit because there had been no witnesses to the jailbreak. Nonetheless, they didn't slow their breakneck speed.

At the south edge of town Nate dropped back a few yards to let Little Joe lead. Five miles later Little Joe slowed to a walk, cut left off the road into what, in the darkness, looked to Nate like underbrush, but after a short distance developed into a narrow trail. They followed it for about a mile and halted.

Turning his horse to face Nate, Little Joe asked, "Now, who are you?"

"Jack Coe."

"Why'd you bust me out?"

"Thought it might be a good way to join the Gannon Brothers Gang."

Little Joe rode closer to peer at him in the darkness. "How old are you?"

"Sixteen."

"For Christ's sake, you're just a kid."

"Man enough to bust you out of jail," Nate said.

After a short silence Little Joe said, "You were that."

"You're not much older," Nate said. "I saw a 'Wanted' poster saying you were only nineteen."

"That was a year ago. I'm twenty."

"Big accomplishment. Everybody gets to be twenty if he lives long enough."

"We'll discuss it in the morning," Little Joe said. "Right now we better put some distance between us and Sheriff Wayne."

He turned his horse and led on. They rode all night, penetrating deep into the mountains. At dawn they halted by a narrow stream and made camp.

Over Nate's objection, his mother had packed four sandwiches for him to carry in his saddlebag. Now he was glad he had lost the argument. He split them with his companion for breakfast.

By the time they had finished eating, it was fully light. They looked each other over carefully. Little Joe Hensen's poster description had been accurate only to a point, Nate thought. He was blond, with blue eyes, of average height and weight, and had a narrow face. What the poster hadn't mentioned was the expression in his eyes. They were as emotionless as a dead carp's.

"You're not so little," Nate said. "Why do they call you Little Joe?"

"Big Joe was my old man. Actually the son-of-a-bitch was littler than me after I grew up, but he could still wallop me up to the day I took off."

"He still living?"

"Who knows, or cares? I told you he was a son-of-a-bitch. Where you from?"

"San Jose."

"Run away from home?"

Nate had mentally rehearsed his assumed background in detail. He said, "Not exactly. Got kicked out."

"For what?"

"Some fool neighbor claimed I raped his daughter. I didn't. It was her idea."

"Why didn't you fight it?"

"They always believe the girl. Also I'd been in trouble before, and it was kind of the last straw for my old man."

"What kind of trouble? More girls?"

"Some. Then I killed a couple of fools in a gunfight."

"A *couple*? At the same time?"

"Uh-huh. They started shooting first. The county coroner called it self-defense."

"How old were you?" Little Joe asked.

"Fourteen."

"Jesus," Little Joe said. "Maybe you are up to riding with the rest of us."

"Did you really kill that old lady in the bank?" Nate asked.

"Why? You got scruples?"

"I lost them the day my old man kicked me out. I was just curious."

"She didn't move when I told her to. We better get an hour's sleep and let the horses rest."

"Why only an hour?" Nate said. "Sheriff Wayne doesn't know where the hell we are."

"I want to get to the hideout. I feel sort of bare without a gun, and I got a spare in my room. Used to carry two when I was a green kid and thought that looked tough."

"What changed your mind?"

Little Joe laughed. It was a strange laugh, because it sounded genuinely amused, but his eyes remained as bleak as ever. "Two things. I got tired of carrying around the extra weight, and I could never hit anything left-handed. Let's get to sleep."

With the sun up, it was not only warm, but getting hot. Nate spread his blanket in the shade of a tree and both slept on it.

Nate, who possessed a mental alarm clock, woke in exactly one hour. When he shook Little Joe awake, the outlaw looked at him blearily, got up, went over to lie face-down at the edge of the stream and plunged his face into the water.

When he rose to his feet, he said, "I think I can stay awake until we get there now."

They rode for most of the day, winding deeper and deeper into the mountains. Nate was not exactly sure where they were, but by periodically checking the sun he knew they were riding generally northeast.

About four that afternoon they emerged from a shallow valley and stopped at the foot of a path leading up the side of a low, flat-topped mountain. Little Joe hooked his two little fingers into his mouth and emitted a shrill whistle.

After a short wait it was answered by a similar whistle from above.

"Follow me," Little Joe said, and started up the trail.

At the top the path went between two large boulders onto the flat mountain top. After they passed between them, Nate found himself covered by a rifle held by a man standing to one side. From the description on his "Wanted" poster, Nate knew it was Manny Villanova.

"Hold real still, señor," the dark, mustached outlaw said.

Little Joe said, "He's all right, Manny. He busted me out of jail. He wants to join the gang."

Lowering his rifle, Villanova said. "For all I knew, he had a gun on you, amigo. I saw you had none."

"They take them away when they throw you in jail. This is Jack Coe, Manny. The famous Manuel Villanova, Jack."

"I've seen your 'Wanted' posters," Nate said.

"Everybody has," Villanova said.

The three of them continued on together, Nate and Little Joe walking their horses at a slow pace so that Villanova could keep up on foot beside them. A hundred feet beyond, shaded by tall pine, was a large, ramshackle frame house with an outhouse and a corral holding four horses behind it. Three men stood on the porch and watched them approach.

Nate recognized the men as Cole and Jubal Gannon and Willie Dobbs. He managed to conceal the hate that frothed up within him beneath a wide smile.

"Who's the kid?" Cole asked as the horsemen and Villanova stopped before the porch.

"Jack Coe," Little Joe said. "He wants to join up. He's only sixteen, but he's hell on wheels. Already got two killings and a rape charge hanging over him."

"Hey," Nate said. "The coroner called those killings self-defense, and that rape charge was never proved."

"Sorry I blackened your reputation. This is Cole Gannon,

Jube Gannon and Willie Dobbs, Jack.'' He pointed to each as he named him. ''Jack busted me out of jail, Cole.''

''How?''

When Little Joe described how, all four of the other outlaws regarded Nate with amused admiration. Jube said, ''You're pretty bright, kid. Maybe we'll let you plan our next job.''

Little Joe and Nate rode on to the corral and unsaddled their horses. The other four had gone inside when they mounted the porch steps.

The front door of the house led into a large room running the width of the house and serving as both a kitchen and sitting room. The half-dozen doors off it presumably led to bedrooms.

As Little Joe and Nate entered, Nate pushed his flat-topped black sombrero off the back of his head so that, suspended by the chin strap, it rode on his back.

Cole was standing at the table, where he was opening a bottle of whiskey, and Jubal was getting glasses from a cupboard, while the other two outlaws stood waiting for the bottle to be opened. Little Joe disappeared into one of the bedrooms and returned buckling a gun belt about his waist.

''Now I feel dressed,'' he said.

Cole said to Nate, ''You old enough to drink, kid?''

''Depends on the time. My daddy always said, 'Never drink until the sun's over the yardarm.' What time is it?''

Cole took out a watch with a dried-up, withered object tied to its stem by a leather thong. ''Four-thirty. I think that's when the sun goes over the yardarm.''

''Funny watch fob you have there, Mr. Gannon,'' Nate said as Cole put the timepiece away.

Jube set six glasses on the table and Cole began to pour. He gave Nate a wide grin.

"Ear of a little bastard who sassed me once."

"That's what I figured," Nate said. "It's mine." He smoothed back the hair on the right side of his head.

Cole set down the bottle and stared at him. Nate said, "You cut it off just after killing my father, and just before you and your brother raped my mother. I'm Nathan Cook."

All five outlaws were now staring at him in astonishment. Aware from his words that he must have come there gunning for Cole, they couldn't comprehend why he was being so suicidal about it. It never crossed any of their minds that he could match any of them, let alone survive all five.

Cole was reaching for his gun when a .41 caliber slug severed his penis and drilled through his testicles. Jube had his gun half out when the second slug ripped through his genitals. The other three actually got their guns all the way out, and Willie Dobbs had his leveled, when bullets slammed into their chests, killing them instantly.

Cole and Jubal were both on the floor groaning and feebly groping for their groins. Both still had their guns in their holsters, Cole never having touched his and Jubal's falling back in when the shock of the bullet made him release his grip. Nate kept his eye on both as he swung out the cylinder of his revolver, ejected the spent cartridges and reloaded.

Both Cole's and Jubal's right hands began to creep toward their gun butts. Nate blew away their elbows, then, on the off chance that they might try to reach across with their left hands, blew away their left elbows, too.

Through his pain Cole tried to say something, but the words were too low for Nate to make out. Bending over him, Nate said, "What?"

This time he heard the whisper. "Finish it, for God's sake."

"Why?" Nate said. "You'll die when you've lost enough blood."

He sat at the table to clean and oil his gun, then went back to look at the two brothers. Still conscious, but unable to move, and nearly mad with pain, they gazed up at him in silent plea to kill them.

Nate began to search the house. In three separate caches he uncovered a total of nearly eight thousand dollars, and dropped it into a gunny sack he found in a kitchen drawer.

He went outdoors, saddled all six horses, stuck the gunny sack in one of his saddlebags, led the horses over in front of the porch and tied them to the porch rail. One by one he dragged the three dead men onto the porch and heaved them belly-down across three of the saddles.

Inside again, he took the watch from Cole's pocket, fingered the dried ear and looked to see the time. Only half an hour had passed since the shooting.

He brought a chair over from the table, swung the back toward the two dying men, straddled it, rested his arms along the back and settled down to watch them die.

It took another hour and a half.

He started down the mountain at six-thirty, leading the train of five horses tied together behind him. There would be only another hour and a half of light, and he didn't know exactly where he was, but he was sure he could find his way home. He believed he was closer to San Buenaventura than to Santa Barbara because of his and Little Joe's steady angling to the northeast, and he figured that a due-south course would take him, if not directly home, at least to some area he recognized.

A bright moon allowed him to continue after dark, but at midnight it set and he had to stop. He built a fire, unloaded and unsaddled the horses, and sat awake all the rest of the night, guarding the bodies against animals. At dawn he resaddled and reloaded the horses and continued on.

When he rode into San Buenaventura at nine that morning, he brought stares from the citizens on the boardwalks and collected a train of curious children.

He found his uncle at his desk. The sheriff looked up and said, "You look half-dead."

"I feel fine," Nate said. "Got nine thousand dollars handy?"

"What?"

"I have nine-thousand-dollars worth of merchandise outside, plus eight thousand in recovered loot. Come take a look."

CHAPTER VI

Nate's obsessive gun practice had been for one purpose. Once he was avenged, he lost interest in his gun. When he left for school in September of 1873, one month short of seventeen years old, he wore no gun belt, although he carried it along in his suitcase.

By now Nate had reached his full physical development. He had grown no taller, but he had finished filling out to a solid one hundred and ninety pounds. While his face was still that of a teen-ager, his body was that of a grown man.

The new village of Berkeley was merely a small cluster of shops and businesses and a few houses surrounding the university. The students hardly swelled the population, as there were only seventy-five, nearly half of them in the freshman class and only twelve of them seniors.

There were five boarding houses near the school, ranging in price from fifteen to twenty-five dollars a month. Nate was not going to school poor. In addition to nine thousand dollars in bounties for the Gannon Brothers Gang, he had received an eight-hundred-dollar reward for the recovered loot he had turned in. While most of the money had given to his mother, he arrived in Berkeley with fifteen hundred dollars. Assuming that the most expensive house would have the best food, he chose it. He arrived in Berkeley on Sunday, September first, the day before school opened, and was moved in by three in the afternoon.

It was a huge, three-story frame house of twenty rooms. Downstairs there was a large parlor, a large dining room with a long table that would seat sixteen, a kitchen, a summer kitchen, and three bedrooms. The summer kitchen, designed to avoid overheating the house when cooking in warm weather, was really just an enclosed porch off the main kitchen with removable storm windows. On the second floor there were seven bedrooms and on the third six.

The landlady was a widow in her mid-thirties named Lois Sherman, a quite pretty, slightly plump brunette with pale, creamy skin and slanting, deerlike eyes. Nate's destruction of the outlaw gang had made the papers all over the Pacific coast, and Mrs. Sherman was so flattered to have him in her house that she gave him the only available room on the first floor, even though he was a freshman and there were eight upperclassmen in the house, including two of the twelve seniors. The other two downstairs bedrooms were her own and a guest room she kept vacant for visits by her brother and sister-in-law from San Francisco.

"My brother set me up here after Everett drowned and left me destitute," she told Nate. "Not out of the goodness of his heart, but because of what the neighbors might think if he let me starve. I already disgraced him once by marrying a common fisherman. He's attorney for, and a director of, the Southern Pacific Railroad, and he has about half the money in San Francisco."

All fourteen student rooms were singles, which was one of the reasons the rent was higher. It was the only rooming house where students didn't have to double up.

Nate's room was large and airy, with a double bed, a
mirrored dresser, an easy chair by the window, a washstand with a basin and pitcher, and a writing desk and
chair with a long shelf on the wall above them that was
more than adequate for the two dozen books he had brought
along in a wooden box.

The landlady asked if he needed help unpacking and,
when he said no, stood in the doorway of his room and
watched him unpack. When he hung his gun belt at the
back of the closet, she said, "That the gun that wiped out
the Gannon bunch?"

"Yes," Nate said, embarrassed.

"You shouldn't blush," she said. "That was a proud
thing you did."

He made no reply to that because he couldn't think of
one.

When he'd finished unpacking his suitcase and began
uncrating his books and setting them on the shelf, Mrs.
Sherman went over to look at the titles.

"Four volumes of Shakespeare," she said. "*The
Tragedies, The Histories, The Comedies* and *The Sonnets.*
You must like him."

"Doesn't everybody, ma'am?"

"You don't have to call me ma'am," she said, bringing
a momentary memory of the prostitute Kitty in Santa
Barbara. "I plan to call all my boys by their first names,
and I prefer they call me Lois. Can I call you Nathan?"

"Everyone calls me Nate."

"All right, Nate. Will you call me Lois?"

"Sure, Lois."

She looked over the other titles as he continued to
shelve books. "Some of this is pretty deep stuff. Homer,
Aristotle, Galileo Galilei—whoever he is—Francis Bacon,
Keats, Shelley. Don't you read any novels?"

"Yes, I just didn't bring any along."

"I like romances myself, particularly the Brontes. I know you're not considered high-class unless you rave over Dickens, but he never has any diddling going on in his books."

Nate gave her an astonished look.

"I don't mean the Bronte sisters ever outright said anything you couldn't quote to a Methodist preacher, but if you read between the lines, you know Jane Eyre was getting diddled by half the men she met, and Heathcliff in *Wuthering Heights* wasn't the sort to keep his peter in his pants if there was a pretty lass available to stick it in."

Looking around and catching Nate's shocked look, she said, "I talk too frank, don't I? I embarrassed you."

Only part of Nate's shock was from embarrassment. Mostly it was from her imaginative reviews of the Bronte sisters' books. If she found that much sex in their works, it must be because she fantasied sex in everything she read. He wondered if she could find some in Aristotle.

He said, "No, I'm just surprised you're so well-read. I know a lot of women who don't read at all."

"I bet you know a lot of women, whether they read or not," she said, looking him up and down with the evident approval. "I bet you're a pretty hot bedroom jockey."

That embarrassed him so much, he didn't know what to say or where to look. She gave him a wide grin.

"If you're not, you might be by the time you get out of here. I could teach you more than any of them professors over at the school." She went out, saying over her shoulder, "Supper at six sharp."

Her parting words before the supper announcement not only flabbergasted him; they also gave him an erection, a phenomenon of increasing frequency during the past year. He didn't know whether to take what she had said as an invitation or merely as an earthy joke. If the former, he had every intention of accepting the invitation, despite her being double his age. Ever since his meeting with Kitty at the Lucky Tiger in Santa Barbara, he had periodically fantasied about what it would have been like if he had accepted her invitation to go upstairs. He had only a general idea because he was still a virgin, a state he had been ready to relinquish for some time.

At supper he met his twelve fellow boarding-house guests. All the rooms but one on the third floor were filled. The two seniors, three juniors and two sophomores were on the second floor, and freshmen occupied five of the six rooms on the top floor. The students all knew who he was, and treated him with a deference he found as embarrassing as the earthy comments made by his landlady while he was unpacking.

During the following days he encountered the same deference at school, not only from his fellow students but even from some of his professors. He entirely escaped the traditional hazing that the other freshmen had to suffer, but instead of feeling relief, his exclusion made him uncomfortable. Because he was essentially good-natured, and also quite shy, before long he began to be accepted as an equal, both on campus and at the house.

While he was on friendly terms with all the students at the house, the two seniors became his particular friends because they were closest to his intellectual level. Byron Moody was a lanky, stoop-shouldered, studious twenty-year-old majoring in Greek and Latin and planning to become a college professor. His father ran a hardware store in Bishop, in eastern California. Twenty-one-year-old Emilio Pizzaro, nicknamed Hank, a suave, handsome ladies' man, was from an ancient Spanish family that owned a huge land grant ranch in the San Jaoquin Valley.

Though from the richest family of the three, he had the smallest spending allowance because his father believed that austerity bred character. Nevertheless, he had plenty of money because of his skill with cards. Unknown to his father, he had accumulated a thousand-dollar poker stake during his three years of school at Oakland, which he used to back his play with other wealthy students on more generous allowances. He needed the income, since his main social activity other than poker was lavishing money on girls. Hank was majoring in literature and was taking the easiest courses he could get.

Nate was not yet majoring in anything as the first two years at the university were general, with mostly required courses, and he would not have to choose a major until his junior year. One of his required courses was a foreign language. He chose French.

Hank Pizzaro taught Nate poker. Nate already knew the basic rules from playing penny ante with childhood friends, but what Hank taught him was the vastly different game of saloons and gambling houses, table stakes. Hank had already taught Byron Moody, when they were roommates at Oakland. Byron had accepted the tutoring only as a mental exercise, for he never gambled. However, he was willing to assist in Nate's training, and the three of them spent many hours during the first two weeks of school playing three-handed draw for valueless chips while Hank lectured on each hand.

At the first session Hank said, ''The rules for winning at either table stakes or no-limit are simple. First, play with amateurs. Every duffer thinks he's the world's best poker player because being good at poker is supposed to be a symbol of manhood, like getting clap. So it's easy to shear the sheep. But recognize your limitations, and never sit in a game with players better than you, or even equal to you.

Second, wait for cinch hands. I never open a pair unless it's aces, nor do I call an open with less. Keep in mind that one good pot during the whole game can make you a winner, and it doesn't cost anything but the ante to pitch in your cards without calling the first bet. The average player figures he's risking only a dollar by drawing to a small pair, and that maybe he'll hit three of a kind, but when the game runs two hundred hands, those tossed-away single dollars add up. Third, bluff early in the game and hope to get caught. If you aren't, keep bluffing till you do get caught.''

''Why?'' Nate asked.

''Because if everybody thinks you're only a cinch player, your big bets will never be called. Once you're caught, you'll get calls the rest of the game, but you never again bet anything except cinch hands. Fourth, know every cardsharp trick there is.''

Nate was aghast. ''I would never cheat.''

''Neither would I, but if you don't know how to second-card or stack a deck, how you going to tell when you're being cheated?''

Whereupon he showed Nate every crooked technique cardsharps used, from deck-marking to mirror rings which reflected the value of each card to the dealer as it came off the deck. ''You don't have to worry about such stuff in on-campus games,'' Hank said. ''But if you ever walk into a strange game, you better be able to recognize the signs, or you could end up the lamb instead of the shearer.''

At the end of his two-week training period, Hank took Nate to one of the student games he played in, and Nate was astonished at how well his few simple rules worked. Despite an evening-long run of poor cards that allowed him to win only two pots out of approximately two-hundred, he won thirty dollars. He didn't play often after that, because he never neglected homework for a game, but when he did, he either won a goodly amount or lost very little.

At the evening meal on October fifteenth, which fell on a Wednesday, the dessert Lois Sherman brought out was a cake with seventeen flaming candles. As she set it before Nate, he said, "How did you know it's my birthday?"

"I know all my boys' birthdays. Nobody in this house will ever have a birthday pass uncelebrated."

"How do you find them out?" Byron Moody asked.

"From the university registrar."

Nate was touched that the landlady would go to so much trouble. Later that night he was even more touched when she awakened him from sound sleep by lighting the lamp on his writing desk. His eyes popped open, he rolled onto his back and regarded her with anticipation as she approached the bed. She was wearing a long bathrobe and was barefoot.

Sitting on the side of the bed, she said, "Only twenty minutes of your birthday is left, so I brought you a present."

"What?"

"Me."

She bent down, enveloped his lips with hers and thrust her tongue into his mouth. He couldn't put his arms around her because they were pinned beneath the covers. He just lay there and succumbed to the kiss.

After a long time she sat up and looked at the center of the bed. The blanket there resembled a tepee for dolls. She put her hand on the tentpole and said, "Umm."

Standing, she stripped off her robe, tossed it onto the easy chair and smiled down at him. Her plump body was smooth all over, her large breasts firm, and despite her plumpness she was shapley. What excited him even more than her nakedness was the expression in her slanting, doelike eyes. They made him think of a hind in heat.

The nights were not yet chill, and he had been sleeping nude beneath only a sheet and one thin blanket. Lois whipped both over the foot of the bed.

"My," she said, examining him. "Looks like I'm the one getting the present."

Kneeling on the bed, she began to kiss him all over, in places using her tongue. When he was groaning with excitement, she suddenly mounted him and pierced herself clear to his scrotum.

For the next few minutes he felt as though he were being ridden by an insatiable demon as she gasped and pushed and squealed and showered his face and lips with kisses. Then she let out a high-pitched scream and her body convulsed in a series of gradually lessening spasms.

After lying quietly atop him for a few moments, she said, "Do me some more."

Do what some more? he thought. All he had done so far was lie still and hang on to her buttocks to keep her from flying off into space.

As though reading his mind, she said, "Then I'll do you some more."

She sat erect, raised herself a few inches, sank back down again, said, "Ah," and went into a second demoniac dance ending in another convulsion. Twice more after that she climaxed before he finally exploded within her. She lay atop him until he went soft, then rolled over, reached down to pull the covers over both of them and nestled in his arms. The still-burning desk lamp brightly illuminated the room. With her face so close, he could see small crow's-feet beginning to form at the corners of her eyes.

"Like your birthday present?" she asked.

"Loved it."

"First time?"

"Was I that raw?"

"You were like Casanova, but diddling isn't a learned skill; it's a natural talent. The talent can be honed, though. I plan to give you a complete course in advanced diddling."

"I look forward to it."

"It was the first time, wasn't it?"

"Is that important?" he asked.

"Not vital, but they say a man never forgets his first woman, and I'd like to be remembered."

"I can guarantee that."

She started to run her fingers through his thick hair, then tensed. "What's the matter with your ear?"

He had long since adjusted to his loss, and while he didn't flaunt it and combed his hair to conceal it from general view, he wasn't ashamed of it. He said, "It's at home, attached to a watch."

She sat up, pushed aside the hair on the right side of his head and looked. "You don't have any."

"Disgust you?" he asked.

She bent to kiss the place his ear had been. "You poor darling. What happened to it?"

"Cole Gannon cut it off when I was twelve."

"My God, is that why you went after him?"

"No, a couple of other reasons. I asked if it disgusted you."

"I didn't answer because it's a stupid question. Don't ever ask it again."

"Want to see the one I still have?" he asked, turning his head.

After pushing aside his hair, she bent to kiss his good ear. "It's pretty enough for both."

Lying down, she again snuggled against him. A few

minutes later she felt downward with an exploring hand. "My God, you're ready again so soon?"

Kicking off the covers, he rolled onto his back.

"This time you do the work," she said, pulling him over on top of her.

CHAPTER VII

Over the Christmas holiday Nate went home, but during the four-day mid-semester break in early February there wasn't enough time. There was insufficient time for Byron Moody to go all the way across the state to Bishop, too. The San Jaoquin Valley, though, was only a ferry ride and a short train ride away. Hank Pizzaro invited both home with him. Byron accepted, but Nate, visualizing a four-day frolic with Lois in the near empty house, declined with thanks.

At the last minute Nate discovered there would be no frolicking. He had borrowed the landlady's barouche to take his two friends to the Oakland ferry. As they were loading Hank and Byron's luggage, Lois returned from her daily walk to the post office.

"Glad I caught you," she said to Nate. "I just got a delayed letter, mailed a week ago from only across the bay. My brother and his family are arriving on the same ferry Hank and Byron are taking. You can bring them back. Try to be subservient."

"Why?"

"I told you he was rich. He likes people to kowtow."

Nate contemplated changing his mind and going along with Hank and Byron, but the time it would take him to pack might make them miss the ferry, and he would have to ask Lois to drive them, so the reason for his change of mind would be too obvious.

He said, "What's your brother's name?"

"Georges Delavigne."

"Delavigne was your maiden name?"

"Yes."

"I knew you were French," he said.

She made a face at him. "His wife's name is Georgia. You won't have trouble spotting them because he's six-feet-four and skinny, and Georgia's a four-foot-ten butterball." As he climbed up on the high driver's seat and took the reins, she said in afterthought, "My niece's name is Denise."

They reached the dock at the Oakland Inner Harbor fifteen minutes before the ferry docked and a half hour before it was due to leave again.

The Delavignes were among the last off. Nate instantly recognized them from Lois' description. He gave them only a brief glance, as his attention was centered on the girl with them. Slim and brown-eyed and so blonde her hair was nearly white, his first thought was that she was beautiful, but he scratched that as insufficiently descriptive. She was a goddess.

Hank Pizzaro said, "Jesus, if that's the landlady's niece, the trip is off, Byron."

"Get aboard the ferry," Nate said. "I saw her first."

He went over to the trio and said to the man, "Your sister sent me to pick you up, Mr. Delavigne. I'm Nate Cook."

Setting down the large suitcase he was carrying, Delavigne

offered his hand and said, "Sis wrote of you. I'm honored to meet the famous captor of the Gannon bunch." Indicating the butterball woman and the girl with him, he said, "My wife Georgia and my daughter Denise."

Nate must have acknowledged his introduction to the girl's mother, although later he couldn't recall saying a word to her. He was too numbed by the lovely smile the blonde goddess gave him. She was about his age, he guessed, and had averaged out between her father's tallness and her mother's shortness to a perfect five-feet-four.

"The famous Sir Nate," she said. "Slayer of dragons."

All he could manage in reply was an adoring look that made her brown eyes dance with amusement. Naturally, she was used to adoring looks, he thought, humbly accepting what he took to be ridicule as proper punishment for gawking at a goddess.

Denise was looking beyond him with a curious expression on her face. Turning, Nate found Hank and Byron standing there with their bags at their feet, openly admiring the girl.

"Excuse me a minute," he said to Denise. "I have to help these fellows aboard."

Picking up both bags, he headed for the gangplank. Hank and Byron had no choice but to follow him. Nate dropped the bags on deck and said, "Have a good trip, gentlemen."

"I hope she gives you crabs," Hank said.

Nate went back down the gangplank and directed the three visitors to the barouche. After setting the suitcase on the seat facing rearward, so that Mr. and Mrs. Delavigne could ride facing forward, and helping them in, he recovered his voice enough to ask Denise if she would like to ride up with him.

"Love it," she said, agilely scrambling up onto the high seat before he could offer to help.

Jumping up beside her, he slapped the reins on the horses' backs.

As they drove off, he examined her from the sides of his eyes. She was as lovely in profile as from the front. Against the February chill she wore a cloth coat over a blue-and-white checkered dress, and her gleaming silvery hair was tied into a ponytail with a blue ribbon.

The folding top of the barouche was up, cutting off her parents' view of them and leaving them practically alone. He tried to think of something to say, but was unable to come up with anything that could possibly interest her. With distress he contemplated the hour's drive in dead silence.

She delighted him by breaking the silence. "Aunt Lois wrote that you attend the university."

"Yes."

"What year?"

"Just a freshman."

"You look older," she said, which at his age was flattering.

"I'm only seventeen."

"I will be in May. I'm a freshman, too."

"Where?"

"The Notre Dame Junior College for Women at Belmont."

"Where is that?"

"Twenty miles south of San Francisco. Haven't you heard of Notre Dame?"

"Only the men's school in Indiana."

"My school is older than yours by a year. We opened in 1868."

Conversation lapsed and he frantically tried to think of

some way to renew it. Finally he had an inspiration. "Is your school Catholic?"

She gave him an amused sidelong glance. "Notre Dame? What did you think, Buddhist?"

"I'm Catholic, too."

"My parents are only nominal Catholics," she said. "Father sent me there because it's the only women's school nearby."

He was overjoyed that they had something in common. "I'm nominal, too, although my mother never misses mass. My father used to joke that a nominal Catholic was one who believed everyone else should regularly attend mass."

"That's my father and mother both. I can't remember when they last went. I attend every day."

"I've been thinking of doing that," he said, instantly becoming devout.

"We have to at school. I wish I could get out of it. Karl Marx says religion is the opiate of the people."

Nate had never before met a girl who thought of things more serious than a new dress. He said, "Are you a Communist?"

"No, they want to blow up people. I'm thinking of becoming an agnostic, though."

He underwent another religious conversation. "I've been thinking of becoming one, too."

There was another long silence as he tried to think of something to say. Finally he said, "Lois—your aunt says your father is a lawyer and a director of the Southern Pacific."

"Yes."

"I suppose you live on Nob Hill."

"Yes. What does your father do?"

"He's dead."

"Oh, I'm sorry. I read that in the paper when they wrote about you and the Gannon gang. They killed him, didn't they?"

"Yes, on my twelfth birthday. He was a doctor."

By now he had conquered his shyness enough to be able to converse without anxiety. He asked what courses she was taking, and she said music and art and Spanish and literature and history, and religion, of course. She said she had just read *Jane Eyre*, which reminded him of Lois, which in turn gave him a guilty feeling. He wondered if, should he and Denise ever marry, having copulated with her aunt would legally constitute incest.

By the time they reached Berkeley, he was deeply in love, and she was chatting so antimately that he was sure she at least liked him.

Lois assigned her brother and sister-in-law to the guest room and moved Denise in with her. Nate was more relieved than disappointed by that, relieved because he would be unable to visit his landlady's room in the middle of the night, as he was expected to periodically, and because he assumed she wouldn't visit his. His room being between hers and the guest room, and her performance in bed involving considerable noise, he didn't see how she could expect to get together while the guests were there. That relieved him further, because he had resolved to stop making love to her. He was going to save what purity he had left for Denise.

What disappointed him about the arrangement was that Denise was so heavily chaperoned and he would have difficulty getting her alone.

The mid-term break was from Wednesday, February fourth, through Sunday the eighth. Aside from Nate, only three boarding-house residents were still in town, all nineteen-year-old juniors on the second floor. All three tried to monopolize Denise during Wednesday night supper, and all three simultaneously offered to show her around the university the next day.

Nate was mentally kicking himself for not having thought of that before dinner, when Denise surprised and delighted him by saying, "Sorry, gentlemen, but Mr. Cook has all my time tied up while I am here."

When he showed her the campus the next morning, it was more of a peripatetic conversation than a tour, because their attention was too focused on each other to get in any sightseeing. Hand in hand, they wandered all over the campus without him pointing out a single landmark.

By the time they started back to the boarding house, they not only knew each other's history back to birth, but also how they felt on all important subjects. Nate discovered that religion was not the only thing on which she held radical views. She was also a woman suffragist and a believer in sexual equality.

"You men make all the rules," she said. "You've probably diddled a hundred girls, but if we got married, you would expect me to be chaste."

"Are we going to get married?" he asked, delighted.

"I was just using that as an example."

"Oh. I haven't diddled any hundred girls."

"Fifty?"

"What makes you think I've diddled any? I've been saving myself for you."

"Hah," she said.

It was only ten in the morning when they got back to the boarding house. Nate steered her along the alley and they went in the back way. No one was in either the summer kitchen or the main one. They stood looking at each other in the main kitchen, and suddenly he had her in his arms.

Their first kiss lasted a long time. When it finally

ended, he kept his arms about her and said, "I fell in love with you when I saw you walking down the gangplank."

"You're too impetuous," she said. "I didn't fall in love with you until we were halfway here."

"Before we go any farther, I have to show you something that may make you fall out of love again."

Looking up at him, she said, "Because it isn't very big?"

It took him a moment to get that, and he burst out laughing. Then he turned the right side of his head to her and pushed aside his hair.

"Your ear is gone," she said, fingering the scar.

He faced her again. "Since I was twelve."

She pushed back his hair on the other side. "This one is in place. You thought I might stop loving you over a silly ear?"

"Not really. I just wanted you to see."

"How did it happen?" she asked.

"Cole Gannon cut it off the night he killed my father. Do you think your father will object?"

"To what?"

"To us getting married."

"We can't get married."

"What?" he said, astounded.

"I mean now. I have another year of school and you have three."

He looked stunned. "Wait three whole years?"

"We don't necessarily have to wait."

"You mean wed secretly?"

"No, no. I want a big church wedding, with bridesmaids and everything."

"I thought you were thinking of becoming an agnostic."

She stood on tiptie to kiss his chin. "It has nothing to do with religion, silly. Every girl wants a church wedding."

"Then what do you mean, we don't have to wait?"

"To—you know what I mean."

"To diddle?"

"Don't be crude, darling."

"I'll try to phrase it more delicately. Make love?"

"That's what I meant."

This had an instant physical effect, apparent to her because she was leaning against him. Backing from his arms, she said, "I didn't mean right now, here in the kitchen."

He took her hand and tried to pull her toward the door into the hall, but she held back.

"Where are you going?" she asked.

"My room."

"No, someone might hear us."

His gaze touched the door to the back stairs off the kitchen, and he pulled her that way.

"Now what?" she said, still holding back.

"Nobody will bother us on the third floor. All the tenants are gone."

She let him pull her that way.

Lois came into the kitchen and looked at the clock. It was half past ten. Now would be a good time to change sheets, she thought, as Nate was showing Denise around the university, Georges and Georgia were making a tour of the village, the three boys on the second floor were off somewhere, and probably none of them would be back before noon. She filled her wash basket with folded clean sheets and carried it up the rear stairs.

On the third floor she pulled the bottom sheets from all five of the freshmen's beds, put the top ones on the bottoms and spread fresh sheets on top. She was starting downstairs again when she heard a feminine voice say from the unused sixth bedroom, "Oh God, you're going to make me do it again."

Her immediate thought was that one of the juniors had sneaked a girl into the house—a violation of house rules, but not a breach she took too seriously. Setting down the basket, she went over to press her ear to the door.

The feminie voice rose to a higher pitch. "You're doing it! You're making me come again!"

This time, recognizing the voice of her niece, she threw open the door. Although the knob banged against the inner wall, the naked couple on the bed was too engrossed to hear it. Denise, her thighs raised so high that they pressed against her breasts, was squealing like a female cat being raped by a tom, and Nate's body was shuddering in the throes of orgasm.

Lois stood in the open doorway, staring, while the spasms subsided. Neither lover noticed her. Denise gave Nate a gentle kiss and said, "I love you."

"I love you, too," he said.

He was pushing himself to his knees when the eyes of both jumped to the doorway and Lois said, "Oh my God, you popped her cherry."

Nate looked down at his shrinking penis, saw it was bright red, climbed off the bed and dug a handkerchief from a pocket of the trousers draped across the dresser. Denise sat up and, swinging to face her aunt, crouched on her knees; with her bare breasts hidden by one arm across them and her crotch by the other hand, she gazed at her aunt in fear.

"You're dripping on my blanket," Lois said. "Get off of there."

Denise scrambled from the bed and stood crouched over, still trying to hide her naked breasts and crotch.

"Don't move," Lois said, running from the room.

Denise gave Nate a frightened look. He had finished wiping away the blood and was starting to dress. He said, "The worst they can do is make us get married."

Lois came back carrying a pitcher and a towel from one of the other rooms. Setting the pitcher on the floor, she lay the room's wash basin next to it and poured water into it.

"Squat over this and wash yourself," she said. "And stop holding your arms in that silly way. Think that will keep me from seeing you're bare-ass naked?"

Denise squatted over the basin. When the water turned bright red, Lois emptied it into the room's slop jar and refilled the basin. It took another basinful after that before the bleeding stopped. Meantime, Nate had finished dressing.

As Denise dried herself with the towel, Lois said to Nate, "Got anything to say, lover boy?"

"We love each other," he said. "We want to marry."

"Don't be idiotic. You've known each other twenty-four hours and she's only sixteen."

"I'm only seventeen."

Denise was hurriedly dressing. "Are you going to tell my father, Aunt Lois?"

Lois looked at her. "What do you think he'd do?"

"I don't know. Make us get married?"

Her aunt gave her head a slow shake. "More likely shoot lover boy and put you in a chastity belt."

Denise turned pale. "Please don't tell, Aunt Lois."

"Whether I do or not depends on your reaction to some rules I'm going to lay down."

Denise looked so relieved that for a moment her aunt thought she was going to run over and kiss her. But she merely said, "I'll do anything you say, Aunt Lois."

Lois waited until she was dressed before setting down the rules. Then she said, "First, I want a promise from both of you that this won't happen again."

"I promise," Denise said.

Lois looked at Nate. He said, "We won't come up here again."

"You won't do it anywhere."

"All right, nowhere in the house."

The landlady glared at him. "Don't push me, Nate. Your promise is that it won't happen anywhere—not in some other building, not outdoors, not on the moon. Otherwise we'll go downstairs right now and have a conference with Denise's parents."

"I promise," he said.

"Second, I don't want to hear any more talk about marriage. Denise, I want your guarantee that you won't run off somewhere and get married."

"Ever, Aunt Lois?"

"Until you're eighteen."

"All right, Aunt Lois. We weren't planning to marry before then anyway."

"Unless you show up pregnant," Lois said. "In which case we'll reopen discussion."

When neither said anything to that, Lois turned to Nate. "The third condition I will tell you privately later on."

"Why can't I hear it?" Denise asked.

"Be glad I'm being so lenient, girl. I don't want you to ask afterward, and Nate, I don't want you to tell her. Do I have both your promises?"

Nate had an idea that whatever it was, he wouldn't want Denise to know anyway. "You have mine," he said.

"All right, Aunt Lois."

Since Lois hadn't forbidden them to be together, after lunch Nate and Denise took another walk. They sat under a tree on campus and talked all afternoon, planning their future.

"I don't want to wait three years to get married," he said.

"Daddy would never permit it now, darling."

"I'm not talking about now. Did you say your birthday's in May?"

"May sixteenth."

"Then you'll be eighteen when you graduate from Notre Dame, and I'll be nearly nineteen. We can get married then."

"How about your schooling?"

"Nothing says you have to be single to attend the university. We'll rent a cottage here."

Her eyes lighted. "Even if Daddy objected, which he couldn't possibly to such a fine catch, I won't need his permission after I'm eighteen."

"Then you will?"

"Of course."

He looked around to see if anyone was in sight, saw no one and leaned over to kiss her.

They plotted how they could see each other again after school resumed. There was no way they could get together by his coming to Belmont, she said, because students were too heavily chaperoned by the nuns. But he could visit her in San Francisco over Easter vacation.

"Better tell Aunt Lois you're going home over Easter," she said. "Will you write me?"

"Of course."

She gave him both her school and home addresses.

Again they entered the boarding house by the back door. They paused in the summer kitchen when they heard voices from the main kitchen. Denise squeezed Nate's hand in fright when she realized it was Lois and her father talking.

"You know I appreciate what you've done for me,

Georges," Lois said. "But do you have to keep rubbing it
in?"

"I'm merely trying to give you some business advice,
Sis. You have no financial sense. If you did, you would
have married Max Golden instead of that penniless
fisherman."

"I couldn't stand Max Golden."

"That's water over the dam," Denise's father said.
"The present issue is the way you run this house. How do
you expect to make a profit when you serve the ridicu-
lously costly sort of meal you did last night?"

"I don't know how to cook cheap."

"Learn, or you'll never be able to pay back what you
borrowed."

"Borrowed?" Lois said.

"Did you think it was a gift? Of course, I'll never press
you, and there will be no interest, but I certainly expect
eventual repayment."

Since the conversation didn't concern them, Nate was
not interested in eavesdropping further. He steered Denise
outside and around to the front door. As they went in, she
said, "I wish Daddy wasn't such a Shylock. He's rich and
poor Aunt Lois has nothing."

As Nate was washing up for supper, Lois stuck her head
in his room and said, "Meet me in the kitchen after
everyone else is in bed."

"All right," he said.

Despite the overheard conversation in the kitchen, Nate
could detect no lessening of quality in that night's supper.
Afterward everyone sat in the parlor talking. At ten o'clock
Denise's parents went to bed, and her father suggested it
was time for her to go too. That left Nate, the three juniors
and the landlady. When Lois announced she was going to

bed, Nate went to his room also. A few minutes later he heard the three juniors go upstairs.

Shortly after that there was a light rap on his door. When he opened it, no one was there, but he saw a dim light coming from the kitchen. The rest of the house was dark.

Lois stood in the kitchen, barefoot and in her bathrobe, holding a lighted candle. "Take off your boots," she said.

"Why?"

"So the boys on the second floor don't hear us when we pass the landing."

"We don't have to go upstairs for you to tell me what you have to say."

"That's true, but we have to go upstairs afterward. What I have to say is that the incident this morning is not going to change our relationship."

"Yes, it is," he said. "I love Denise. I'm sorry, Lois, but we're not going to do that anymore."

She moved past him toward the hall.

"Where are you going?" he asked.

Pausing in the doorway, she said, "First to waken Denise and tell her how many times you and I have been to bed together. Then to waken my brother and tell him what happened this morning."

He gazed at her indignantly. "You would stoop to blackmail?"

"I doubt that anything else will work." Turning, she continued into the hall.

"Lois."

Coming back to the doorway, she said, "Yes?"

He sat on a kitchen chair and began to remove his boots.

CHAPTER VIII

After the Delavignes returned to San Francisco, Nate had a heart-to-heart talk with his landlady. He told her that he liked her a lot, which was true, and that he appreciated her keeping silent about him and Denise, and that he enjoyed making love to her, but that in good conscience he couldn't continue because he loved Denise and making love to any other woman made him feel he was betraying that love. Lois, who was really quite amiable and had resorted to blackmail only because she was also quite horny, understood and stopped pressing herself upon him. Actually, she seemed rather touched by his fidelity.

Two nights after this conversation Nate heard squeals of ecstasy coming from the bedroom next door. They kept him awake for a long time, and when they finally ceased, he got up and cracked open his door and stood waiting. After several minutes Hank Pizzaro, wearing a bathrobe and carrying a lighted candle, emerged from Lois's room. He went past Nate's door toward the front stairs.

Two days after that Lois moved Nate to the second

floor, into the room where Hank had been sleeping, and moved Hank into Nate's vacated room.

Berkeley
February 15, 1874

My darling Denise:

The short time we have been parted has dragged like aeons. You are on my mind night and day. I can hardly wait for Easter vacation, so that I can again hold your beautiful body in my arms. I plan to kiss you all over, from your perfect little nose to your cute little toes.

Write instantly, so that I may at least endure the days by carrying your words next to my heart.

All is well with me. I live to see you again.

All my love,
Nate

Belmont
February 25, 1874

My dearest Nate:

Your first letter arrived today, and already I have read it ten times. Such a short letter. I want to know what you do each minute, how many times a day you think of me, who you talk to, what you learn in class, everything that happens from the time you waken until you go to sleep.

I have some slightly bad, but not disastrous news. You cannot come to visit me at home over Easter vacation. When I told my parents I had invited you, Daddy quite definitely put the kibosh on it. At first I was terrified that Aunt Lois had told on us, but his reaction would have been stronger if she had. I think he just noticed how we looked at each other, which, in retrospect, I suppose was like a couple of lovesick sheep, and he thinks I am too young to be that serious, particularly with a boy of whom he doesn't entirely approve.

Let me hasten to assure you that he likes you, as who wouldn't, and admires your brave capture of the Gannon gang. He just doesn't approve of you for me. I couldn't pin him down as to exactly why, but he seems to think you possess some kind of killer instinct. When I told him you were the kindest, gentlest person I had ever known, he said, "The boy is a bounty hunter, Denise, and bounty hunters are not gentle." It did no good to explain that you had not gone after the Gannon brothers for the bounty, but for what they had done to your father and mother. He just kept saying that it was not normal for one so young to wipe out five men in a gunfight with such deadly efficiency.

Although he didn't mention it, I suspect money is a factor too. Daddy has never forgiven Aunt Lois for not marrying a rich man he had picked out for her, and I suppose he wants me to marry someone rich, too.

Not only is his judgment faulty, so is what he considers a solution to the problem. He thinks that by parental decree he can keep us apart.

The situation requires alternate planning. Between now and Easter vacation you must take the ferry over to San Francisco, arrange some place to stay, then write me where you will be. I will not be able to see you on Easter Sunday because I could not possibly get away, but we can be together all day long on other days. Daddy will be at his office, and he never gets home before six. Mother is no problem. She will believe whatever I tell her, that I am going shopping, going to visit a girl friend, or even going to mass. We will be unable to be together evenings, but we can make up for that with love-filled mornings and afternoons.

Write as soon as you have made arrangements.

All my love forever,
Denise

The following weekend Nate ferried over to San Francisco. He rented a hansom to take him to Nob Hill, had it drop him in front of Grace Cathedral, and walked to Taylor and Sacramento to look at Denise's home. It was an elegant two-story house fronted by a tall wrought-iron fence.

Walking back down the hill, he explored the area on all sides for hotels or rooming houses. In this exclusive residential area there were none, but three blocks south of Nob Hill, on Sutter Street, he saw a FOR LET sign on a small cottage. The sign gave an address on Post, an additional block south, to make inquiry.

When he had seen the inside of the cottage and learned that it rented furnished for twenty-five dollars a month, he rented it for two months, which would more than go through Easter vacation.

As soon as he got home Sunday evening, he wrote Denise.

Berkeley
March 2, 1874

Darling:

I have rented a nice little furnished cottage only four blocks from your house, at the northeast corner of Sutter and Jones. You will love it. It is white with green trim and has a white picket fence. There are only three rooms, but the important one, the bedroom, has a large feather bed into which we can sink together.

School here lets out on the Thursday before Easter and resumes the Thursday after. I plan to take the ferry over Wednesday night, and if your schedule is the same, hope to see you on Thursday morning.

All my love,
Nate

Denise's reply said her schedule was the same as his, and he could expect her about ten on the Thursday morning before Easter. The letter gave him such an erection, he almost wished he hadn't been so noble with his landlady.

When he left on Easter vacation, Nate didn't have to make a point of convincing Lois he was going back to San Buenaventura as she didn't express any interest in his plans. He overheard her questioning Hank Pizzaro in detail about how he expected to spend his vacation, though.

Hank was going home, this time alone because Byron Moody had time to get back to Bishop. Hank and Nate rode over on the ferry together. Nate had not confided his real plans to his friend, and Hank assumed he was going home. They parted at the dock, Hank taking a hansom to the railroad depot and Nate taking one to his cottage.

Thursday morning Nate rose early and went shopping for a supply of food. When he returned and finished stowing it away, he bathed and dressed in his best clothes. Then he waited.

Denise never appeared. He was afraid to leave the cottage for fear she would come while he was gone, but when it grew dark, he knew she wouldn't, and walked up the hill to look at her house.

There were lights on the first floor. She must have arrived home too late to leave the house that day, he thought, and returned to the cottage.

Denise failed to appear on Friday, too. Again he waited all day, afraid to leave, and again climbed Nob Hill after dark. Again, after gazing at the lighted first floor of the house for a time, he returned to the cottage.

When Denise had not appeared by noon Saturday, Nate walked up the hill, opened the wrought-iron gate, mounted the porch steps and knocked on the front door. A tall, dignified-looking Negro in livery opened it.

"Is Miss Delavigne in?" he asked.

"No, sir, the Delavignes are in St. Louis over Easter, visiting Mrs. Delavigne's parents."

Nate felt his heart failing. "When are they expected back?"

"Not until late next Thursday, sir, just in time to drive Miss Denise back to school. Would you like to leave a message?"

"It isn't important," Nate said, turning and almost reeling down the steps.

He spent his entire Easter vacation at the cottage, in the hope that something would cause the Delavignes to return early. They didn't. Thursday afternoon he climbed the hill again and stood across the street from the house, hoping for at least a glimpse of Denise when she arrived home. At five o'clock he couldn't stand it anymore. Again he opened the wrought-iron gate, mounted the steps and knocked. The liveried Negro again answered.

"Have the Delavignes returned from St. Louis yet?" he asked.

"Yes, sir, long ago. Mr. Delavigne had the coachman

meet them at the depot and he and Mrs. Delavigne took
Miss Denise back to school from there.''

"Thank you," Nate said, and tottered down the steps.

The explanation arrived in the mail a week later. Nate
read it before leaving the post office.

Belmont
Thursday night

Dearest Nate:

Disaster has struck. The nuns made one of their
periodic searches of quarters and found all your
letters, even though they were hidden in a hatbox
beneath a hat on my closet shelf. They of course
turned them over to my parents, who accordingly
know all about us: what went on at Berkeley, about
your cottage, and our plot to meet there. The reason
I never appeared is obvious.

If there was any hope of accomplishing it, I would
ask you to come here some weekend and would
sneak out my window to meet you, even though it is
on the second floor. But I am under such tight
restriction that there is no chance of us seeing each
other until the end of the school year. I am allowed
off the grounds only when accompanied by a proctor,
and I have been moved in with one of the nuns,
where I sleep on a cot only feet from her bed.

Your letters will not be delivered to me, and all
other letters will be opened and read before I can have
them. My letters out will be similarly censored. I will
continue to write you when I can, and have the same
girl who is mailing this for me smuggle my future
letters out. There is no point in your writing me again,
though, because your letters will go to my father.

In the event I can get no more letters out, let us lay plans for this summer right now. School here lets out on Friday, June 5th. By then perhaps my parents will think that our affair has been effectively killed. My father is suspicious by nature, though, perhaps because of his profession, and I am sure he will check with my Aunt Lois as to what your plans are when school ends. If you can convince her that the affair *is* over, and that you plan to return directly home, she will relay that on to Daddy and it should ease his suspicions.

Keep the cottage rented. I am sure that once I get home, my restrictions will not be as severe as here, and they may even be entirely lifted. I will come to the cottage at absolutely the first minute I can.

Incidentally, my reference to our relationship as an "affair" reflects only my parents' view of it. I am sure you know I regard it as an enduring love greater than Antony and Cleopatra's, greater than Romeo and Juliet's, greater than any in history.

> My total love forever,
> Denise

Nate's first thought was that he should be unable to send Denise a present for her birthday in May, or even a birthday greeting. His second was that if her father was as suspicious as Denise said, he probably wouldn't be content with merely writing his sister about Nate. His legal mind would tell him to check whether Nate still rented the cottage. He knew of it, including its location, because he had read all Nate's letters.

Instead of going upstairs when he got back to the boarding house, Nate went up to his former room, where he found Hank Pizzaro studying at his desk.

"I need a favor, Hank," he said.

"You have it, my friend."

"Could you go over to San Francisco with me Saturday?"

"That sounds more like fun than a favor. Sure."

"Not for carousing," Nate said. "I have a cottage rented until the end of this month. I want to keep it, but not under my own name. I'll tell the landlord I don't want to renew, and then, after I leave, you show up and rent it for the whole coming summer. I'll give you the money to pay in advance."

"Sounds conspiratorial," the handsome Spaniard said. "Do I rent it under my own name?"

"No, make one up."

"How about Wolfgang von Clabbertrap?"

"Let's keep it believable."

"All right, how about Jose Lopez? That's the Spanish equivalent of John Smith."

"Better," Nate said.

"Do I get to know what this is about?"

"No."

"I sense a señorita in the woodpile, or perhaps a señora with a jealous husband."

"We'll catch a noon ferry," Nate said as he headed for the door. "I'll arrange for Byron to drive us to Oakland and pick us up in the barouche."

Toward the end of the school year Nate wrote his mother that he would be staying in San Francisco for a while after school ended, and she could write him in care of General Delivery there. His plan was to spend the month of June with Denise, go home to visit his mother for the first two weeks in July, then return to San Francisco to spend the rest of the summer with Denise.

He moved into the cottage on the afternoon of Friday,
June fifth, within hours of the time the university officially
closed for the summer. By that evening he had it thoroughly cleaned and stocked with food and supplies. He
rose early on Saturday, bathed and dressed and waited for
Denise.

By noon he had resigned himself to having to wait until
Monday, assuming she wasn't going to be able to get away
today and sure she couldn't get there on Sunday. Then
there was a knock on the door. When he answered, Denise
fell into his arms.

He hardly noticed what she was wearing. It didn't matter because, two minutes after she arrived, she wasn't
wearing anything. Their first hour together they had no
conversation at all, except for the inarticulate exchange of
hard breathing and moans and cries in the language of
love.

For another hour they lay in each other's arms, bringing
each other up to date on what had happened to them.
Denise told him that her father seemed to believe that what
he kept referring to as her "lewd relationship" with Nate
was permanently over and that she was properly penitent—
beliefs she had deliberately fostered in order to get him to
relax restrictions. While she was still not allowed out at
night, she thought she would have no trouble getting away
from home daytimes, except on Sundays.

When Nate told her how he had arranged things so that, if
her father checked with the owner of the cottage, he would
discover it was now rented by a Spaniard named Jose
Lopez, Denise put her hand to her mouth and said, "I
never thought of that. Of course, he would check. You've
saved us from another disaster."

Nate remembered something then, rolled from bed and

brought her a white-wrapped package that was lying on the dresser. "Belated Happy Birthday," he said.

Sitting up, she tore off the paper. It was a small gold pendant in the shape of a heart on a gold chain. He showed her how it opened, and inside her initials were engraved on one side and his on the other.

"I love it," she said, throwing her arms about his neck. "I will never take it off."

She turned her back so that he could clasp it about her neck. Kissing the back of her neck when it was in place, he said, "Next birthday you'll be eighteen and can do as you please."

Turning, she drew him down alongside of her. "I do as I please now. I just don't let Daddy know about it."

"Suppose I pick you up on graduation day and we get married at the Mission San Buenaventura?"

Pushing aside his hair, she stroked the scar where his ear had been. "What about my big church wedding?"

"You'll need a different groom for that. Your father would never accept me."

"Let me work on him, darling. He might come around. He really loves me, you know, despite being an old pooh." Then she jumped, "What was that?"

She looked down to see what had poked her, said, "Oh," and threw her arms about his neck.

Sunday they couldn't be together at all, but Monday through Saturday of the following week they were together from ten every morning to five every afternoon. Then the honeymoon came to an abrupt end.

Nate had gotten in the habit of going to the post office early, so he could be back before Denise arrived at ten. On Monday, June sixteenth, she arrived to find him packing.

"I have to go home," he said, handing her a letter.

It was from his mother and read:

San Buenaventura
June 12, 1874

Dear Nate:

I have terrible news. Your Uncle Philip was killed
yesterday. A man named Jason Quillan, whom your
uncle sent to prison for stagecoach robbery and murder ten years ago, escaped and came back to San
Buenaventura for revenge. He shot Philip in the back
at Wood's Saloon, just walked in and fired without
warning. Quillan then jumped on his horse and fled
town. A posse is out hunting for him.

Martha and little Phil are both devastated. After
the funeral, when things quiet down, I will invite
them to move in here if they wish.

By the time this reaches you, it will be too late for
you to get here for the funeral, son, but please come
as soon as you can. You are the oldest man in the
family now, and we need you to pull things together.

Love,
Mom

Nate had finished packing his valise while Denise read
the letter. Putting her arms about him, she said, "I'm
sorry."

He gave her a brief kiss. "I'll write you when I'm
coming back."

"How can you, honey?"

"I'll address it to Jane Eyre, General Delivery. You'll
remember that, because you had just read the book the day
we met."

"All right," she said, giving him a more solid kiss than
he had offered her. "I will miss you every minute."

"And I you," he said, but the words sounded perfunctory. There was a glitter in his eyes she had never seen before.

Then she noticed something else she had never seen before. He had a gun belt strapped around his waist.

CHAPTER IX

The mare picked her way up the steep, rock-strewn path with dainty steps. Her rider sat with back erect, his gaze sweeping the countryside in all directions. The summer moon was so bright that he could see for miles, and the only sign of life was some dozing cattle.

Despite being four months short of eighteen, the rider was not a youth. There had been no youth for Jamie McKay. On the Texas range you were either a man or dead by his age. Jamie had been a wrangler since fourteen.

Six feet tall, lean but heavily muscled, he was a hundred ninety pounds of bone and sinew. A flat-topped black hat hanging on his back by its chin strap exposed waveless, shining black hair combed straight back, and his half-Comanche blood gave his exceptionally handsome face the sharp classic cast of a warrior.

At the top of the rise, nestled among alamo, was a line shack where in bad weather riders for the Double-D on stray-gathering patrol could hole up. A saddled horse with its reins hanging stood before the shack, and light showed at the edges of the single shuttered window. Before dismounting, Jamie took one last look around to make sure there were no potential interrupters of his tryst.

Inside the one-room shack a coal-oil lamp burned on the table. Seated on one of the two cots was a dark, shapely, cat-eyed girl of Jamie's age, dressed in denims, a flannel shirt and quarter boots. Jumping to her feet as he came in, she threw her arms about his neck and kissed him passionately.

"I thought you weren't coming," she said when she finally broke the kiss.

"I would have to be dead. Little Doe had some chores for me." He never called his mother anything but her Indian name.

He steered her back to the cot, had her sit, knelt before her and pulled off her boots and socks. She giggled when he kissed the bottom of each foot after he'd bared it. She sat still as he unbuttoned and removed her flannel shirt. She wore nothing under it, and her coconut-sized breasts were firm. He kissed each before pushing her onto her back, then unbuttoning and pulling off her denims. She wore nothing under them either.

Scooting over to the far side of the cot, she lay watching as he undressed. When he was beside her, naked, she put her arms about him, pressed her body to his and said, "Do you love me?"

"Forever."

He kissed her deeply, and moved his hands, and made love to her, and there was no more conversation until they were through. Then, lying quietly in his arms, she asked, "Do you still love me after, or only when you're hard?"

"I love you twenty-four hours a day."

"Will you still love me after I'm married?"

He lay silent for a time before answering. That eventuality sickened him when he thought about it, but it was far enough in the future so that most times he was able to avoid thinking about it. There was no chance of Consuela ever becoming his bride, because Don Miguel Derango would never permit his daughter to wed a penniless half-breed. Someday she would have an arranged marriage into a family as rich as her own.

He said, "You're not even betrothed."

"Father's starting to talk about it."

That upset him so much that he rolled off the cot and began dressing. After watching him for a moment, she rose and started to dress also. There was no further conversation until they got outside. He turned out the lantern and followed her out.

As they stood between the two horses, looking at each other in the moonlight, she said, "I hurt your feelings, didn't I?"

"I don't know why we have to talk about it."

Laying her head against his chest, she said, "We won't again. Forgive me?"

Instantly he thawed. As his arms went about her, he said, "I'll love you always."

Looking up at him, she said, "Do you think I'm pretty?"

"If I could write the beauty of your eyes and in fresh numbers number all your graces, the age to come would say, 'This poet lies, such heavenly touches ne'er touch'd earthly faces.' "

"How sweet. Shelley?"

"Shakespeare."

"You're the strangest cowboy I ever knew," she said. "Most can't even read or write, and you quote Shakespeare."

"His library was my father's only legacy. Sometimes I wish he'd left me the equivalent in money."

She gave him a quick kiss, moved away from him and lifted her horse's reins. "Next Saturday night?"

"Of course."

Mounted, she started down the steep trail to the valley below, and he followed. At the bottom they both stopped.

"Don't get caught," he said.

When she laughed, he said, "What's funny?"

"I've been twice. Father couldn't sleep and was smoking a midnight cigar on the porch when he saw me ride into the barn. I told him I couldn't sleep either, and had felt like a ride. All he said both times was he hoped I had sense enough not to ride too far at night."

She rode east toward the ranch house and he turned south in the direction of El Paso.

Jamie's thoughts turned to his father. They often did when he parted from Consuela. Memories of his father were dim, since he had last seen him when he was six. What memories he had were fond, though, except after being with Consuela, when he brooded on the injustice of not being left rich. Ashley McKay had failed at every commercial enterprise he ever tried. He had been a failed horse trader, a failed cattle breeder and a failed storekeeper before, in 1862, homesteading one-hundred and sixty acres ten miles from the little village of El Paso. That might have been a success if he had stayed to run the ranch, but he sowed the seeds of failure in it, too, by enlisting in the Confederate Army and never returning. In a sense he had even failed as a soldier. Instead of dying gloriously in battle, he had been killed by dysentery.

When he wasn't brooding about being poor, Jamie thought of his father as a success in less tangible ways. He had been adored by his mother, whom Jamie considered the most beautiful woman in Texas, and she possibly was the most beautiful in the thirty-five-year-old range. With no formal schooling Ashley McKay had nevertheless been thoroughly educated. In fact, his devotion to knowledge may have contributed to his financial failures, since he had always been able to find money for books when bills were due and had always been able to find time to read them while customers were waiting. He had left a library of five-hundred volumes, mostly classics, every one of which Jamie had read more than once.

Little Doe was as educated as her husband had been. Illiterate and able to speak only broken English when he took her as a sixteen-year-old bride, he not only taught her to read and write, but also to love reading as much as he did. He had started Jamie reading at four, and by age twelve Jamie had made the first of several voyages through all five hundred volumes of his legacy.

Little Doe's dream was for him to go to college, but on their combined wages of eighty dollars a month, that was as impossible a dream as marrying Consuela.

Little Doe had managed to hold on to the ranch until the war's end, but during the early days of the Reconstruction, thankfully now ended three months ago, she had been driven into bankruptcy by a combination of the carpetbagger government seizing cattle for claimed tax delinquency and by the raids of rustler gangs which proliferated in southwest Texas following the war. Only nine when the war ended, Jamie had been too young to help fight either.

Consuela's father had partially come to their rescue. Don Miguel had nothing to do with the foreclosure, but he bought the ranch at the foreclosure auction. While an autocrat, the owner of the five-hundred-thousand acre Double-D was not a cruel man. He allowed Little Doe and Jamie to continue living in the three-room cabin built by Jamie's father, hired Little Doe as a chuck house cook and hired Jamie, when he reached fourteen, as a wrangler.

Like everyone else in southwest Texas except his two children, Jamie was a little in awe of Consuela's widower father. The origin of the Double-D had been a Spanish land grant to a caballero ancestor clear back in 1682, when the first two Spanish missions in Texas was built near the present site of El Paso, and ever since the Derango family had been the law in the area. Although Don Miguel had been an outspoken Confederate sympathizer, even the carpetbaggers had steered carefully clear of him. While ruining many small ranches throughout the state with their demands, the Union military government had never requisitioned a head of cattle from the Double-D.

Despite poverty, Jamie would probably have been happy enough if it weren't for Don Miguel's two children. Consuela, although he loved her, made him unhappy because she was unattainable. Her twenty-year-old brother Raoul made him unhappy because he was an arrogant bigot who treated most of the Double-D riders like servants and considered Indians dirt.

Thought of Raoul made Jamie rein in the mare and reconsider going into El Paso. It was the Saturday night custom for most Double-D riders to gather at Dowell's Saloon on San Francisco Street. Because of his rendezvous with Consuela, Jamie always arrived late, often past midnight, and by then most of the hands were drunk. Of late Raoul Derango had been growing progressively more obnoxious when he drank, and he had taken to making loud remarks about half-breeds in Jamie's hearing. So far Jamie had ignored him, but it was probably only a matter of time before Raoul made some slighting remark about his mother, which would oblige Jamie to break his head and automatically lose his job.

The risk was too great, Jamie decided, and anyway it was no great joy to walk into a room full of drunks when you were dead sober. Turning the mare, he headed for home.

Jamie's father had built the cabin in a tiny valley, next to a spring. Coming from the south, you couldn't see the cabin until you topped the rise just before the valley. Jamie paused to look down. Tied to the hitching rail before the cabin was a saddled horse. Jamie wondered who could be visiting at this time of night. The incredulous thought occurred to him that perhaps, after all these years, Little Doe had acquired a beau.

He let the mare feel her way down the slope, rode her into the barn, lit a lantern, unsaddled her and gave her a quick rub-down. After turning out the lantern, he walked to the house.

As he opened the door, he heard a drunken male voice say, "You goddamned squaw, will you relax?"

Two fast steps took him to his mother's bedroom door. No lantern burned in the room, but the hanging oil chandelier in the combination kitchen-dining-room-parlor cast plenty of light through the door. Little Doe was on her back on the bed, her wrists lashed with cords whose other ends were tied to the bedposts. Her flannel nightgown was ripped down the front to leave her naked except for her arms. Raoul Derango, still wearing his shirt, was nude from the waist down. He knelt on the bed next to Little Doe, unsuccessfully trying to pry apart her legs.

Jamie took two more steps, gripped the man's neck with his left hand and his balls with his right. Although Raoul was six-feet-two and outweighed him by twenty pounds, Jamie lifted him overhead without great effort and slammed him face-down on the floor.

As Raoul lay there stunned, Jamie whipped the knife from his belt sheath and sliced through Little Doe's bonds. Sitting up, she pulled her torn nightgown about her.

"Don't kill him," she said.

"Why not?"

"Please, Jamie. Even though he's in the wrong, they would hang you."

Raoul had managed to get to a sitting position. He was bent over, clutching his crotch and groaning. His pants and underdrawers lay across a chair, his hat and gun-belt hung from its back, and his boots stood next to it. Gathering everything up, Jamie went to the front door, removed the pistol from its holster to hurl it out into the night, then tossed everything else in the dirt just outside.

When he returned, Little Doe was on her feet and had put on a robe. Her long, gleaming black hair tumbled about her shoulders in disarray, and her usually soft eyes were fearful. Again she said, "Don't kill him."

Raoul painfully climbed to his feet and stood glaring at Jamie. Grabbing him by the back of the neck, Jamie dogtrotted him across the central room and propelled him through the front door so violently that Raoul stumbled to hands and knees in the dust.

When he got up, he gave Jamie another glare before looking around drunkenly. Spotting his clothing in the dust, he picked it up and put it on. As he buckled his gun belt, he said, "Where's my gun?"

"I was afraid you might reach for it and get yourself killed."

Moving forward, he drove a fist into Raoul's stomach. As Raoul gasped and reeled backward, Jamie smashed lightning rights and lefts to his jaw, deliberately pulling both punches so as to inflict pain without knocking the man down.

Raoul made a wild swing, which Jamie easily blocked. Then, with sadistic deliberation, Jamie meted out punishment. The bigger man staggered around, throwing occasional haphazard punches which never landed, while Jamie symstematically converted his body from his waist to his neck into one large bruise. When Raoul finally sank to a seated position in the dirt, whimpering, Jamie stood looking down at him.

After a time Raoul recovered enough to look up with hate and say, "You're fired, breed."

"Maybe. We'll see what Don Miguel says when I take you home."

The seated man considered this before saying, "What do you mean, take me home?"

"I plan to deliver you to your father personally, just to make sure he gets the true story."

After considering some more, Raoul said, "I didn't hurt your mother."

"You tried. 'For as he thinketh in his heart, so is he.' Proverbs 23–7. That makes you a goddamn rapist."

Raoul pushed himself to unsteady feet. Licking his lips, he said, "I'll tell him I got in a fight at Dowell's with somebody passing through."

Jamie made his tone sarcastic. "You mean I'm not fired?"

"Listen, McKay, let's just forget it."

"Sure."

Raoul looked surprised. "You're not going to push it?"

Jamie shook his head.

Raoul looked around, saw the glint of moonlight on his gun a dozen yards away, and painfully limped over to recover it. Holstering it, he came back and struggled aboard his horse.

"Raoul," Jamie said.

"What?"

"If you ever come near my mother again, if I ever hear you even mention her, if you ever call me breed or say anything about half-breeds that I can overhear, I'll kill you on the spot."

Raoul looked away. Without answering, he rode off.

Jamie turned to find his mother standing in the doorway. "Thank you, papoose," she said; it was the first time she had used that childhood endearment in years.

"For what?"

"For not killing him."

They went inside and Jamie set the bar in place across the door. "Are you all right?" he asked.

"He didn't hurt me, just tore my nightgown."

Remembering that, Jamie felt renewed rage rise within him. "You should have let me kill him."

"You would have hanged. I lost your brother. It's enough."

Jamie knew that story, but only a few of its details because Little Doe didn't like to talk about it. All he knew was that his older brother by five minutes had been with their Indian chief grandfather at the Prairie Dog Town Fork massacre, where he had been murdered by the cavalry along with everyone else. Jamie decided to take advantage of Little Doe's opening of the subject to see if he could get answers to some of the questions that had always puzzled him.

"How come Fighting Wolf just had Ash with him and not me?" he asked.

"He didn't know about you."

"My grandfather didn't know about me? How could that be?"

"Please don't open that old wound, Jamie."

"It's natural to want to know about my twin brother, Little Doe. Where was Dad when it happened?"

"Fort Worth. He heard about the massacre on the way home, but didn't know Ash was with my father until he got home. He rode a hundred miles back to Prairie Dog

Town Fork to give your brother a Christian burial, but he couldn't find him."

"You mean he might still be alive?"

"No, there is no chance of that."

"Why not, if Dad couldn't find him?"

"Please, Jamie, let's not talk about it anymore."

Jamie was getting more answers tonight than he ever had before, and didn't want to stop. He said, "Just tell me that and I swear I'll ask nothing more."

Little Doe looked sick. "Your father probably did find him. He just couldn't identify him."

"Why not?"

"The carrion-eaters had been there."

Now Jamie wished he hadn't forced an answer.

CHAPTER X

Raoul Derango stayed in his room all day Sunday and had his meals delivered by the black house cook, whom he warned not to let anyone know he was home—under penalty of being skinned. Since he often stayed the weekend in El Paso, he wasn't missed by either his father or sister.

Monday he had to appear. To delay the meeting with his father, he got up at four in the morning, creaked to the bathhouse and soaked some of the stiffness from his body in a hot tub. Most of Jamie's blows had rained on his body, and while his chest and stomach were a mottled purple and yellow, the only marks on his face were a black eye and a swollen jaw. When he was dressed, most of his injuries were concealed.

Consuela had not yet appeared and Raoul was just finishing breakfast when his father came into the kitchen. Don Miguel was a chunky man of fifty with a round, pleasant face, a mass of curling gray hair and a small mustache.

"Morning, Belinda," he said to the cook. "Morning, son."

Both told him good morning.

Don Miguel seated himself across from Raoul, gave him a startled look and said, "What happened to you?"

"Some drifter at Dowell's. You should see him."

Don Miguel merely grunted. In his youth he had been in his share of fistfights, and even in a couple of gunfights, and believed boys should be allowed to sow their wild oats.

"Is Red still out?" Raoul asked. He referred to a cowhand named Red Crowley, who had been injured in a fall from his horse.

"Doc says a couple of weeks yet. Felipe put on a new hand."

"Who?"

"Some fellow named Swain. I haven't seen him yet."

After breakfast Raoul headed for the corral to watch the morning shakedown. En route he had to pass the hands' chuck house, and through the open kitchen door he saw Little Doe scrubbing a pot.

At the corral Felipe Gomez, the foreman, was surrounded by about forty men, to whom he was doling out chores. Among them was Jamie McKay. After a brief glance at Raoul, Jamie ignored him.

The crowd had dwindled to about twenty when Gomez said to Jamie, "You and Jake check the south flat for strays."

Jamie and a cowhand named Jake Fox mounted their horses and rode off.

Eventually only one man was left, a good-looking, solidly-built, clean-shaven man of about Raoul's age. Although Raoul couldn't recall ever seeing him before, there was something familiar about him.

The foreman started to introduce him, then halted to examine Raoul's face. "Fall off a horse?"

"Tangled with a nosy foreman."

Used to arrogant treatment by the ranch owner's son, Gomez shrugged. "This is John Swain, hired temporary to replace Red Crowley. Raoul Derango, Swain, the boss's son."

As the two shook hands, Gomez said to Raoul, "You planning to work today?"

Raoul was, because he hoped the exercise would remove some of the stiffness from his joints. He said, "Yes."

"Peewee spotted a cat last week in Balkers Canyon. Swain says he can track. Show him where the canyon is, and maybe he can pick up some sign."

Although Raoul worked only when he wanted to, when he did work, he followed orders. That was because his father had once heard him talk back to the foreman, and the subsequent blistering had left a lasting impression. In essence, Don Miguel had gotten across that when Raoul worked, he was a cowpoke of the same status as other hands and Felipe was his boss—and if he ever talked back to him again, Don Miguel would beat him senseless.

"Sure," Raoul said. "Got a rifle, Swain?"

"Just this," the man said, pointing to a short-barreled .41 at his waist.

"Follow me."

Raoul led the way to the ranch house. Consuela was breakfasting in the kitchen.

"Morning, Sis," Raoul said as he went by.

"Morning."

As they entered Raoul's bedroom, the new man said, "Who's she?"

"My sister."

"She got a name?"

Raoul looked at him steadily. When he spoke, his tone made it clear that the hired help didn't get formal introductions to his sister. He said, "Yes," then lifted two rifles from a gunrack.

After handing one rifle to Swain, Raoul took a box of .30 caliber shells from a dresser drawer, and both loaded their guns.

As they passed through the kitchen again, Consuela said, "Going hunting?"

"One of the hands spotted a mountain lion," Raoul said.

Just inside of Balkers Canyon they found a dead steer, its throat ripped open and a large chunk of meat gnawed from its haunch. A black vulture and two turkey buzzards rose from the carcass as they approached.

Swain told Raoul to stay back, dismounted a dozen feet from the dead steer and carefully circled it at that distance. Halting on the far side of the circle, he knelt to study the ground, then went over to kneel again next to the steer's carcass.

When he rose to his feet, he said, "Dead at least twenty-four hours. For what it's worth, the cat headed into the canyon."

Raoul said, "If he hasn't eaten for twenty-four hours, he may be back. We could stake out his kill."

The new man shook his head. "Better chance tracking. A puma can smell where a human's been from fifty yards off. He'd come that close, then fade."

"If he came within fifty yards, we could get him from up on the rim of the canyon."

Swain gave him a surprised look. "You got the mind of a hunter. We'll try it."

He remounted, and they backtracked, circled around to a path leading up onto the right-hand rim of the canyon where they picked a spot in the shade of a tree about a hundred yards farther into the canyon than the dead steer.

As they dismounted, Raoul said, "We'll alternate as lookouts and spell each other every hour. You're first."

The new man gave him a curious look and seemed on the verge of suggesting they draw straws, but the arrogant look on Raoul's face dissuaded him. He lay on his belly at the edge of the dropoff with his rifle alongside him. Raoul rested his back against the tree.

Swain said, "The birds are back. They'll make good lookouts. They'll take off again if the cat gets near."

Raoul rolled and lit a cigarette.

Over his shoulder the new man said, "Put that out."

Raoul gazed at him in astonishment. "What?"

"The cat could smell that half a mile away, you damn fool."

Raoul flushed. No Double-D rider talked to him that way. He was about to put the man in his place when he suddenly knew why his face had looked familiar. Stubbing out his cigarette, he sat thinking.

The last time he had been in the town of Comanche, Raoul had seen the picture of the man calling himself John Swain on a poster offering a four-thousand-dollar reward, dead or alive. He was really John Wesley Hardin, the deadliest gunfighter in Texas.

Only twenty-one, Wes Hardin was the named killer in official coroners' inquests into the deaths of ten men and the reputed killer of perhaps thirty more. The crime for which he was wanted in Comanche was the murder of a deputy sheriff there.

Raoul considered what to do. It would be easy to shoot Hardin in the back, but as the eventual heir to millions, four thousand meant nothing to Raoul. All at once it occurred to him how he could use Hardin.

"Wes," he said.

"Yes?" the man said, then his body stiffened.

"I don't have a gun on you," Raoul said. "You can turn around."

Hardin rolled over, sat up and crossed his arms over his raised knees, his left hand dangling just above the butt of his .41 revolver.

"If I meant to take you, you'd already be dead," Raoul said. "I don't need four thousand dollars. I could spend that on a weekend without feeling it."

Hardin said nothing.

"You must be low on money, or you wouldn't be breaking your back for thirty a month. Would a thousand get you safely out of Texas?"

Hardin smiled slightly. "Who do you want killed?"

Raoul smiled back. "Did you meet Jamie McKay?"

"The kid the foreman sent out to the south flats with Jake Fox?"

Raoul looked surprised. "Did you memorize all forty names?"

"I memorize the names and faces of everybody around me," Hardin said. "He the one who beat your head in?"

Raoul let his voice cool. "Let's stick to the part that's your business."

The gunman shrugged. "Tell me about him."

"He's a half-breed, son of the squaw who cooked your breakfast. He doesn't sleep in the bunkhouse. They have a cabin three miles west of the ranch house, in a little valley."

Hardin nodded. "I saw it when I rode in from El Paso."

"I don't want him bushwhacked. That could make me a suspect."

The gunfighter's eyes turned cold. "I'm not an assassin."

"Just thought I'd mention it. It has to be a witnessed gunfight. Best place is Dowell's Saloon on San Francisco Street. He drops in there most Saturday nights."

"You expect me to hang around an El Paso saloon, waiting for him to show? I would be there about fifteen minutes when some bounty hunter would walk in."

Raoul pushed back his hat to scratch his head. "Maybe wait across the street and watch for him to show?"

"Stand around for a couple of hours and tip my hat to the ladies who pass, eh? Should I hang the reward poster around my neck?"

"I'm paying the money," Raoul said. "Suppose you furnish the ideas."

After thinking, Hardin said, "I'll watch his cabin, follow him to town and walk in the saloon a minute after him. I'll pick a fight, get the job done, and be headed out of town five minutes after I get there."

"That ought to do it," Raoul said.

"You'll have to pay in advance."

"Half in advance, half after."

The gunfighter shook his head. "I can't stop to collect after. I'll be in Mexico."

Raoul considered the possibility that Hardin might just pocket the money and run, and decided it was small. The gunfighter had a reputation for keeping his word.

"All right, rap on my bedroom window Saturday evening after chow, and I'll pass it out to you." Raoul raised his eyes skyward. "The buzzards are aloft."

Hardin looked over his shoulder, then rolled on his stomach, crawled to the canyon edge and picked up his rifle. Grabbing his rifle also, Raoul crawled over alongside him.

Down below, at a range of about two hundred fifty yards, a sleek, graceful puma padded in the direction of the dead steer. Both men sighted their rifles.

"Say when," Raoul said.

"When."

The two rifles cracked together. The beautiful cat jumped into the air, half turned, then crashed to the ground to lie still.

Getting to his feet, Raoul said, "Guess that entitles us to the rest of the day off. After we skin him, we'll go back to the ranch for a couple of poles and go fishing."

Jamie and Jake Fox found plenty of steers on the south flats, but no strays. At noon they stopped for a lunch of hardtack and jerky.

Jake Fox was a puzzle to Jamie. About twenty-five, big and blond and good-natured when sober, he turned into an arrogant bully when drunk, with a nasty habit of picking fights with men half his size. He was the only Double-D rider Raoul Derango seemed to regard as an equal instead of an inferior, the two usually appearing at Dowell's Saloon together. Jamie suspected the affinity was that both were bullies when drunk, because he had never noticed any other social grace either possessed when drinking. He was an affable man to work with, though, and Jamie rather liked being paired with him.

Curious about why he hadn't been with Raoul Saturday night, Jamie said, "How were things at Dowell's over the weekend?"

"Never got there," Fox said. "Had a date with a hot tamale over in Juarez."

That was surprising, because usually Jake showed no interest in women, his idea of a good time being to get drunk and beat up someone. Jamie had never seen him pay any attention to any of the occasional women customers at Dowell's.

Now that he thought of it, he realized that Raoul paid little attention to them either. He had been thinking that if Jake had been with Raoul, he might have acted as a deterrent. But perhaps not. The two had so much in common, Little Doe might have had to fight off two rapists if Jake hadn't been in Juarez.

Then he felt guilty for having the thought. He was mentally accusing the man without evidence.

After supper on Saturday, Wes Hardin strolled to the east side of the ranch house, glanced around to make sure no one was watching, and tapped on Raoul's bedroom window. Immediately it opened and Raoul passed out a thin sheaf of currency. Hardin counted ten one-hundred-dollar bills, folded them and thrust them into a pocket.

"Going in to see the show?" he asked.

"I wouldn't come within miles of the place. I'll be right here in bed."

"Sleep pretty," Hardin said, and walked away.

The day had been heavily overcast, and if it didn't clear, the night would be too dark to follow anyone at a distance. In anticipation of having to follow close behind Jamie McKay, Hardin muffled his horse's hooves with burlap.

At this time of year it stayed light until eight o'clock, and it was only six when Hardin took up position in a stand of trees one hundred yards north of the McKay cabin. He was surprised to see smoke coming from the smokestack. It was too warm to require a fire for heat, and since both Jamie and his mother ate at the chuck house, it couldn't be a cooking fire.

Jamie came from the cabin carrying two wooden buckets, filled them at the spring and carried them inside. When he made a second trip, Hardin deduced he was heating water on the stove for a bath. Half an hour later, wearing a different shirt, Jamie carried out a washtub and emptied it.

Little Doe worked later than her son because she had to clean up after serving supper. At seven she drove up in a small one-horse wagon, unhitched the horse and led it into the barn. Shortly after she entered the cabin, Jamie made two more trips to the spring, presumably for his mother's bath, and later dumped the washtub for a second time.

When it started to get dark, Hardin began to doubt that Jamie was going to town that night. A light went on in the cabin. When it grew fully dark, Hardin led his horse to within fifty yards of the cabin. He was in the open there, but it was still overcast, and visibility was about half that distance.

Dropping his horse's reins, he continued on foot and peered in a window. A chandelier lighted the central room, and Jamie and his mother were on opposite sides of the table, reading books. Hardin returned to his horse.

While it looked to the gunfighter as though he were wasting his time, he decided to wait as long as there was light from the cabin. It went out at half past ten. Hardin mounted his horse, then held it still when a dimmer light went on. Jamie came from the cabin carrying a lantern and headed for the barn.

Hardin watched through the open door as Jamie saddled a horse. The lantern went out and he heard the barn door close.

Hardin closed the distance to near visibility range and followed by the sound of the other horse's hooves. Since he could barely hear his own horse's burlap-wrapped hooves, he was sure Jamie couldn't hear them.

After about three miles, Jamie turned west, which was not the way to El Paso. Worried that he might lose him, Hardin closed the distance until he could see the other horse and rider, dimly, and hoped Jamie would not look back.

After another two miles Jamie turned onto a steep path leading to the top of the butte. By the suddenly sharp clip-clop of the horse's hooves, Hardin knew the path was mainly rock. Afraid that even the muffled hooves of his horse would be heard, he dismounted and followed on foot. It was a long, steep climb.

At the top he spotted a crack of light from a small building surrounded by trees. As he neared, he saw that the building was a line shack, and the light came from the edge of a shuttered window. Two horses with dropped reins were in front of the shack.

Hardin peered through the lighted crack. Inside Jamie had a woman wearing riding clothes in his arms and they were kissing with passion. When they finally moved apart and Jamie led her toward one of the two cots, Hardin saw that the woman was Raoul's unintroduced sister.

Retreating, he descended the path, mounted his horse and headed for the ranch house.

Raoul's bedroom window was wide open against the still summer heat. He was awakened from sound sleep by someone lighting his bedside candle. Looking up, he saw Wes Hardin.

"What the devil?" he said, sitting up.

Hardin said, "He won't be at Dowell's tonight."

"You woke me to tell me that?"

"He's in a line shack about seven miles from here with your sister."

Raoul stared at him. "Consuela?"

"If that's her name. You introduced us."

"What are they doing?"

"Fucking about now, I'd guess. Last I saw them, they had just separated from a hot embrace and he was steering her to a cot."

Raoul bounced from bed. He had been sleeping in his underdrawers. Picking up the lighted candle, he strode along the hall to his sister's room at the opposite side of the house. When he found it empty and the bed unslept in, he returned to his own room, quickly dressed and strapped on his gun belt. Then he motioned Hardin to follow him, carried the candle to a door off the central part of the hall, opened it and went in.

Awakening, Don Miguel said, "What's the matter?"

"Jamie McKay's got Consuela in a line shack, screwing her."

Don Miguel sat up. "How do you know?"

Raoul should have expected the question, but it caught him off-balance. Doing some fast thinking, he said, "I suspected she was meeting someone, and had Swain here follow her."

Don Miguel looked up at Hardin, swung from bed and began dressing. When he was dressed, he took a double-barreled shotgun from a gun rack similar to the one in Raoul's room and loaded it.

Jamie and Consuela had finished making love and were lying naked in each other's arms when the door burst inward and Don Miguel appeared in it with a leveled shotgun. Both scrambled off the cot and Consuela jumped between her father and Jamie. Her brother and the new hand who had helped him kill the puma earlier in the week came in behind her father.

"Get out of the way," Don Miguel said, cocking one of the hammers.

Backing against her lover, Consuela said, "Run, Jamie."

There was nowhere to run. While the window was right behind Jamie, its shutter was closed and latched.

Out of desperation Jamie turned and dived at the shutter with outstretched hands. There was the screech of screws being wrenched from wood as the shutter disappeared from

the window, and Jamie went through headfirst. Landing
outside on his hands, he tucked under his head somersaulted
and bounced to his feet running. As he cut around to the
front of the shack, the shotgun roared from the window
and he heard buckshot whistle past.

Mounting his horse with a flying leap, he swept up the
reins and galloped off. Two pistols fired from the doorway,
and he felt the heat of one slug as it whispered past his ear.

The horses of the interlopers had been left at the top of
the path, fifty feet from the cabin. They reared as Jamie
shot by to race headlong down the steep, rocky path to the
valley below.

As he headed for home, he heard the three horses
pounding down the path behind him. Looking around, he
could see them riding three abreast only twenty yards
back. The shotgun roared again and both pistols cracked,
but this time nothing came close.

Crouching low, he dug his naked heels into the mare's
sides, brought an increased spurt of energy from her and
lengthened his lead until he could no longer see his pursuers,
which meant they couldn't see him either. He could still
hear their hoofbeats, though, which meant they could hear
his. He gradually pulled ahead even farther, until he could
barely hear the pursuing hooves.

Halfway to the cabin there was a stand of trees off to the
left. Darting into it, Jamie reined in the mare and stroked
her heaving sides to quiet her. The pursuing hoofbeats
grew louder and the three horses raced by. When the
sound of them faded into the distance, he headed in the
opposite direction at a gallop.

The riders would go clear to his cabin, he was sure. If
Don Miguel hadn't been one of them, he would have
worried about his mother, but despite his homicidal rage
against Jamie, Don Miguel had the manners of a caballero

and was incapable of even discourtesy to a woman, let alone inflicting harm. Jamie was sure Little Doe would suffer nothing worse than polite questioning as to where she thought her son might be hiding.

The door of the line shack was open and the lantern was still burning. Consuela's horse was gone. Jamie hurriedly dressed, strapped on his gun, turned out the lantern, closed the door and headed west. He would have liked to stop at the cabin to tell his mother good-bye, as he knew it would be some time before he'd see her again. But he suspected that by morning every Double-D rider would be searching for him with orders to hang him when caught.

He rode all night, arriving at Las Cruces, in the Territory of New Mexico, thirty-five miles from the ranch, at nine in the morning. He had ten dollars in his pocket. In Las Cruces he bought enough grub to last a few days, an extra shirt, some socks and underwear, a blanket, and headed west.

Jamie thought it wise to put at least a hundred miles between himself and the Double-D. As the town of Deming was a little over that, he stopped in a saloon there to inquire if any nearby ranches were hiring. The barkeep told him that the Lazy-8, five miles west of town, was looking for a couple of laborers.

It was a small ranch, less than a thousand acres. The owner, who acted as his own foreman, was a big Dutchman named Herman Vroos. He needed no riders, but he did need a couple of men to string fence for one month. He had arranged with a neighbor to borrow one of his men as one of them, which left one opening. The pay was thirty dollars and found.

Jamie had two dollars in his pocket and had run out of grub. He took it.

CHAPTER XI

Nate arrived at Port Hueneme on Thursday, the eighteenth of June. As San Buenaventura had no telegraph service, he'd been unable to inform his mother when he would arrive and had to take the stage from there. As usual a small crowd was gathered to watch the stagecoach come in. He knew everyone in the gathering, and he was offered a dozen handshakes and expressions of sympathy.

It was shortly after noon when he got home. Hearing conversation in the kitchen, he dropped his hat and valise on his bed and continued on to there.

His mother was making sandwiches and his Aunt Martha setting the kitchen table, while four-year-old little Phil sat at the table. Abigail set down her bread knife and ran to give Nate a hug. Martha hugged him when she was through, and little Phil jumped up and formally offered his hand.

"I'm sorry about Uncle Phil," he said when greetings were over.

Martha's eyes misted. "I know how much you loved him, Nate. You were almost like a son to him."

"He was almost like my father. Has Quillan been caught?"

Abigail said, "The posse lost his trail between here and Los Angeles."

"Are you going to kill him?" four-year-old Phil asked, looking at his gun.

"Phillip!" his mother said.

"I'll bet he will," the boy said.

Abigail changed the subject by telling Martha to set another place and telling Phil and Nate to sit down.

During lunch there was much talk about Nate's Uncle Philip, what Father Hernandez had said about him at the funeral, what a fine husband and father he had been, and there was much reminiscing by Martha about the good things and the funny things he had done over the years, but there was no mention of the circumstances of his death. Nate didn't ask, knowing that this wasn't important to Martha now, whereas expressing what he had meant to her and how much she had loved him and how much she would miss him was. Nate and his mother mainly listened, interjecting occasional comments merely to show their continued sympathy.

His Aunt Martha and little Phil were staying here now, Nate learned, but permanent plans were still up in the air. Martha rather thought that when she adjusted to her loss, she would move home and support herself and Phil by doing seamstress work.

"We can help financially," Nate said. He turned to his mother. "There must be a good part of the bounty money left."

"Most of it, dear. I've already told your Aunt Martha she doesn't have to worry about finances."

After lunch Nate walked down to the sheriff's office. Pete Dawson, who had been a part-time deputy under

Sheriff Cook, had been appointed acting sheriff until next election. Ventura County, with a total population of less than five thousand, ordinarily had too little crime to justify more than one full-time law officer, but a part-time deputy had been required to take over when the sheriff was ill or out of town. Dawson was a rangy, friendly man of thirty whose regular job was punching cows.

The acting sheriff had been present when Nate arrived on the stage and had already offered his condolences. He said, "Afternoon, Nate, how was college?"

"All right. How'd the posse lose this Quillan fellow?"

"He had a fast horse. About halfway to Los Angeles we couldn't find any sign, so we gave up."

"Tell me about him."

"There's a poster on the wall," Dawson said.

"Nate went over to look at it. It read:

$500 REWARD
DEAD OR ALIVE FOR
JASON R. QUILLAN

Escaped Convict, Killer and Stagecoach Robber
Subject escaped from State Prison May 26, 1874
DESCRIPTION
Age 35, height 6'1", weight 180 pounds, dark,
long hair, brown eyes, sallow complexion, knife
scars on forehead and chin.
Contact Attorney General, Sacramento, California

Returning to the desk, Nate said, "You have a spare poster?"

Dawson drew one from his desk drawer and handed it to him. "The state's added two thousand to that for murdering the sheriff, but the fliers haven't come in yet. I understand they'll have his picture."

Nate folded the poster and put it in his breast pocket. "How did it happen, Pete?"

"It was mid-afternoon, and the only people in Ward's Saloon were two old guys at a table, Andy Parker, the barkeep, and the sheriff. Phil was just standing at the bar talking to Andy—he never drank on duty, you know—when Quillan walked in and stuck a gun in his back. According to all three witnesses, your uncle didn't even know he was there until he felt the gun. He looked over his shoulder and Quillan said, 'Afternoon, Sheriff, remember me?' Phil said, 'Yes, you're Jason Quillan,' and Quillan pulled the trigger. Then he jumped on his horse and lit out southeast. By the time Andy spread the word and a posse got organized, fifteen or twenty minutes had passed and he was probably five miles out of town."

"Think he went clear to Los Angeles or cut off somewhere?"

"If I was him, I wouldn't even stop in Los Angeles. I'd keep going right into Mexico."

There was only one stagecoach a day to Los Angeles, leaving at noon. The next day Nate was on it. The stage made the sixty-five-mile trip in five hours. Nate got a room over a cantina near the stage depot, had supper there and made a tour of the town.

Los Angeles was a growing town of six thousand, mostly Mexican, with the reputation of being the most lawless community in the Southwest. There were sometimes as many as four gunfights in a single night, and lynchings were so common that it was estimated there had been fifty-five in the past twenty years.

Nate went from cantina to cantina showing the reward poster to barkeeps, asking if they had seen anyone answering Jason Quillan's description. All he got from most was uninterested shrugs. A couple thought they might have

seen him, but couldn't recall when and had no idea where
he was now.

When he had visited every cantina in town, he started
over, this time talking to the girls working the male
customers. By now it was past ten and a lot of patrons
were drunk. A fistfight broke out in the first place he
entered during his second round, and two drunks in the
next place drew and fired at each other; both missed, and
were knocked unconscious with a bung starter by the
barkeep before either could fire again.

None of the girls he talked to recalled seeing anyone of
Quillan's description. At midnight he gave up and returned
to the cantina where he was staying.

He had shown the flier to the barkeep there, but that had
been at six o'clock, and there had been no girls working
that early. There were now two girls and a different bar-
tender was on duty, all three Mexican. Both girls were
slim and pretty and in their mid-twenties.

The place was crowded. One girl sat at a table with
three men and the other stood at the bar, flanked by two
more. The barkeep was too busy to be interrupted at the
moment. Nate touched the arm of the girl at the bar.

When she turned, he said, "Excuse me, señorita—"

That was as far as he got when the man to her right, a
heavyset mustached man who looked like a bandido, swung
around and said, "She is taken, chinche."

Ignoring the insult, Nate said, "I just want to ask her a
question, señor."

The man, who was quite drunk, put his hand on his gun
butt. Not wanting to get involved in a gunfight, Nate
whipped a left hook to his jaw so fast that no one saw it
except the girl and the man on the other side of her. The
bandido's eyes crossed, his back hit the bar, and he slowly
slid to a seated position on the floor and went to sleep.

Nate took the flier from his breast pocket, unfolded it and showed it to the girl. "Ever see this man, señorita?"

She glanced down at the man at her feet, gave Nate a fascinated look, then studied the poster. The man on her other side looked at his friend seated on the floor, glanced at Nate and looked away.

"Scars on his forehead and chin," the girl said. "He stayed here last week, muchacho."

Nate felt the satisfaction of labor rewarded. "Know where he is now?"

"No, he was with Tina."

"Who's Tina?"

She pointed to the girl at the table. "Gracias," Nate said, starting that way.

"Uno momento," the girl said, laying a hand on his arm. "One of her amigos is the jealous type. I will get her."

She went over to the table, bent to speak to Tina; the girl glanced Nate's way, then rose to come over. One of the men began to get up too, but the first girl pushed him down, said something to him and he relaxed.

Tina halted before Nate, gave the man on the floor a curious glance and said, "Señor?"

Nate showed her the circular. "Your friend says you know this man."

After studying it, she said, "Yes, his name was Jason."

"Do you know where he is?"

"He said he would go to San Diego."

"How long ago?" Nate asked.

Tina thought. "We were together last Friday and Saturday. He left Sunday."

This was Friday, which put Nate only five days behind him.

Tina said, "You look young for a bounty hunter."

"I'm not a bounty hunter," Nate said. "What time does the stage for San Diego leave?"

"Six a.m. You are a cute niño. Are you old enough to like girls?"

"Love them, but I have to rise early."

Shrugging, she started to walk away, but was stopped by the other girl, just returning from the table, who said, "I told Carlos he was your hermano, Tina."

"Gracias," Tina said, and returned to the table.

The other girl said to Nate, "I am Carmella."

"How do you do, Carmella. I'm Nate. Thanks for the help."

"You are welcome. You stay here?"

"Just tonight."

"You would like company in your room, perhaps, muchacho?"

"I am flattered, señorita, but I must be up at dawn."

"You are flattered?" she said, smiling at him. "It was not to be a gift, enamorado."

"I am still flattered. Good night."

As he walked toward the stairs, the man seated on the floor regained consciousness, pushed to his feet and leaned against the bar.

Carmella said to him, "You wish to buy me another drink, amante?"

Although only half the size of Los Angeles, San Diego called itself a city. It matched Los Angeles in one respect: it had just as many cantinas. Nate toured them for two days before he finally found a girl with whom Jason Quillan had spent the night. Quillan had told her he was going to Mexico.

The search was narrowing. There was only one town of any consequence on the Baja peninsula, Ensenada, eighty miles south of San Diego on the Pacific coast.

Until now he had traveled by stagecoach because he wanted to move fast. From here on he needed mobility more than speed. In San Diego he bought a horse and saddle, a horse blanket, a sleeping blanket and a canteen, then transferred the contents of his valise to the saddlebags and left the valise in the care of the hostler from whom he had bought the horse and saddle. He stocked up with food and water and headed south.

At the border the two bluecoats supposed to be guarding the American side and the two Mexican soldiers supposed to be guarding the other side were all seated around a small table in the shade of a tree, playing cards. They gave him uninterested looks as he rode by.

The crossroads called Tijuana, sixteen miles south of San Diego, was so small that all strangers were noted and remembered. Six days before Jason Quillan had passed through heading toward Ensenada.

Nate was now in no hurry. If Quillan had continued beyond Ensanada into the mountains south of it, there would be little hope of finding him and it wouldn't matter how soon Nate reached the seaside town. But the pattern Quillan had been following suggested he wouldn't want to be too far from cantinas and girls, and there was no reason the outlaw shouldn't think he was safe in Mexico.

Taking his time, walking his horse, Nate took three days to ride the sixty-five miles. In late afternoon of the third day, on the outskirts of town, stopped at an adobe hut where a lean, middle-aged woman was washing clothes in the yard and a plump, middle-aged man sat in the shade of the hut watching her.

Halting, Nate said, "Buenos dias."

The woman looked at him impassively and went on working. The man said, "Buenos dias, señor."

"Habla Ingles usted?"

"Si, señor."

"A gringo, tall, with long dark hair and scars on his forehead and chin. Have you seen him?"

The man looked thoughtful. "I may have, señor. I am trying to remember."

Nate flipped him a silver dollar. Expertly plucking it from the air, the plump man said, "My memory is slightly improved."

When Nate flipped him another, the man said, "I almost remember now. Not quite."

"When you remember, you get a third dollar," Nate said. "Not before."

"Pasqual's Cantina on the beach, señor. He will be there now."

"How do you know?"

"He sits there each afternoon with Pasqual's daughter and drinks wine."

Nate tossed him the third dollar and rode on.

The cantina was a small adobe building facing the ocean at only fifty yards back from the water. Nate tied his horse to the hitching rail and went over to lean his back against the building alongside the bat-winged door and to close his eyes against the glaring sun. He lounged there for five minutes with his eyes closed, then suddenly turned to push through the bat wings and pop his eyes open inside. With his eyesight instantly adjusted to the dim interior, he swept his gaze over the room.

The floor was dirt and the bar was two heavy boards laid across carpenter's horses. A half dozen Mexican men wearing sombreros were seated around a large circular table sharing a jug of wine. At a smaller table near the rear wall a man and a girl had wine glasses and a bottle before them. The girl looked about nineteen and the man answered the description on the flier.

"Señor?" the middle-aged barkeep said.

"Nothing, thanks," Nate said, crossing to the small table.

The scarred man gazed up at him from narrowed eyes. "Something on your mind, boy?"

Nate spread the "Wanted" poster on the table before him. "This you?"

After a bare glance at it, the man pushed his chair back from the table and let his hands drop onto his thighs. "They're sure sending 'em young these days. Bounty hunters from north of the border got no jurisdiction down here, kid."

"I'm no bounty hunter," Nate said. "I'm Sheriff Philip Cook's nephew."

Jason Quillan's right hand slid from his thigh to his gun butt. Nate let him get it all the way out before driving a bullet into his chest. The chair went over backward and the dead man lay there, still seated in it, his knees raised and his calves dangling over the front edge of the seat.

The girl screamed. Nate put away his gun and walked over to the bar. "What do you have to drink?" he asked.

In a shaking voice the barkeep said, "Only wine and tequilla, señor."

Nate had never tasted tequilla. As a matter of fact, since the watered whiskey his mother had forced on him when he was twelve, on the night his father was killed, he hadn't tasted anything alcoholic except a little beer at the campus poker sessions Hank Pizzaro had taken him to. He had heard stories of tequilla's dynamite power, though.

"Wine," he said, laying a dollar on the bar.

The barkeep poured a glass of red wine. "No charge, señor," he said, still shaking.

"Consider it a tip," Nate said.

He looked around the room. The six men at the large

table and the girl at the small one were all watching him
warily. The girl rose and disappeared through a door at the
back.

"What will you do with him?" Nate asked, nodding
toward the body.

"I don't know, señor. I suppose I should send for the
undertaker."

"If there is a charge, I will pay it."

"That is kind of you, señor."

Nate sipped his wine and disliked the vinegary taste. It
wasn't until then that the bounty, the two-thouand five-
hundred dollars, on Jason Quillan occurred to him. Up to
that moment nothing but revenge had been on his mind.

It would be silly to pass up two and a half thousand, he
thought. But there was the problem of getting the body
across the border. The border guards were not likely simply to watch him go by leading a horse with a dead man
draped over it, and besides it would take five days under a
torrid sun to get to San Diego, the nearest spot where he
could claim his reward, and by then the body might be
bloated beyond recognition.

He had an idea. "Send someone for the undertaker," he
said.

Six days later, driving a small, mule-drawn dray with a
seven-foot pine box on it and his riding horse tied behind
it, Nate drew up alongside the four card-playing soldiers at
the border. All four came over.

"What is in the box, señor?" one of the Mexican
soldiers asked.

"My brother," Nate said.

The soldier lifted the hinged lid, and he and his comrade
and the two bluecoats all gazed at the wax-like face of the
embalmed body and the wax-like hands crossed on the

chest. The two Mexican soldiers crossed themselves and the American soldiers tried to look sad.

"The family plot is in the cemetery at San Diego," Nate said.

The soldier who had opened the lid closed it again. "Our condolences, señor."

"Thank you," Nate said, and drove on.

He delivered the body to the city marshal of San Diego. By now the new circular containing Jason Quillan's picture and offering a twenty-five-hundred-dollar reward was out, and the marshal telegraphed Sacramento that he had positively identified the body and that Nate deserved the reward. At Nate's request he asked in the telegram for the money to be sent to San Buenaventura. A telegraph message came back that a bank draft would be mailed in care of the sheriff on Ventura County.

At a small loss Nate sold back his horse and saddle to the hostler from whom he had bought them, sold his mule and dray at a small profit, reclaimed his valise and caught the stage back home.

On Wednesday, July eighth, he walked into the sheriff's office in San Buenaventura to claim his reward. After Pete Dawson handed him the bank draft, he went over to look at the posters on the wall. A new one caught his eye.

$3000 REWARD
DEAD OR ALIVE FOR
BRODERICK (BRAD) COLLINS
Rapist and Murderer of two 15-year-old Girls
at San Jose, California on June 17, 1874
DESCRIPTION
Age 29, height 5'10", weight 240 pounds, light
hair worn short, blue eyes, fair complexion.

There was a head-and-shoulders picture of a round-faced, sullen-looking man, and below that was the usual notice to contact the attorney general at Sacramento.

"This Collins sounds like a delightful fellow," Nate said over his shoulder.

"Yeah," Acting Sheriff Dawson said. "How'd you like to invite him home for supper?"

That evening Nate wrote a letter to Denise, the first he had found time to write since he left her in San Francisco.

Every morning for a month Denise had called at the post office to inquire if there was mail for Miss Jane Eyre. She had a key to the cottage, and daily she went there, too, to see if perhaps Nate had unexpectedly returned without writing. On Tuesday, July fifteenth, she finally got a letter. She tore it open before leaving the post office.

> San Buenaventura
> July 8, 1874

Darling:

I am sorry I have been away for so long, but family business necessitated it. I will be a little longer because I have some business in San Jose. The minute that is completed, I will write when I expect to be back in San Francisco.

I miss you terribly and count the days until I can hold you in my arms again. Only the most urgent business keeps us apart. I love you eternally.

> All my love,
> Nate

The letter left her numb. What business could he have in San Jose to keep them apart when there was only six weeks left of the summer? It couldn't be family business, for he'd never mentioned having relatives there.

When she got home, Hendrix the butler told her that her mother was attending a ladies' tea and would be gone until mid-afternoon.

"The *Chronicle* is in the parlor if you wish to see it, Miss Denise," he said.

She carried the newspaper up to her room, then twice reread Nate's letter before looking at it. When she finally began reading the paper, an item on the second page caught her eye.

MURDERER JASON QUILLAN KILLED

Information has been received that on July 2nd the body of murderer and escaped convict Jason Quillan was turned in to the city marshal of San Diego for the $2500 bounty offered by the State of California. The bounty hunter was Nathan Cook, nephew of the murdered sheriff of Ventura County, Philip Cook, for whose murder the bounty was offered.

This is the second time young Nathan Cook has collected bounties. Two years ago, at the age of only 16, he hunted down and killed the notorious Cole Gannon, who four years earlier had murdered young Nathan's father, Cole's equally notorious brother Jubal and three other gang members. For that feat he collected a total of $9000 in bounties and an $800 reward for recovering some bank robbery loot. Now, not yet 18, he has avenged the murder of another close relative and has collected a second fat bounty.

The *Chronicle* suggests that the shortest route to Boot Hill for any outlaw who is suicidally inclined would be to harm some other member of young bounty hunter Nathan Cook's family.

Why does the reporter keep calling him a bounty hunter?
Denise thought. The bounties had been only incidental.

Then it struck her that the horrible rape murders recently
reported in the *Chronicle* had been at San Jose. She wondered if that had anything to do with Nate's business there.

CHAPTER XII

In mid-July Jamie McKay decided to risk a visit home. In case Don Miguel was still feeling homicidal, he timed his arrival for late at night. It was midnight when he topped the rise just above the cabin and looked down at it. The moon was bright enough for him to see clearly. The cabin was dark, as he had expected it to be at that time of night. When he saw no sign of anyone, he rode down into the valley.

Finding the door barred from inside, he went around to his mother's bedroom window and tapped. When Little Doe's face appeared at the window, it broke into a smile of joy. She disappeared, and when, a moment later, he saw lantern light in the central room, he rounded to the front door and waited for the bar to be removed.

When the door opened, Little Doe, in a nightgown and robe, threw her arms about him.

"Hey," he said. "I'm alive.

She drew him inside and over to the table. She had not lighted the chandelier, but only a lantern. Jamie worked the cord that lowered the chandelier, lighted it and turned off the lantern. They sat on opposite sides of the table and smiled at each other.

"You're looking fit," she said. "Who's been feeding you?"

"The wife of a Dutchman near Deming, in New Mexico Territory. I strung five miles of wire for him. Did Don Miguel give you a bad time that night?"

"Of course not. Or since. I'm still his chuck house cook. But he's still awfully angry at you. What did you do?"

"Nobody told you?"

"Nobody knows, except the three who were here that night. Your crime is a big secret. Incidentally, that third man was Wes Hardin."

"John Swain was Hardin? Has he been caught?"

"No, it didn't come out until after he was gone. They think he fled to Mexico. What did you do to Don Miguel?"

"Nothing. He just found out that Consuela and I were in love."

Her eyes widened. "For that he put a hundred-dollar bounty on you?"

"He has a bounty on me?"

"Dead or alive. I've been terrified that someone would find you. Why would he do a thing like that just because you love his daughter?"

"It's a little more than that, Little Doe. He caught us together."

She gazed at him, shocked. "Together like—"

When she couldn't finish, he said, "Yes."

"Jamie, how could you?"

"You sound like Don Miguel," he said. "We're in love. It's perfectly natural for people in love to get together."

"But you couldn't ever marry her, Jamie. You've ruined her."

"This is 1874, Little Doe. There is no longer such a thing as a fallen woman. You're over-Christianized."

"What do you mean by that?"

"If my father hadn't converted you to Catholicism, you wouldn't disapprove. The Comanche don't mind young people in love getting together."

"We're not living on the reservation, Jamie. This is the white man's world, and when in Rome, you have to do as the Romans do."

"You should have told me before it happened. Do you know how Consuela is?"

"I haven't seen her," Little Doe said. "I hadn't thought about it until now, but she must be confined to the house. See what you've done to her?"

"You want me to atone by turning myself over to Don Miguel?"

That made her cry. Rounding the table, he held her head against him and said, "If you want me to feel guilty, I'll try, Little Doe, but I can't see anything wrong with being in love."

Pulling away from him, she wiped her eyes. "Maybe Don Miguel and I just don't understand the younger generation. In any event, you can't stay here. You would be killed." She looked up at him, trying to smile. "Don't think just because I scolded you that I don't love you anymore."

He bent to kiss her forehead. "I love you, too, Little Doe. I had better go now, if I want to be out of the area by dawn."

"Where will you go?"

"I think I'll try Arizona Territory. There doesn't seem to be much work in New Mexico. I'll write you."

"Do you need some money?"

"No, I told you I've been working."

Little Doe insisted on filling a sack with food. While she was packing it, he brought in his saddlebags and blanket roll and packed some of the clothing he had left behind. From the bookshelves in the central room he chose two books to put in a saddlebag: Shakespeare's *Sonnets* and Plato's *Dialogues*. He also took his rifle and its saddle scabbard.

Little Doe clung to him when they parted and said, "Good-bye, papoose."

"Good-bye, Mother," he said.

It was one a.m. when he arrived at the Derango ranch house. Leaving his horse behind the barn, he walked around to its west side, which was in shadow and allowed him a view of the west side of the house, and gave the secret owl-hoot signal: three hoots, a pause, two more, another pause, then a single hoot.

Five minutes passed. He was on the verge of repeating the signal when he saw a figure in white climb from Consuela's bedroom window. As she ran across the moon-lit patio, he saw that she was in her nightgown. Darting into the shadow, she threw herself into his arms.

After a month's separation their physical need for each other was stronger than their need for words. They kissed long and deeply, without speaking, and his hands moved over her body until she began to moan. Taking her hand, he led her behind the barn to a pile of new-mown hay, and they made love there in the moonlight.

When they were finished, she pulled down her nightgown, he pulled up his pants, and they cuddled.

"You'll have to be careful," she said. "Father has a hundred-dollar bounty on you."

"Little Doe told me. There's no danger; I'm going away again tonight."

She emitted a sigh, accepting that it was the only thing he could do. "You just came back to see me?"

"And Little Doe."

"Where have you been and what have you been doing?"

It took only two sentences to tell her that. Then he said, "What about you? Did your father punish you?"

"Not physically. I'm restricted to the house until I'm married, which won't be long, because he's in the process of arranging a marriage."

Jealousy gripped him. "With whom?"

"A rancher near Laredo named Juan Cassando, a widower with two daughters and two sons, all older than me. I haven't met him."

Outraged, he said, "How old is he?"

"Fifty."

"Why is Don Miguel doing this? Punishment?"

"Practicality," Consuela said. "I'm not a virgin, which reduces my marketability as a bride."

Little Doe had not been able to make Jamie feel guilt, but this did. "My God," he said. "I did ruin you."

"Don't be silly. If I can't marry you, do you think I care who I marry?"

He pressed her close. "Come away with me."

Rolling from his arms, she sat up. "How much money do you have?"

His face assumed a wry look. "Twenty dollars."

"Senor Cassando has something like two million."

There was no point in pursuing the subject. All he could offer was poverty, and possibly even starvation. Getting to his feet, he took her hand, pulled her erect and kissed her. Both knew it was a kiss of good-bye.

"I'll always love you," she said.

"And I you."

"After I'm married, Father will probably lift the bounty

on you, since I'll be living in Laredo. You could come back.''

''To what? With you gone it won't be home, and I couldn't even get a job around here. Your father sure as hell wouldn't hire me back.''

''I have to go in,'' she said.

He stood in the shadow of the west side of the barn and watched her run across the patio and climb back through her window. Then he mounted his horse and rode west.

CHAPTER XIII

On August twelfth Denise got another letter from Nate, her first since the one nearly a month before. It was from Virginia City, Nevada, and said he would arrive in San Francisco in five days. As it had been written on the ninth, that meant he would be there the next day.

She was so excited that she nearly fainted in the post office. She went directly from there to the cottage, thoroughly cleaned it, then went shopping to lay in a supply of food.

The next morning she was at the cottage at ten. En route she picked up the *San Francisco Chronicle* so that she would have something to do while she waited. After making herself a cup of tea, she sat at the kitchen table to read the paper.

Again an item on the second page caught her attention.

YOUTHFUL BOUNTY HUNTER STRIKES AGAIN

For the second time in a little over a month young bounty hunter Nathan Cook has brought a dastardly criminal to justice. In July he shot and killed escaped convict Jason Quillan, who had murdered his uncle, Ventura County Sheriff Philip Cook, with a cowardly shot in the back. For that deed he earned a bounty of $2500, plus the satisfaction of putting his uncle's murderer permanently out of circulation.

A few days ago at Virginia City, on August 8th, he shot and killed rapist-murderer Brad Collins, wanted for the brutal rapes and murders of two young girls at San Jose in June. The bounty this time was $3000.

There was more to the item, but Denise couldn't read it because she started to cry. At that moment the front door opened and closed, she heard footsteps crossing the parlor, and Nate appeared in the kitchen doorway. She was instantly in his arms, still weeping.

"Hey," he said, kissing her. "You're supposed to be happy."

"Oh, Nate," she said. "Oh, Nate, there's only two and a half weeks left until school."

"Then we'll make love for two and a half weeks."

Scooping her up, he carried her into the bedroom. She was so glad to see him and so starved for his love that she postponed thinking about what had caused her tears, dried them and submitted herself to him completely. It was an hour before their searing passion subsided, then even more time passed without conversation as they lay exhausted in each other's arms and thought of nothing but their mutual contentment.

Finally he said, "I love you."

"I love you, too," she said.

"Then why did you cry when you saw me?"

That brought back all the thoughts she had postponed.

She began to cry again. Pulling her head onto his shoulder, he stroked her silver-hued hair.

"What's the matter, darling?"

"You—you left me all alone to go bounty hunting."

She could feel his body stiffen. "How do you know?"

"It's in today's *Chronicle*. I was reading it when you came in."

"I had to do it," he said.

"Is money more important than me, Nate?"

"It wasn't the money, Denise, at least not entirely. The man raped and murdered two innocent young girls. I couldn't sleep until he was dead."

She drew back to give him a puzzled look. "You're not God, darling."

"A strange remark for an agnostic. The man was a monster, honey. He would have raped and killed other young girls if he had gone on living. I had to save them from him."

"Hypothetical victims? Girls you'll never know you saved, if in fact you did?"

"Whoever they are, I know they're safe from that particular predator. I slept better the night he died than I had in a month."

"You can't kill all the evil people in the world, Nate."

"I can eliminate some of the worst."

She sat bolt upright. "You mean to do more bounty hunting?"

"Only for monsters, for the back-shooters, the killers of women and children, the rapists and torturers. I'll leave the horse thieves and rustlers and burglars to hunters who are in it only for money."

Her voice went high. "Nate, I don't want to be married to a bounty hunter."

Nat sat up also. "Honey, we'll be far richer than if I became a college professor."

"Oh my God," she said, putting her hand to her mouth. "You're not going back to school."

She began to cry again. Pulling her against him, he gently patted her back and, as a result, only made her weep harder.

After a time she pulled away, hopped from bed and got a handkerchief to dry her eyes. He continued to sit on the bed, looking at her.

"You'll probably leave me a widow," she said. "Look what happened to your uncle."

"You think I'd be immune to death as a professor? Look what happened to my father, who never harmed a soul in his life. You can fall off a horse and get killed, honey."

"You're twisting things. You know your uncle was murdered in revenge for sending a man to prison. What makes you think you couldn't be shot in the back?"

"Nobody cames back from the grave to get revenge."

Her face turned white. "You mean you'll kill them all?"

Swinging himself off the bed, he took her by the shoulders to look down into her face. "Do you think anyone I've killed deserved to live?"

She spaced her words distinctly, letting each hang in the air for an instant before enunciating the next. "I - do - not - want - to - be - married - to - a - killer."

"You mean you no longer want to marry me?"

"What would you say if I made it an ultimatum?"

"I would say my heart was broken."

"You would let me go?"

"I would hope you wouldn't leave."

Throwing her arms about his neck, she said, "Nothing you did, nothing you wanted to be could make me leave you. I love you forever. But you can't ask me not to worry. What if some day you run down a killer with quicker reactions than you?"

"There aren't any," he said.

CHAPTER XIV

A wooden sign at the edge of town was lettered *RIMFIRE—POP. 1132*. There was a single street, lined on both sides with false-front buildings, and boardwalks ran the length of the town. No one was on the street, which wasn't surprising, as it was noon in mid-August, the temperature was 105, and it was Monday, when all the ranch workers in the area would be hard at work.

The first building Jamie McKay passed as he entered town was a church on his left. After that there were several houses on each side of the street, then the buildings immediately following all had signs on them. He read them as he rode by. On his left was *Denton's Hardware Store*, and across from it was *Appleton's General Store*, which also had a sign on it reading *U.S. Post Office*. A Chinese laundry was next to the hardware store, and the town marshal's office next to the general store. Then came a leather-and-saddle shop across from a shoemaker. Next on his left was the *Palace Saloon* and the *McCarthy Hotel*, and across from both of them was *Hank's Blacksmith Shop and Livery Stable*. He only rode as far as the livery stable, but beyond it he could see a barber pole, a midwife sign and a gunsmith sign. Then there was another string of houses on both sides of the street, and at the far end was a peaked-roofed red schoolhouse. The first house beyond the blacksmith shop and livery stable was larger than any other in town, three stories high, and had a sign affixed to the roof of its porch reading *Mrs. Schraft's Boarding House for Children.*

Through the open front of the blacksmith shop Jamie could see a large, muscular man wearing a leather apron over his bare chest and shaping a glowing horseshoe on his anvil. Dismounting, he waited until the man finished and had thrust the horseshoe into a bucket of water before saying, "You Hank?"

"Right, young fellow."

"I'm Jamie McKay. Know if any ranches around here are hiring?"

After looking him up and down, the blacksmith said, "All will be before long, for the fall roundup. Meantime, you could probably pick up work busting broncs."

"Where?"

"Most anywhere. They all bought new horses for roundup."

"Any suggestions?"

The blacksmith pursed his lips. "Circle-K, ten miles north, has the best cook."

"Thanks," Jamie said. "Can I board my horse a few days?"

"See Izzy in the stable. If he's drunk, just boot him awake."

Izzy turned out to be a skinny old man. He wasn't drunk, but he smelled of whiskey. Leaving his horse with him, with instructions to water her carefully, then rub her down, Jamie shouldered his saddlebags and blanket roll, withdrew his rifle from its scabbard and crossed the street to the McCarthy Hotel.

A plump, middle-aged woman who introduced herself as Miss Emily McCarthy, slightly stressing the *Miss*, registered him and gave him a key to a second-floor room.

"That will be fifty cents, Mr. McKay," she said.

"Do you have a bathtub?"

"Bathhouse is out back. That's another fifty cents."

Jamie gave her a dollar.

There was a dining room off the small lobby, and through an archway between them Jamie could see a number of people eating. "How late do you serve?" he asked Miss McCarthy.

"Nine p.m."

"I mean lunch."

"We call it dinner. Any time you want, except after five we call it supper."

Jamie carried his gear up to his room, and came down again carrying his last clean change of clothing. He soaked in the tub for a long time, scrubbed thoroughly and washed his hair. When he got back to his room, he tied all of his dirty clothing in a dirty shirt and carried it up the street to the Chinese laundry.

"Not tomollow, next day," the laundryman said.

Before going into the dining room, Jamie went up to his room to get one of the two books he had with him. The dining room was empty when he entered, it now being nearly two o'clock. He took a table by a window, where the light was good. A young Mexican girl brought him a glass of water.

"We got good beefsteak today, señor," she said. "Fried potatoes, corn, bread and butter, coffee or milk. Fifty cents."

"All right. Medium rare and black coffee. Hold the coffee until I finish eating."

Jamie opened his book while he was waiting. A lanky, middle-aged man wearing a pinstriped shirt with sleeve garters came in, looked around and said, "Howdy."

Jamie glanced up long enough to say, "Howdy," then resumed reading.

The man seated himself at the table next to Jamie's and the Mexican girl came from the kitchen with a glass of water.

"Hi, Maria," he said. "The usual."

"Beefsteak rare," she said. "Hold the potatoes. Coffee after. We got corn today."

"All right."

When the girl went back into the kitchen, the man said. "I'm Amos Appleton, owner of the general store, which is also the stage depot. I'm also the town mayor and the postmaster."

Smiling at him, Jamie said, "Glad to meet all of you, sir. Jamie McKay."

"Just passing through?"

"Looking for work. Blacksmith across the street says the ranchers around here are hiring."

"Yes, fall roundup will be starting soon."

Jamie went back to his book, but closed it and put it aside when his meal came. Amos Appleton got his at the same time.

"Sure hot," the mayor said.

"It is that."

"Always hot this time of year. We're less than a hundred miles from the Painted Desert.

"Never been there," Jamie said.

Conversation lapsed while both ate. But when they were

finished and Maria brought both coffee, Appleton said, "Mind if I join you?"

"Be pleased," Jamie said.

The mayor carried his coffee cup over and sat across from Jamie, who watched fascinated as he shoveled six teaspoons of sugar into it.

"Never eat dessert," Appleton said. "Get my sweets this way. What's the book you're reading?"

"Plato's *Dialogues*." He handed the book across the table.

The mayor looked at the cover without opening the book, and handed it back. "Essays of some kind?"

"Sort of. He was a Greek philosopher. Pupil of Socrates."

"That's wrote in Greek?"

"No, I don't read Greek. It's a translation by Benjamin Jowett, an Oxford don."

When Appleton looked puzzled, Jamie said, "A professor at Oxford University in England."

"Oh. You sound like an educated man."

Jamie had never thought of himself as one, but the statement made him pause. After considering, he said, "I'm familiar with most of the classics."

"You do sums?"

Bemused by what seemed a switch of subjects, Jamie said, "Yes."

"Both add and subtract?"

"Yes."

"Multiply and divide?"

"Yes."

"Know fractions?"

"Yes, but you've reached the limit of my arithmetical knowledge. I've never studied higher mathematics."

Appleton took a sip of his coffee. While waiting for

enlightment of what this was all about, Jamie sipped his, too.

Setting down his cup, the mayor said, "Ranchers around here pay thirty dollars a month and found. How would you like to earn fifty, plus room and board?"

The only job Jamie could think of that would pay that kind of money was town marshal, which would also explain the questions about sums. The town marshal would have to keep books on fines, the cost of feeding prisoners and other expenses. Most marshals were hired more for their skill with guns than their arithmetic, though.

"I'm not a gunfighter," he said.

Appleton looked at him blankly. "Some of our kids are tough, but we don't need a gunfighter to teach school."

Jamie's expression turned equally blank. "You want me to teach school?"

"It's supposed to open in two weeks, and our former teacher wrote he ain't coming back."

"I've never taught school," Jamie said. As a matter of fact, he had never even attended one.

"You sound to me like you could. We got a town council meeting at my home at seven p.m. Think you could be there?"

"Sure."

"Last house north on the west side of the street, right next to the schoolhouse." In afterthought the mayor said, "Get there at six and have supper with us."

"Thank you," Jamie said. "I will."

The mayor's wife, Martha Appleton, was a motherly woman who stood a head shorter than her husband but was twice his girth. They had a seventeen-year-old daughter named Melissa and nicknamed Missy, a stocky girl built along the general lines of her mother, who clerked for her father at the general store. During dinner Jamie learned they also had a twenty-two-year-old son who was a corporal in the United States Cavalry, stationed at Fort Bliss. It was his room Jamie would occupy if he were hired as the schoolmaster, he discovered, as the board and room offered as part of the deal was at the Appleton house through arrangement with the town fathers.

Mrs. Appleton was an excellent cook. They had roast chicken, three vegetables, potatoes, cornbread, and apple pie for dessert. Jamie flattered his hostess by stuffing himself, then further flattered her by telling her that her cooking was far more inducement for taking the teaching job than the salary.

The council meeting after dinner took place in the parlor. Present were hardware merchant Abraham Denton, the town treasurer; Miss Emily McCarthy from the hotel, the secretary; blacksmith Hank Ford, whose title was merely councilman; and City Marshal Jess Pinter, who was not on the council, but whom, Jamie gathered, attended all council meetings in an ex-officio status. The town treasurer was a dour man in his forties, the city marshal a lean, weathered man of about the same age with cold eyes and a quiet manner.

Jamie had already met Hank Ford and Miss McCarthy. After introducing him to Denton and Marshal Pinter, the mayor said, "We'll table regular business until we discuss the reason I've invited Mr. McKay here, then take it up after he leaves, if that's all right with everybody."

There was a general murmur of assent. Miss McCarthy wrote on a note pad.

"Mr. McKay is a real educated man," Appleton said. "Knows all the classics, like Plato's *Dialogues*, and can do sums, including fractions."

"You suggesting him to replace Percy Ellison?" Denton asked.

"Yes."

"The hardware merchant looked at Jamie. "How old are you, young man?"

"Eighteen in two months."

"Pretty young. What's your educational background?"

"Just reading, sir. I haven't been to college, if that's what you mean."

Emily McCarthy said, "Are you familiar with Shake-speare?"

"Yes, ma'am. Read everything he wrote. I have the sonnets with me, but not the plays, because I've been traveling light."

Hank Ford said, "What's nine-times-eight?"

"Seventy-two."

"Can you quote any Shakespeare?" Miss McCarthy asked.

"Some. I'm not a believer in memorizing passages from anything, including the Bible, just to show off, but some things stick just from reading them over and over."

"Know the balcony scene from Romeo and Juliet?"

" 'He jests at scars that never felt a wound. But soft, what light through yonder window breaks? It is the east, and Juliet is the sun. Arise, fair sun, and kill the envious moon, who is already sick and pale with grief, that thou her maid art far more fair than she.' Want more?"

"That's enough." She looked around the room. "Gentle-men, I'm satisfied."

Hank Ford said, "Fine with me."

Denton said, "Before we vote on it, what salary are we talking about?"

"Same as Ellison," the mayor said. "Fifty, plus room and board."

"Percy Ellison was a regular schoolmaster," the town treasurer said. "I think thirty would be adequate."

Appleton said, "I already told McKay fifty."

"You had no authority to do that, Amos."

"Beggars can't be choosers, Abe. School won't even open if we don't hire a teacher fast, and if we don't get McKay, who do we get?"

"I can settle the argument," Jamie said.

When everyone looked at him, he said, "I came here looking for a wrangler's job, and was sidetracked into this by His Honor the Mayor. If you're only offering cowhand wages, I'll get a cowhand job."

Marshal Jess Pinter laughed, his first and only contribution to the discussion. Miss McCarthy said, "I move we hire Mr. McKay at fifty dollars a month, plus room and board with our usual arrangement of paying Mrs. Appleton ten a month to compensate her for the extra expense."

"Second," Hank Ford said.

The motion was unanimously carried, although Abraham Denton managed to look disapproving while voting approval.

CHAPTER XV

When Jamie stepped out on the front porch, Missy Appleton and another girl were seated in the porch swing. The sun had just set, but there was still enough light for him to see that she was a slim, pretty redhead with a mass of freckles and wearing a ruffled gingham dress.

"Mr. McKay, this is Cricket Denton," Missy said.

He didn't have to remove his hat because he was wearing it, as he always did after sundown, hanging by its chin strap on the back of his neck. He said, "How are you, Miss Denton?" and she said, "Fine, thanks."

"Are you Mr. Denton's daughter? The town treasurer, I mean."

"Yes."

She looked him over so thoroughly, he was embarrassed. Finally she asked, "Get the job, Mr. McKay?"

"Yes. I don't suppose you'll be one of my pupils?"

She laughed. "I finished my schooling long ago. Missy says you're staying at the hotel."

"Yes."

"I have to stop by the store, so I'll walk you home."

"I'll be honored."

When she jumped down from the swing, he saw that she was only a little over five feet tall, coming barely to his shoulder. They both told Missy good night and went down the steps together.

"Do I have to call you Mr. McKay?" she said.

"Make it Jamie. I assume Cricket is a nickname."

"My real name is Nancy. My parents say when I was a baby, I used to make a noise like a cricket to get attention. Do you have some Indian in you?"

"My mother is Comanche; my father was Irish."

"You must get those dark good looks from your mother."

He was not used to compliments from girls, for he was conditioned to think men did all the flattering. He said, "You must get those pretty freckles from your mother."

"I do take after her." They reached the hotel and stopped. She said, "I always hate going in that dark store by myself."

"I'll go with you."

At the hardware store she led him around to the back door, opened it with a key and told him to wait. Moments later a lantern was lighted inside and she said, "Come on in."

He entered a storeroom. It was apparent why she had him wait until she lighted the lantern. The floor was littered with boxes and kegs to stumble over in the dark.

"Close the door," she said.

When he had closed it, she opened a door into the main part of the store and carried the lantern in there. He followed. Setting the lantern on a counter, she went behind it, stopped to reach beneath it, held up a small packet for him to see, then put it in the pocket of her dress.

"My mother asked me to bring home some needles after work, and I forgot."

He had the curious feeling that she was making that up as an excuse for bringing him to the store. He said, "You help out your father here?"

"I'm clerk, bookkeeper, inventory taker and purchasing agent."

"Sounds busy."

She led the way back into the storeroom and he closed the door after them. She set the lantern on a box.

"This is where we keep all the screws and nails," she said, indicating a row of bins along one wall.

"I see."

"Nuts and bolts are over there." She pointed out a similar row of bins along the opposite wall.

"Very orderly."

Pointing to a half empty bottle of whiskey and two shot glasses on a shelf, she giggled. "That's one of the Reverend Wilson Stenton's secret vices."

When he gave her a blank look, she said, "I see my father and the preacher coming out of here sometimes on Sunday mornings, and afterward the bottle is down. I think Daddy brings him in here to sneak a little snort."

"Oh. What are the reverend's other vices?"

"I think he fornicates with members of the ladies auxiliary."

"Actually?"

She giggled again. "Just a fantasy I have."

She stood looking at him, now out of excuses for lingering in the storeroom. It didn't take a bang over the head for him to recognize an invitation. He took her into his arms and kissed her.

Instantly she turned to fire, thrusting her tongue deeply into his mouth, rubbing her body against his and breathing heavily. Although he was aroused, things were going too fast for him. Releasing her, he stepped back.

"I better walk you home before your mother starts worrying."

"She won't worry. She thinks I'm at Missy's."

If he had not been burdened by the guilt of what he had done to Consuela's life, he would have accepted the unveiled invitation, but he had no wish to start his new life in a new town by ruining another girl within eight hours of his arrival, particularly the daughter of one of his employers. Pulling open the back door, he turned out the lantern.

There was nothing she could do but follow. She locked the door and they went around front.

"Where do you live?" he asked.

"Other side of the street, first house after the gunsmith's."

They crossed the street in silence. As they went past the shoemaker's shop, she said, "You think I'm forward, don't you?"

"I think you're very nice." It was the truth. He liked the girl. He just didn't want to seduce her twenty minutes after meeting her.

"I was never kissed like that by a boy before."

Her expertise made that a patent lie, but he was diplomatic. "I shouldn't have been so bold on such short acquaintance."

"I'm not mad," she said, generously letting him take the blame. "Boys can't help their exuberance. Nature designed them that way."

"I suppose," he said. "It helps preserve the species."

When they reached her house, she asked him in, introduced him to her mother and explained to her who he was. Cricket had not lied about where she had gotten her looks. Lydia Denton was an older replica, with the same freckles, still slim and attractive in her mid-forties, and with her red hair just beginning to gray. Jamie noted that Cricket didn't offer her the needles she was supposed to have gotten for her.

Mrs. Denton invited him to have tea.

"I don't want to put you out," he said.

"It's all made. My husband's due home any minute, and he likes a cup before bed."

"In that case, thank you."

Cricket went to get the tea while Jamie sat in the parlor with her mother.

"You seem young for a schoolmaster," Mrs. Denton said. "Have you taught before?"

"No, ma'am, this is my first try. I think they hired me in desperation."

"You're too modest, Mr. McKay. I'm sure you're a fine teacher. Where are you from?"

"Near El Paso."

Cricket rolled in a tea cart containing tea and cookies. Pouring a cup, she said to Jamie, "Milk, sugar or lemon?"

"Plain, please."

She gave him a cup, poured her mother's and her own, and carried the cookie dish to Jamie. He accepted one, nibbled it and said, "Which one is the master baker?"

"Cricket," her mother said. "She's a wonderful cook."

Cricket gave Jamie a resigned look and said, "Mother keeps trying to marry me off. Don't pay any attention to her."

"Cricket, what a terrible thing to say!" After a moment she said, "She did bake the cookies, though."

The front door opened and Abraham Denton came in. He looked surprised to see Jamie.

"Mr. McKay was kind enough to walk me home," Cricket said.

"I see. Nice of you, McKay."

Denton took a chair, and while Cricket poured him tea, he lit a cigar.

"Aren't you going to offer Mr. McKay a cigar?" his wife asked.

He gave her a disapproving look. "He's the school-master." To Jamie he said, "You don't smoke, do you?"

"No, sir."

"We don't like the teacher to smoke. Bad influence on the children."

Mrs. Denton said, "It's just as bad an influence for the town treasurer to smoke."

"Please, Lydia," he said, looking pained.

Finishing his tea, Jamie stood up and said, "Thanks for the refreshments. I better be going."

"You only had one cookie," Cricket said.

"They're too delicious. Afraid I'd become addicted."

"I think you're all Irish instead of just half," she said. "You've kissed the Blarney stone."

Her mother said, "Why don't you invite Mr. McKay to the church picnic, dear?"

Cricket looked pleased by the suggestion. "It's this Sunday, right after church, Jamie. Would you like to go?"

"Love to, thank you."

"Church is at eleven. You can pick me up at ten forty-five. Don't wear a coat. This hot, nobody does."

He hadn't contemplated attending church. Although raised Catholic, he hadn't been to mass in years, and had never been in a Protestant church. There was no way to decline with grace, though. He said, "All right."

As he crossed the street to the hotel, he decided he had better tread cautiously, or he might find himself pushed into marriage. He increasingly liked Cricket, and his side-stepping her advances was solely a matter of prudence, not because she didn't hold physical appeal for him. But since the only woman he wanted for a wife was the unattainable Consuela, he had decided on lifelong bachelorhood.

An early riser, Jamie was having breakfast at seven a.m. when Amos Appleton came into the hotel dining room.

"Hoped to catch you before you ate and invite you to the house," the major-postmaster-storekeeper-stage depot manager said.

"I get up with the chickens. Sit down, Your Honor."

"No, got to get to the store. We open at seven-thirty. Me and the wife talked it over last night and decided there's no point in you paying a high hotel bill for the next two weeks until school starts. Since you'll be moving in then, if you want, you can move in now for a half month's room and board. That would be five dollars."

As Jamie was down to fifteen dollars and was contemplating looking for some bronco-busting work to tide him over, this was a godsend. "Mighty kind of you, sir," he said. "I'll move in this morning."

After breakfast Jamie checked out and carried his gear to the Appleton house. Mrs. Appleton seemed disappointed that he had already breakfasted. He paid her five dollars and was shown his room on the second floor. It was a large room with a double bed, a big closet, a marble-topped dresser, a writing desk with a China lamp, and a washstand with a pitcher and basin on it and a slop jar under it.

When he had stowed his gear, he walked next door to the schoolhouse. Finding it unlocked, he went inside. It was one large room with twenty-four student desks and a desk for the teacher. There was a blackboard and a pointer behind the teacher's desk. In the corner to the left of the teacher's desk was a high stool with a dunce cap sitting on it. Hanging by a leather loop from a nail in the same corner was a willow switch with a taped handle.

At the back of the room was a pot-bellied stove showing little sign of use. Jamie was surprised that it had been used at all. While at home winters were sometimes quite cold and there was even occasional snow, it had been his understanding that here in eastern Arizona Territory the weather was warm year-round.

There was a storage closet in which he found paper and pencils, notebooks, twenty-four copies of the McGuffey *Eclectic Reader*, twenty-four spelling books and twenty-four arithmetic primers. He took one of each to read.

After dropping the books at his room, he walked down to the general store, which he found empty except for Appleton and his daughter.

"Just checked the schoolhouse," he said to Appleton. "There seem to be adequate supplies, but when I run low, how do I get more?"

"Give me a list. I'll fill the order and bill the town."

Jamie said, "There are twenty-four desks. Are there that many schoolchildren here?"

"Usually about twenty. They come in from the ranches, and from as far away as Goose Flats, twenty miles from here."

"When is enrollment?"

"First day of school, September first, unless that's on a weekend." He looked at a wall calendar. "It's a Tuesday, just two weeks from today."

Jamie could think of no further questions to ask at the moment. He went home to read his textbooks.

Saturday night the town exploded as cowhands streamed in from ranches in all directions. At nine o'clock Jamie walked into the Palace Saloon, his first visit to it. Typical of most small-town saloons, there was a long bar, at the moment crowded with customers, a piano player, a couple of poker tables, and no girls. Unless it was a wide-open town, it had been Jamie's experience that dance-hall girls were seldom seen in smaller communities, because righteous citizens refused to tolerate prostitution.

Spotting Marshal Pinter at the far end of the bar, Jamie went over next to him. The marshal had a glass of beer before him.

"Evening, Schoolmaster," Pinter said. "Buy you a drink?"

"Thank you. Whiskey."

Pinter called the order to the barkeep and laid down fifteen cents when he delivered it. Jamie raised his glass in a toast as the marshal raised his beer, and both sipped.

As he set down his shot glass, barely touched, a voice at Jamie's elbow said, "What are you doing here?"

Jamie turned to look into the disapproving face of Abraham Denton. "Beg pardon?"

"And drinking whiskey. The schoolmaster is supposed to set an example for our youth, Mr. McKay."

Jamie examined him thoughtfully. "The other evening you suggested I shouldn't smoke, which I don't. Now you're saying I shouldn't drink, which I do, in moderation. I thought I was being hired as a teacher, Mr. Denton, not a preacher."

"A schoolmaster should be as above reproach as a preacher, young man."

Jamie turned back to Jess Pinter. "Do you feel that way, Marshal?"

"I bought you that drink, didn't I?"

Denton said, "You're not on the council, Jess. You have no say in this. You're also wearing a gun, McKay. Do you think that seemly for a schoolmaster?"

Spotting blacksmith Hank Ford at one of the poker tables, Jamie went over. Ford was out of the pot. He looked up and said, "Evening, McKay."

Jamie said, "Do you have any objection to me being here?"

The blacksmith looked puzzled. "I don't understand the question."

"As the new schoolmaster, I mean. Mr. Denton seems to think I should behave like a preacher—not smoke, drink or wear a gun, but just walk around looking pious."

"Denton is an old maid." Then he looked beyond Jamie, smiled sheepishly and said, "Hi, Abe."

Jamie spotted Amos Appleton coming in the door and headed him off en route to the bar. "Evening, Your Honor."

"Hello, young fellow."

"Mr. Denton thinks I set a bad example for my prospective pupils by being here. Do you agree?"

When Appleton frowned past him, Jamie realized Denton was still trailing him. The mayor said, "Abe, I wouldn't be surprised if the rules you set didn't drive Percy Ellison away. You want to end up teaching school yourself?"

"He can't," Jamie said. "He smokes."

Appleton laughed and slapped him on the shoulder. "I'll take this up at the council meeting Monday night, Jamie, and see if we can resolve it. Meantime, consider your personal life your own affair. Within limits, of course. I go along with Abe that the schoolmaster should be a little circumspect, like not showing up at church drunk and throwing up on the preacher."

If either Ford or Appleton had agreed with Denton, Jamie had been prepared to resign then and there. Appleton's words mollified him enough at least to postpone his resignation.

He returned to his place at the bar and tossed off the rest of his whiskey. Noticing the marshal's glass was empty, he reordered and paid for drinks for both of them. As they were delivered, he saw Denton farther up the bar, eyeing him with disapproval.

Within his mind Jamie said, *Keep pushing, mister, and I'll diddle your daughter.*

Sunday morning Jamie crossed the street to the Denton house and walked to church with the whole family. He wore his usual range garb, having nothing else with him, but at least it was clean, since he had picked up his laundry on Wednesday. He left his gun at home, figuring it would be out of place in church. Cricket and her mother both wore light cotton dresses, Abraham Denton a white shirt with a string tie and blue sleeve garters.

In his dour way the city treasurer was cordial enough. Perhaps he thought he had won his point the previous night because Jamie had become so annoyed by his disapproving looks that he had gone home at a quarter of ten, only forty-five minutes after entering the Palace. Or perhaps he thought he would get his way at the council meeting tomorrow night. In any event he seemed to have tabled his animosity.

The church, which seated five hundred, had every pew filled, and there were several standees at the rear. Jamie suspected the large attendance was only because it was the sole church in town, since he couldn't believe that all the congregation could be as harshly fundamentalist as the preacher.

About forty, the Reverend Wilson Stentor was gauntly handsome, but he fitted Jamie's mental image of a Spanish inquisitor. Wearing a long black coat in the stifling heat, he was a rip-roaring evangelist who preached eternal damnation for sin, which Jamie gathered was anything that was fun. In view of Cricket's suggestion that he was a secret drinker, it was bemusing that one of the sins he railed against was drinking. Jamie spent most of the service plotting how to get out of attending future services.

After church the Dentons introduced Jamie to virtually everyone there, few of whom he could remember five minutes later. The blur of names and faces eventually blended into a drone of unintelligible sound and the two blank faces of Everyman and Everywoman.

When the ordeal was over, Cricket asked Jamie to walk home with her to get the the picnic basket. The picnic was to be in a grove just behind the church.

"How did you like the service?" Cricket asked as they walked along.

Afraid of offending her beliefs, Jamie made a neutral comment. "The Reverend Stentor sure lays down the law."

"Isn't he awful?"

He looked at her. "You go because your parents make you?"

"They don't make me. They can't stand his preaching either."

"Then why do any of you go?"

"What else is there to do on Sunday?"

It had always puzzled Jamie why so many people flocked to church to hear that they were going to hell. Maybe, in one sentence, Cricket had given the answer.

Cricket said, "Personally he's very nice. It's only in the pulpit he's so boring. We often have him over for dinner, and he can be quite witty, poor man."

"Why poor man?"

"He has to sleep alone. His wife died a year ago."

"That why he fornicates with members of the ladies auxiliary?"

Cricket giggled. "That was just a joke, silly. My sweet mother belongs to the auxiliary."

When they got back to the picnic, Jamie began to

understand that Cricket's explanation of why she and her parents went to church had been over-simplistic. Except for the preacher, who still wore his black coat in the hot sun, everyone seemed to be having an enjoyable time. There were probably many other social events sponsored by the church, he thought. It was the social hub of the town, and perhaps the one hour a week of chastisement they suffered was regarded by members of the congregation as the dues they had to pay for the socializing and fellowship they enjoyed.

He ate with Cricket and her parents on a blanket spread next to the Appletons. Afterward Jamie and Cricket walked over to the edge of the picnic grounds and sat in the shade of a tree.

"Mama says you told her you were from El Paso," Cricket said.

"Near there. I worked on a ranch."

"Leave a sweetheart behind?"

"Yes."

Cricket looked disappointed. "Is she pretty?—Cancel that dumb question. Of course, she'd be pretty."

"She's beautiful."

"You plan to return and marry her?"

"She's going to marry someone else."

Cricket gave him a surprised look. "She chose someone over you?"

"Her father did the choosing. It's an arranged marriage."

"They still have those in this day and age?"

"It's an old Spanish family," Jamie said. "Goes back to the conquistadors. Don Miguel believes money should marry money, and I was just a thirty-dollar-a-month cowpoke. As a matter of fact, it was his ranch I worked on."

"I know who he is. A rancher from Mexico, fifty years old, with four grown children, all older than Consuela."

"How terrible! How could her father do that to her?"

"He didn't. I did."

"You arranged the marriage?"

Jamie wished he hadn't told so much. He said, "I made the arrangement necessary. Let's talk about something else."

"You can't take me to this point of your Romeo-and-Juliet story, then drop it."

"I shouldn't have told any of it. A gentleman doesn't talk about his love affairs."

"You won't be slandering her as I have no idea who she is. I'll die of curiosity if you don't finish the story."

He was silent for several seconds while she waited expectantly. Finally he said with an embarrassed expression on his face, "She wasn't a virgin. That's important in Spanish families. No younger man wanted her."

"My God, this is from the Middle Ages. You think it's your fault just because you diddled her?"

When he looked pained, she said, "Excuse the language. I forgot you were a gentleman. I don't know why, because I distinctly remember your gentlemanly behavior at the store."

"I've already ruined one girl. I'm not going through life laying waste."

She gave him a curious look. "We're not all descended from conquistadors."

"You don't understand. I could never marry another girl. I still love her, and always will."

"You think if you diddle a girl, you have to marry her. Sorry, there I go again."

"I used to think virginity wasn't important. But since

I've ruined Consuela's life, I think a man assumes some responsibility when he deflowers a girl.''

''What makes you think you'd deflower me?''

Jamie gazed at her for a long time before saying, ''Want to take a walk to the hardware store tonight?''

''No, tomorrow night.''

Now that he had given in, Jamie was eager to consummate the union. In fact he was concealing a sudden erection.

''Why not tonight?''

''Mother invited the Appletons for dinner, and wants me to invite you. Tomorrow night will be better anyway.''

''Why?''

''Daddy will be at the council meeting and won't know I'm out of the house. I'll tell my mother I'm going to Missy's and meet you behind the store at seven-fifteen.''

''All right,'' Jamie said, exerting mental effort to put down his erection.

It didn't occur to Jamie that there was no place to lie down in the storeroom until Cricket lighted the lantern. When she saw the expression on his face as he looked all around, she said, ''If you're thinking what I think you are, don't worry.''

Locking the back door, she pointed to a barrel with a lid on it marked LIME a few feet from the back door and said, ''Move that over flush against the door.''

''Why?''

''Because there's no room along any of the walls.''

That was true. The walls on either side were lined with bins, and the other two had shovels, picks and other tools hanging from them. His question remained unanswered, though. What he had meant was why did she wish it moved at all? He didn't want to waste time discussing it, however. Tipping the barrel, which felt about half full, he rolled it in front of the locked back door.

"Flush against it," she said.

He put his shoulder to it and shoved until it touched the door.

Moving into his arms, she put hers about his neck and thrust her tongue into his mouth. She was wearing the same gingham dress she had on the night they met, and he could feel nothing beneath it. She began to breathe heavily the moment his hands moved over her.

Breaking the kiss, she unbuttoned her dress, pulled it off over her head and kicked off her shoes, which left her naked, as she had on no undergarments or stockings. She had a cute little bosom, and her pubic hair was as bright red as her head. Draping her dress over a box, she hoisted herself to a seated position on the lime barrel.

He got the idea then. Quickly stripping, he walked between her spread thighs and entered her standing up. When she leaned her back against the door and elevated her knees, the height was just right. He went in clear to his scrotum.

For the next few minutes there was nothing on his mind but her writhing body. But after they were finished and were redressing, it occurred to him that the barrel trick couldn't have been impromptu. Either some other man had devised it for her, or she had devised it for some other man. Maybe several other men.

The council meeting was still going on when Jamie entered the house at eight o'clock. As he passed the archway off the entry hall which led into the parlor, he heard Miss Emily McCarthy say, "Abe, you have a head like a rock. If we don't compromise, we're going to lose him."

He climbed the stairs to his room and was studying his

arithmetic primer when Amos Appleton came up at nine o'clock. The mayor paused in the open door.

"Got a minute, Jamie?"

"Yes, sir, come on in."

Appleton came in and sat on the bed. "We had quite a session, but the two old maids finally agreed to a compromise."

"Oh?"

"Miss McCarthy and Denton both think there should be a code of conduct for the schoolmaster, that he shouldn't smoke, wear a gun or frequent the Palace Saloon. Hank Ford and I—and probably Jess Pinter, but he never says anything—think we have no business telling you what to do. The compromise we arrived at was that you're not to smoke, which you don't anyway, and stop wearing a gun. Can you live with that?"

"I'll think about it."

"All we're really asking you to do is stop wearing a gun, which lots of men don't. I don't carry one, Denton don't, and neither does Hank Ford. Is somebody after you?"

"Not really. I'd need it in El Paso, but not here."

"Then what's the problem?"

"None, I guess. Tell them I'll go along."

Appleton looked relieved. "One more thing, but this is only a suggestion. They think it would be seemly if you bought a suit to wear in class."

"No."

Jamie's tone was so definite that Appleton said, "All right, it was only a suggestion. I'll tell them."

CHAPTER XVI

Enrollment was scheduled to begin at eight o'clock a.m. on September first. When Jamie opened the schoolhouse door at 7:45, a crowd of pupils and their parents was already waiting. Jamie invited everyone in and seated himself at his desk.

A few of the parents and children he already knew because they lived in town. Most, however, were from outlying areas. After introducing himself to the crowd, he asked the parents to form a line with their children and come to the desk one at a time. He recorded each child's name in a notebook, along with age, the grade level already attained, the names of both parents, home address and, if necessary, weekday address. This last was necessary in the case of children who lived a considerable distance away as they would be staying at Mrs. Schraft's Boarding House for Children during the week and returning home only on weekends.

The first parent was a giant named Thaddeus Thudd, owner of the Circle-K ten miles north. He had with him his equally enormous son, Norval, a sullen two hundred-

pound sixteen-year-old with shoulders and arms like a
gorilla. Norval, his father said, had completed first grade.

"Schoolmaster Ellison couldn't learn him nothing at
all," Thaddeus Thudd said. "I opine that he spared the
rod too much. You got my go-ahead to lambast the boy as
much as you need."

Jamie had stored the willow switch in the supply closet.
He had a fleeting, but immediately discarded impulse to go
get it when Norval gave him a belligerent glare that was an
overt challenge to "learn" him anything.

He said, "I don't think it will come to that, Mr. Thudd.
Norval and I will get along fine."

Norval's sneer said, *That's what you think*.

The next pupil was Faustina Monet, a slender, gawky
thirteen-year-old with a pixie face and impish eyes. Her
father, a funny little man sporting a pointed, waxed
mustache, a French accent and a beret, introduced himself
as Armand Monet and said he was the proprietor of the
Hotel Parisian in Goose Flats.

Faustina said, "You're being pretentious again, Father.
Mr. McKay, it's really just a saloon with rooms upstairs."

Spreading his hands in a Gallic gesture of despair, her
father said, "I have reared a child of mockery, Monsieur
McKay. Perhaps you can teach the *juene-fille* respect. His
criticism was belied by a beam of pride.

After recording the girl's and her father's names, Jamie
said, "Her mother's name?"

"Alas, she is departed these many years," Monet said.

As Jamie started to write *Mother Deceased*, Faustina
said, "By departed, my father just means gone. She ran
off with a whiskey drummer when I was two."

Jamie erased and changed it to *Mother Away*.

The school curriculum was geared to take pupils only

through the sixth-grade level. Her father said Faustina had passed that when she was ten.

"What am I supposed to teach her, Mr. Monet?" Jamie asked.

"Monsieur Ellison, he gave her special instruction in many thing, such as science and astronomy. She has her own textbooks."

Jamie was relieved to hear that. If he could borrow them, perhaps he could stay one jump ahead of her.

"This is to be her last year."

Jamie was also relieved to hear that. It was going to be awkward having a pupil in school smarter than he was.

The little man said, "I have enroll Faustina in the Bessie Tift Women's College in Georgia next year, but she must pass examinations because she be only fourteen then, and the college usually takes no younger than sixteen. I bring her to you in the hope you may prepare her for such tests."

Jamie was not relieved to hear that. It seemed a lot to expect of a man who had never spent a day in a classroom as a pupil.

Faustina was going to stay at Mrs. Schraft's Boarding House during the week as Goose Flats was twenty miles away.

Altogether there were twenty-one enrollees, eight from Rimfire and the rest living anywhere from a mile to twenty miles away. Six lived far enough to have to board at Mrs. Schraft's. The age limit was from two six-year-old boys to sixteen-year-old Norval Thudd.

After the parents left, Jamie told the pupils to sit anywhere they wanted today and he would assign them permanent desks tomorrow. Faustina Monet took a desk in the front row, Norval Thudd one at the back.

Jamie had designed three tests to determine present

levels of performance in reading, writing and arithmetic. He explained that the tests would not be graded and that no one should worry about passing or failing.

"These are only to let me know at which grade levels to assign you," he said. "Anything you can't do, just don't do it."

First he passed out copies of McGuffey's *Eclectic Reader*, telling the pupils not to open their books until he gave the word. Seating himself behind his desk, he laid his watch on it and said, "When I say 'Go,' open your books and read the first story as fast as you can, but not so fast that you can't absorb what you are reading, because afterward I'm going to have you write down what the story was about. As soon as you finish, close your book and raise your hand." He looked at his watch and said, "Go."

While his pupils were reading, he started to transpose names from his enrollment notebook to a sheet of paper in alphabetical order. He had entered only six names when Faustina Monet's hand shot up.

He looked at his watch. She had taken a minute and a half.

He completed his alphabetical list and had entered Faustina's time behind her name before the next pupil finished, a twelve-year-old boy. His time was four-and-a-half minutes.

Subsequent times ranged from eight to twenty minutes. At the end of twenty minutes only the two six-year-olds and Norval Thudd had not raised their hands. The books of all three were closed.

Jamie said to one of the six-year-olds, "You're finished, Albert?"

"No, sir. I can't read. My mommie sent me here to learn."

A titter ran through the classroom. Jamie said to the other six-year-old, "Can't you read either, Joseph?"

"No, sir."

Jamie said to the oversized boy at the back, "How about you, Norval?"

"Didn't feel like reading today, teacher."

Jamie said nothing. Rising, he passed out sheets of paper to everyone, then returned to his desk.

"Now, keeping your books closed, I want you to write what the story was about. When you finish, print your name at the top of the sheet and bring it to me. Albert, Joseph and Norval can draw pictures while everyone else is writing."

Faustina took five minutes to finish. The longest time, an eight-year-old boy, was thirty minutes. Albert had drawn a stick man, Joseph a lopsided horse. Jamie complimented both on their skill. Norval had folded his paper into a ship.

"Very talented, Norval," Jamie said when the boy laid it on his desk.

Jamie passed out more paper, went to the blackboard and picked up a piece of chalk. "Now I'm going to write some simple arithmetic problems on the board. Copy them down and work as many as you can."

He started to turn toward the board when some extrasensory alarm sounding within his head made him glance around. Norval was half standing, his body bent forward, his right arm extended, and a small, round, red object was hurtling at Jamie.

Sidestepping, Jamie's left hand flashed up to pluck the object from the air. It was an apple full of worm holes. Even though Jamie's palm was calloused from years of roping steers, the force of the throw was enough to sting his hand. If the apple had hit the back of his head, it could have knocked him out.

Reseating himself, Norval gave Jamie a smug grin. "My old man said maybe I'd get a good grade if I gave the teacher an apple."

There was a little nervous laughter, but most of the class seemed shocked.

Setting the apple on his desk, Jamie lifted the dunce cap from the high stool and set it on the desk also. As he walked toward Norval, the boy's eyes glittered a challenge. Jamie went past him and around behind his desk, gripped his neck with his right hand and jerked him to his feet. With his left hand he gripped his belt, pulled him upward out of the space between his desk and his seat and heaved all two hundred pounds of him overhead. Holding him in that position, Jamie marched to the front of the room and slammed him down onto the dunce stool so hard that his teeth clicked together audibly. Spinning him around to face the class, Jamie clapped the dunce cap on his head, picked up the apple and handed it to Norval.

"Eat it," he said.

Gazing at him in fright, the boy said, "It's full of worms, teacher."

Jamie leaned forward to whisper in his ear. "If you don't start eating it right now, I'm going to bend you over the stool, pull down your pants and ram it up your ass."

Norval gulped, stared at the apple sickly and began to eat it. Jamie said to the rest of the class, "Recess, twenty minutes."

When Norval finished his apple, Jamie told him he could go to recess too. As the boy started out the door, Jamie said, "Norval?"

Turning, Norval said, "Yes, teacher?"

"You wouldn't think of cutting off and not coming back, would you?"

"No, sir."

"If you do, know what I'll do?"

"No, sir."

"I'll ride out to the Circle-K with another apple. That one you won't get to eat."

"Yes, sir."

"Go to recess."

As the boy scurried out, Jamie sat at his desk to look over the story descriptions. Surprisingly, all had gotten the gist of the story, but most of the writing was atrocious, and some of the spelling was so inventive that it made Jamie chuckle. Faustina's report was written in a neat copperplate script with perfect spelling, and her account struck Jamie as being considerably better written than the story itself.

After recess Jamie conducted his arithmetic test, and discovered that Norval could do simple addition and subtraction. While the rest of the class was taking a slightly more advanced arithmetic test, Jamie gave the boy a chance to take the earlier tests he had skipped. His reading of the story took the rest of the morning, and after lunch it took him an hour to write his report. He understood the story, though. Unsurprisingly, his handwriting, spelling and grammar were the worst in the class.

At three o'clock Jamie pulled the cord that made the bell outside over the door clang, and there was a general rush for the door. Jamie stopped Faustina.

"Yes, sir?" she said, looking up at him.

"Where are these special textbooks your father mentioned, Faustina?"

"We left them at the boarding house when Daddy registered me, before we came here. He said he was sure I wouldn't need them today."

"I see. Have you already studied them?"

"No, sir. Daddy had to send away for them to New York, and they only arrived a few days ago."

At least that didn't put her ahead of her teacher, Jamie thought. "Would you mind if I borrowed them to look over?"

"No, sir."

"Wait until I gather my papers and I'll walk to Mrs. Schraft's with you."

As they walked along the boardwalk, she said, "You are very strong, Mr. McKay."

"But not very self-controlled. I'm not really proud of that performance."

"I thought it was masterful. Norval had Mr. Ellison frightened out of his wits. That's probably why he didn't come back."

"Oh? I thought it was because of some pedagogical rules."

"What, sir?"

"Just thinking aloud."

"I know that pedagogical means, but I don't understand what you meant."

Jamie was not surprised that she knew the meaning of the word. He would have been surprised if she hadn't. He said, "It's not important."

When they arrived at the boarding house, he waited outside while she ran in to get the books. There were five—four of them college level textbooks on science, world history, English literature and philosophy, and the other a recent book by the English astronomer, John Couch Adams, not a textbook, but a report on his studies.

Jamie suspected he was going to learn more this year than any of his students except Faustina.

"Thank you," he said. "Which subject would you like to start on tomorrow?"

"Whichever you prefer, sir."

Since he had read a considerable amount of philosophy, he said, "We'll start with philosophy. Are you familiar with Plato's *Dialogues*?"

"I know of them."

"I happen to have a translation. I'll loan it to you tomorrow."

"Thank you, sir."

"Do you mind if I keep the other books for a few days while we work on philosophy?"

"Of course not."

"Your father is very proud of you, isn't he?"

"I am very proud of him, too. He has read nearly everything."

"I suspected it ran in the family."

She giggled.

"What's funny?" he asked.

"He is. That French accent, for instance, and the French gestures."

"I thought both were charming."

"They are, which is why he cultivates them. My grandparents were born in France, but he was born in New York. He doesn't even speak French."

In mid-September Little Doe got a letter from her son.

Rimfire, Arizona
September 5, 1874

Dear Little Doe:

Hold your hat; I'm a schoolmaster.

This came about through the coincidence of Rimfire's mayor seeing me reading *Plato's Dialogues* two weeks before school opened and right after he had learned that last year's schoolmaster wasn't coming back. I was a choice of desperation, it either being me or no school. I earn the magnificent salary of $50 a month, plus room and board.

I have twenty-one pupils and have divided them into six grades, plus what I'm calling seventh grade, but which is really a graduate seminar. Two six-year-olds are in first grade, a thirteen-year-old girl genius preparing for college is the sole member of the seminar. I am supposed to instruct her in history, science, English literature, philosophy and astronomy, and it looks as though much of what I teach her I will have to learn the night before class.

To assist me in tutoring her in English literature, please send me the following books from the library: Lyly's *Euphues*, Nashe's *The Unfortunate Traveller*, Swift's *A Tale of a Tub*, Richardson's *Pamela*, Smollett's *Peregrine Pickle* and Sterne's *Sentimental Journey*. If this seems a strange selection because it doesn't include some of the above author's more important works, and leaves out Bunyan, Defoe, Fielding and all the novelists since Fielding, it is because the young lady either has read all of those, or they are available in her father's library.

This is a pleasant community, although the weather is a bit hot for my blood. I am well and hope you are also. Write me the news.

Love,
Jamie

Toward the end of September Jamie received the books, along with a letter.

Double-D Ranch
El Paso, Texas
September 18, 1874

Dear Jamie:

I am pleased and proud of you in your new
profession. Perhaps you will be able to save enough
to attend college like your little girl pupil.

Consuela Derango had a big bethrothal party at
the ranch house last Saturday, and I had to help
Belinda cook for it. She is marrying a rancher from
Laredo named Juan Cassando, a nice looking, genial
man, but much older. He is a widower, and Belinda
says he has grown children. Consuela looked so
unhappy at the party, I felt sorry for her.

Don Miguel has not lifted the bounty on you, but
perhaps will after the wedding, which will be in
November. If he does, I hope you can come home
for a visit next summer.

I am well, and hope you remain so. Where you
are, I can't give you the motherly advice to stay
warm, but will you stay out of trouble?

Love,
Little Doe

Since the only expenses Jamie had were laundry and a
dollar-a-week board for his horse at the livery stable, his
ten dollars lasted him until he received his first month's
pay. Saturday was two days later, and that night he made his
first visit to the Palace Saloon since the night of his run-in
with Abraham Denton. His only recreation had been some
church social events, to which he had escorted Cricket,
and a couple of sessions a week with her in the storeroom

at the hardware store. He was a little worried about getting her pregnant, but she assured him she was taking precautions.

The saloon was packed. After having a drink at the bar with Marshal Pinter, Jamie went over to watch one of the poker games. Hank Ford was in the game and gave Jamie a cordial greeting.

The game was table stakes draw. Jamie had never been able to afford anything steeper than nickel poker, but he had played lots of that in the chuck house at the Double-D. He had also watched many table games at Dowell's Saloon in El Paso, where cowboys sometimes blew a month's wages in a few hands, and he had come to the conclusion that very few players in such games had even the basic skills of poker. He had seen hopeless hands drawn to, calls made that should never have been made, and obvious bluffs go uncalled.

The professional gambler banking the game was a slender, sleek man with a dark mustache. He was dragging a white chip from each pot and two from the big ones. He and Hank Ford struck Jamie as the only two competent players in the game. The other six were cowboys in various stages of drunkenness.

As he watched, one of the cowboys went broke by calling a straight with a pair of queens. As the man made a disgusted noise, got to his feet and lurched to the bar, the banker looked up at Jamie and said, "Sit in, young fellow?"

Jamie had all of his fifty-dollar pay in his pocket. "What are the stakes?" he asked.

"Table stakes, size of the pot, twenty-dollar buy-in, dealer antes two dollars but nobody else does. Jacks or better. One joker in the deck, good for aces, straights or flushes."

Deciding to risk twenty dollars, Jamie took the vacant

seat and traded two tens for twenty white quarter chips, ten red fifty-cent chips, and ten blue dollar chips.

It happened that the busted cowboy had last dealt, which meant Jamie wouldn't have to ante for the first seven hands.

The first hand he drew a pair of tens; somebody opened and he threw them away. The second hand he drew a four-card inside straight and pitched it in. The third hand he drew a pair of jacks and, when Hank Ford opened, threw them in. He considered it a basic principle of poker never to stay on anything that couldn't beat the opener going in. The house man dealt next. He dealt Jamie a bust, and again he threw in.

The next dealer, a drunken cowboy who had difficulty shuffling, said, "You waiting for four aces, mister?"

"I'll stay on three," Jamie said.

He was dealt four spades; the two players before him passed, as did he, and the man to his left opened for two dollars. When it came around to Jamie with two callers and no raises, he called and drew one card. It was the joker, giving him an ace-high flush. The opener and the two other callers each drew three.

The opener bet ten dollars and the other two callers folded; Jamie called and pushed in his remaining eight as a raise. The opener called and showed a pair of kings.

Sucker, Jamie thought. *Ever hear of a check?*

Jamie didn't play again for two rounds, after which he won a pot on three aces. He then hit a short lucky streak where he drew openers four times in a row, the lowest being a pair of kings and the highest three treys. On the kings he folded and showed his openers after another player bet into his check. The other three pots he won.

After pitching in the next six hands, he drew to an open straight, hit it, but collected only a small pot when he bet into the opener's check and everyone folded. The players were getting the idea that he played only cinch hands.

He waited for the opportunity to jar them out of that notion, and it came on his next deal. He drew a pair of jacks, everyone passed around to him, and he opened. Three players stayed, all drawing three cards.

Jamie stayed pat and bet ten dollars. The three stayers folded.

The house rule was that the opener had to show his full hand. When Jamie spread his, one of the folders said, "Jesus Christ, I pitched three tens."

Jamie wouldn't have particularly cared if the man had called. It would have been worth the investment to show the table that he was capable of bluffing. For the rest of the evening he never pulled another bluff, but he had no trouble getting called. He ended winner by $112.

That started a weekly habit. Almost always he won, sometimes not much, but once, on his eighteenth birthday, October tenth, he won two hundred dollars. His rare losses were small. Even on second-best nights, when he repeatedly drew good hands which lost to better ones, his losses were never heavy because he had sense enough to pull out of the game as soon as the pattern for the evening became obvious to him. During October and November he won a total of six hundred dollars, for a monthly average of six times his schoolmaster's salary.

CHAPTER XVII

Just before Christmas vacation Cricket told Jamie that she and her parents were going to her grandmother's in Tucson over Christmas. The Appletons were going to Fort Bliss to spend Christmas with their son. Jamie contemplated a Christmas dinner alone at the McCarthy Hotel.

Christmas was on a Friday that year, and school let out for the holiday on the previous Friday. As had become the custom, Faustina's tutoring session lasted beyond the dismissal bell, so she and Jamie were always the last two in the schoolhouse.

As she picked up her books and he gathered his papers, she said, "What are you doing over Christmas, Mr. McKay?"

"Nothing."

"You must be having Christmas dinner."

"Yes, at the hotel."

"You mean all alone?"

"Yes."

They had started out the door together, but she stopped and said, "You are not. You're coming to our house for dinner."

He stopped also. "Thanks, but I wouldn't dream of putting your father out."

"You wouldn't. Who do you think cooks Christmas dinner?"

"You?" he asked, surprised.

She grinned. "The foreman of our ranch. We don't live at the hotel. Will you come?"

"You had better check with your father first. When's he coming for you?"

"Five o'clock, but I don't have to check. Who do you think is boss in our family?"

"You?"

She grinned again. "My father, but he would be delighted. Please come, Mr. McKay."

She was too bright to invite him unless she was sure it would be all right. He said, "I would be most happy."

They continued out and he closed the door. "Come Christmas Eve," she said. "The ranch is beyond Goose Flats, so come to the saloon. Daddy plans to close at five, and he'll lead you to the ranch."

"All right," he said.

Jamie carried on a weekly correspondence with his mother. On the Monday before Christmas he received a letter saying that Consuela had been married on Saturday, November twenty-first. That night he went to the Palace Saloon, which on Mondays was practically deserted, and quietly got drunk for the first time in his life.

Christmas Eve Jamie rode into Goose Flats at four in the afternoon, carrying two presents in his saddlebags. One was a bottle of wine for Armand Monet, the other a new book he had ordered from New York some time back, which had just arrived, and which he had decided to give to Faustina and reorder for himself. It was Lewis Carroll's sequel to *Alice in Wonderland*, *Through the Looking Glass*.

He knew Goose Flats was small, but he hadn't realized how small. It was only a crossroads. There was the inevitable livery stable, combined with a blacksmith shop, a general store, the saloon-hotel and three houses. The saloon-hotel was between the livery-stable-blacksmith-shop and the general store.

A long sign on the balcony of the hotel's second floor read: HOTEL PARISIAN—MONSIEUR ARMAND MONET PROPRIÉTAIRE. There were two horses tied to the hitching rail in front. Jamie tied up his mare and went inside.

The only difference from any other saloon Jamie had been in was that, to the right, stairs led up to a balcony, off which he could see seven doors. A bar ran along the rear of the room; there was a piano against the left wall and a number of tables, among them a single poker table.

Two cowboys were seated at the bar. Armand Monet, in a white shirt and white apron, was behind it. An elderly, unshaven man with a drinker's red face was sweeping the floor.

"Monsieur McKay," Monet said, reaching across the bar to shake hands. "Merry Christmas."

"Same to you, sir. I hope Faustina told you I was coming."

"*Certainement*. We are honor to have you. What may I give you to drink?"

"Nothing, thanks." Jamie never drank before evening, and not much then, except for the previous Monday.

Looking pointedly at the two cowboys, Monet said, "I will close and take you to the ranch as soon as the last customer leave."

One of the cowboys said, "You posted a notice saying you were open until five today, Frenchy."

"I envisioned a packed house."

The other cowboy said, "You said five, Frenchy."

Reaching beneath the bar, Monet brought up a quart of whiskey and set it in front of the two men. "There, I give you a Christmas present. Only you must drink it elsewhere."

"Hey, you're all right," the first cowboy said, picking up the bottle. "Let's go, Colorado."

As the two men went out, Monet took off his apron. "We are close, Lolly," he said to the man sweeping the floor. "Go out back."

As Lolly carried his broom through the back door, Monet said, "He sleep in the shed. If I permit him to sleep here, he drink the bar dry. I be with you when I have lock the back door."

Two miles north of town they came to a sign alongside a lane lettered: IDF RANCH—MONET.

"What's IDF stand for?" Jamie asked as they turned into the lane.

"Ile de France. I am not a rancher, Monsieur McKay. I buy this to make a home for Faustina."

"Your cattle look healthy," Jamie said, spotting a small herd of steers off to the right.

"I am bless with superb help. I hire one foreman and two wrangler."

A hundred yards along the lane there was a large adobe one-story ranch house shaded by trees, a small bunkhouse, a corral, a barn and a couple of other outhouses. Faustina, in a checkered gingham dress, came running from the back door as the men dismounted at the barn.

"Hi, Mr. McKay," she said. "Merry Christmas."

"Same to you, Faustina. My, you're looking pretty."

Blushing, she gave him a curtsy. The men led their horses into the barn and Faustina returned to the house. As they were unsaddling their horses, two Indians in flannel shirts, denim pants and cowboy boots came into the barn;

one was long and spare, the other squarely-built and moon-faced.

Monet introduced the tall, spare man as Bigfoot Harry and the chunky one as Bucking Horse. As he shook hands with them, Jamie said, "Apache?"

"Once," Bigfoot Harry said. "We converted to white."

"I'm Comanche," Jamie said.

The two Indians regarded him dubiously. Monet said, "You are Indian?"

"Half, and half-Irish. Didn't Faustina tell you?"

"She know I am believe the only good Indian is a dead one," he said, looking at his employees deadpan.

"Got a coin?" the lanky Bigfoot Harry said to Bucking Horse.

"Why?"

"To flip to see who scalps the little Frog."

"Let us repair to the house," Monet said to Jamie.

"I have to rub down my horse."

"The savages will care for the animals. Come along."

As the Indians each led a horse to a stall, Jamie shouldered his saddlebags and followed his host to the house. They went in by the kitchen door. A large black man was stuffing a turkey and Faustina was cutting cookies.

Monet said, "Um, the dinner of tomorrow. Monsieur McKay, this is our foreman, Monsieur Mortimer Brown, who avenges his former slavehood by tyrannizing this household."

The black man used a towel on his hands before offering a handshake. Faustina said, "He was never a slave, Mr. McKay. His parents were free colored. My father likes his little joke."

Mortimer Brown said, "Put Mr. McKay in the northwest bedroom."

"See?" Monet said. "I am but a lackey in my own

house. Is what comes of the late Monsieur Lincoln's proclamation. Come along, Monsieur McKay.''

The pseudo-Frenchman certainly had an unusual employer-employee relationship with his men, Jamie thought as he followed Monet from the kitchen. He began to understand where Faustina got her odd sense of humor.

They ate the evening meal together in a large dining room, the black foreman doing the cooking and Faustina serving. Afterward they went into the parlor, where there was a Christmas tree covered with paper decorations, to open presents beneath the tree. Jamie went to his room to bring out his two and place them with the rest.

Faustina and her father and the three hands all exchanged gifts, all of them simple except the ones for Faustina. She got a braided leather belt from Mortimer Brown and hand-crafted silver-and-turquoise jewelry from the two Indians. Big Foot Harry gave her a ring and Bucking Horse a bracelet. Her father gave her a heart-shaped pendant on a golden chain.

The men's gifts were all shirts and socks.

When Monet opened his gift of wine, he held it up to the light to examine its color and said, "*Magnifique*. I am desolate that I bought you nothing, monsieur."

Faustina said, "He is not, Mr. McKay. I told him you would probably bring gifts, but would be embarrassed if you got any from anyone but me. It was a conspiracy among the five of us."

Monet said, "I am plagued by honesty from all sides."

When Faustina opened her gift from Jamie, she burst out laughing. While he was trying to figure out the joke, she handed him a package of similar size. It was also a copy of *Through the Looking Glass*.

"Two minds with but a single thought," she said.

After opening the presents, Monet, trailed by his daughter,

showed Jamie his library. It was a separate room with the walls solidly lined with books. There must have been fifteen hundred.

"No wonder your daughter is so learned," Jamie said. "How many of these have you read, Faustina?"

"About a fourth. I will get to them all."

Monet said, "Your teaching have helped her much, monsieur. I have faith that she will pass her entrance tests at Bessie Tift."

Christmas dinner, served at two p.m., was so bountiful that it left all but the two youngest diners logy. Faustina's father fell asleep on the parlor sofa and the three ranch hands went to the bunkhouse to take naps.

After gazing at her sleeping father, Faustina said to Jamie, "Want to go fishing?"

"Where?"

"There's a creek nearby."

"All right," he said.

She got two fishing poles and a spade from the barn and watched him dig a half-dozen worms. Then she led him to a narrow stream two-hundred yards from the house and along its bank to a large pool formed by a log-and-mud dam.

"I didn't know there were beaver this far south," Jamie said.

"Bigfoot Harry and Bucking Horse were the beaver. They meant it as a swimming hole for me, but it's also good fishing."

They baited their hooks, threw out the lines and sat on the bank under a tree, watching their wooden floats. There was a bright sun in a cloudless sky, only a light breeze, and the temperature was about seventy-five.

"Could you fish this time of year where you came from, Mr. McKay?" Faustina asked.

"In an overcoat."

"You're from the north?"

"El Paso."

"Isn't that strange? That's south of here."

"It has to do with elevation and prevailing winds," Jamie said.

Faustina gave him an admiring look. "You're so smart, Mr. McKay."

The child was practicing coquetry on him, Jamie realized with astonishment. The remark was blatant feminine flattery.

Previous instances of her regarding him as more than a teacher, unnoticed at the time but apparently absorbed by his subconscious, suddenly emerged: the time he had looked up from a book they had been studying side by side, to catch her gazing at him with what he now realized had been near adoration; the time he had accidentally touched her hand and she had jumped as though stung; the way she had blushed yesterday when he complimented her appearance.

The kid had a schoolgirl crush on him.

CHAPTER XVIII

Between the time Denise went back to school in September and Christmas, Nate collected two more bounties totaling seventy-five hundred dollars. During his travels he also played a considerable amount of poker, and Hank Pizzaro's tutelage, plus a natural talent, made him a consistent winner. He used two thousand dollars to buy the cottage he had been renting and banked the rest.

Since it was believed both by her parents and the nuns at the junior college that Denise no longer had any contact with Nate, her restrictions at school had been lifted. Nate wrote to her as "Miss Jane Eyre," c/o General Delivery at the Belmont Post Office. So that they wouldn't be found during one of the periodic room searches, Denise carried each letter from him around with her, rereading it over and over until the next arrived, and then destroyed it.

Her Christmas vacation created a problem. She would be out of school from Wednesday, December twenty-third until Monday, January fourth. Four of those days she would be unable to get away from home: Christmas Eve, Christmas Day, New Year's Eve and New Year's Day. All these were scheduled as family celebrations, with numerous out-of-town guests. Nate's mother wanted him home for Christmas, and as much as she begrudged sacrificing any of the little time available to them, Denise was unselfish enough not to want him to spend Christmas alone. When she wrote urging him to go home, he arranged to take the packet boat the day before she got out of school and to return on the evening of the twenty-ninth. That gave them only one day together before New Year's and one after.

They made the most of it. They hardly got out of bed either day.

They did as much talking as love-making, mostly about their future. They would be able to see each other briefly during the mid-semester break in February and again for several days over Easter vacation. After that it would be less than two months until Denise graduated.

"Are you going to break the news about us to your father on your eighteenth birthday?" Nate asked.

"Yes, I've already rehearsed what I'm going to say."

"What?"

As usual they were in bed. She raised herself on one elbow, assumed a daughterly expression and said, "Daddy, I'm pregnant."

"Good God, are you?"

She giggled. "No, but that ought to end all argument. What do you think?"

"I think he'll come after me with a shotgun."

"No, he wouldn't want to make his grandson an orphan."

"Is it going to be a boy?"

"You weren't listening," she said. "It's only a make-believe pregnancy."

"Let's make it for real. We'll need a bigger house, won't we?"

"I don't want a bigger house. I love this one. When the time comes, you can add on a nursery."

"Let's start something to keep in it," he said, pulling her down against him.

During the two days they had together, neither mentioned bounty hunting. By tacit agreement that had become an unmentionable subject both in correspondence and in conversation. But at their final parting on January second she said, "Please be careful, darling," and he knew what she meant.

During the between-semester break they had three wonderful days together, but two days before the start of Easter vacation she got a letter from Oregon saying he would make every effort to be in San Francisco when she got there, but might be held up. Every day while she was home she went to the cottage and also checked at the post office for letters to Miss Jane Eyre, but he never appeared or wrote. When she got back to school, she daily bought the San Francisco *Chronicle* for a time and read it thoroughly, hoping to learn why he had been in Oregon and at the same time dreading to know. She found no mention either of Nate or of any outlaws recently captured or killed in that state.

Just before her birthday she got both a letter and a small package from him. In the package was a gold ring with a half-carate blue diamond. The letter read:

Carson City, Nevada
May 10, 1875

My darling:

Happy 18th birthday, my love. I hope this arrives before the 16th. The present, in case you are puzzled, is your engagement ring. I know you can't wear it now, but you can hang it on the same chain as your heart locket, and I will transfer it from there to your finger the day you graduate from that jail. There is no chance I will miss that day, no matter how far I have to come.

Next time you go to mass, you might light a candle for a generous gentleman named Nevada Johnson, who contributed the price of your engagement ring during a poker session at the Lucky Dollar Saloon in Carson City.

Now that you are of age, screw up your courage and tell your parents about us, so that we may be married as soon as possible after you graduate.

I love you deeply and count the days until we can be together permanently as man and wife.

Love always,
Nate

As overjoyed as she was to hear from him, she couldn't help feeling a twinge of disappointment that he made no apology for not seeing her over Easter vacation. His oblique reference to it by assuring her he would not miss the day she graduated was evidence that he hadn't simply forgotten it, and it hurt her that he didn't seem to feel it necessary to offer any explanation.

Then she decided that perhaps that stemmed from their tacit agreement not to mention bounty hunting, because the explanation would involve breaking the agreement.

When Nate got back to San Francisco at the end of May, he found a letter waiting for him.

Belmont
May 20, 1875

Dearest Nate:

When my parents came to visit me and take me out to dinner on my birthday last Sunday, I used the opportunity to drop bomb number one. I told them that you and I had never broken contact, that we were in love, and that we planned to marry when school let out.

Predictably Daddy's reaction was an angry no, plus threats to have the school reimpose restrictions and to lock me in my room at home after graduation until I came to my senses. Instead of pointing out that I was now of legal age and had to submit to no such treatment, I dropped bomb number two by announcing I was pregnant.

Daddy got apoplectic and my mother cried right in the cafe, but eventually they settled down and accepted the situation because they had no other choice. To make a long story short, I have transferred my engagement ring to my finger, our engagement announcement will appear in the *Chronicle* this weekend, and we are to be married at a huge church wedding at 2:00 p.m. on Saturday, June 19th.

I will arrive home from school on Saturday, June 5th. You are ordered by my father to appear at our house at 2:00 p.m. on Sunday the 6th for your formal welcome into the family. Please dress up and don't wear a gun.

Darling, we are actually going to be together, married and living in our own little cottage twenty-four hours a day instead of only a few days out of the year from 10:00 until 5:00. I love you deeply and forever,

All my love,
Denise

On Sunday, June sixth, at two o'clock p.m. Nate raised and dropped the brass knocker on the front door of the big house on Nob Hill. He was dressed in a new suit and a starched collar with a string tie; he wore no gun and carried a bowler in his hand. The Negro butler answered the door.

"Miss Delavigne, please," Nate said. "Tell her Nathan Cook is calling."

"You are expected, sir."

The butler stepped aside, closed the door after Nate was in the large entry hall and held out his hand palm up. It took a moment for Nate to understand what he wanted, but then he quickly handed over his hat. The butler hung it on a hook, said, "Follow me, sir," and led the way through an archway into an enormous parlor.

The black man said, "Mr. Nathan Cook," and went away.

Denise's six-foot-four father and her short, round mother, reminding Nate of a cue and billard ball, stood with their backs to an empty fireplace at the far end of the room. The railroad lawyer wore a frock coat, pinstriped trousers, a wing collar with a black necktie, and a pearl gray vest. His wive wore a golden gown. Denise, looking beautiful in an ankle-length blue gown, her silver-hued hair done in an upsweep and pinned with a jeweled comb, stood next to her mother.

The distance from the entry hall to the fireplace, actually about sixty feet, seemed endless as Nate marched toward them. Georges Delavigne glared at him with controlled rage as he neared, and his wife looked as though she might cry. Denise was smiling radiantly.

Halting three feet away, Nate bowed formally and said, "Good afternoon, sir. Good afternoon, Mrs. Delavigne. Good afternoon, Denise."

Denise said, "Afternoon, darling." Georgia Delavigne dabbed at her eyes with a handkerchief. Denise's father said, "Young man, you have violated my daughter."

Denise said, "Daddy!"

Nate said, "I don't consider it a violation, sir. I love her."

"It was a violation." His Adam's apple bobbed as he swallowed twice in an effort to control himself before he said in a more normal, but still unfriendly tone, "However, the deed is done and we must accept the situation. I understand Denise has written you about the wedding plans."

"Yes, sir, two weeks from yesterday."

"The reception afterward will be here. Do you plan to invite guests?"

"Yes, sir, my mother and an aunt and a five-year-old cousin, my best man and a college friend from Bishop."

"Who will be your best man?"

"Emilio Pizzaro."

The lawyer's lip curled. "You are having a Mexican for your best man?"

"They call themselves Spanish, sir, but perhaps that is just a snobbish way of saying Mexican. His father is Don Simon Pizzaro."

His future father-in-law looked startled. "The San Joaquin Valley rancher?"

"Yes, sir."

"Will you have room to put him up?" the lawyer asked in a much friendlier tone, implying that if Nate hadn't, he could find room in the mansion.

"Yes, sir," Nate said. "For both him and Byron Moody. That's my guest from Bishop. I'll just spread feather ticks on my parlor floor. I'm planning to put my mother and aunt and cousin in a hotel."

"They can stay here," Denise said. "I want to get to know your mother anyway."

George Delavigne frowned at his daughter, obviously not as interested in hosting Nate's relatives as he had been in putting up the son of California's richest rancher. Before he could say anything, his wife said, "Yes, please tell them they're welcome here, Nate."

Her husband and daughter looked as surprised as Nate at the use of his nickname. Sensing her husband's displeasure, she gave him a defiant look. "He is going to be our son-in-law, Georges. I have no intention of calling him Mr. Cook."

Her husband's face developed a sour look. "You are right, of course, my dear, but I think I'll wait until the wedding day."

Georgia said, "The children will want to talk, dear. Shall we leave them alone?"

Nate suddenly began to like his prospective mother-in-law. Denise's father grunted something Nate took to be a good-bye and walked from the room. Giving both Nate and Denise a wan smile, Georgia followed.

As soon as her parents were out of sight, Denise flew into Nate's arms. After a long kiss, she said, "Don't be upset by Daddy's way, darling. He'll learn to like you. I think Mother already does."

"I just started to like her, too," he said. "What explanation are you going to make when no baby arrives?"

"None."

"You'll have to say something."

"No, I won't. It happened when we were together during the mid-semester break. I'm four months pregnant."

CHAPTER XIX

When school ended on June fourth, Jamie had a sense of accomplishment. The two youngest pupils, now seven, could read, write a little and knew their multiplication tables up to ten-times-ten. Norval Thudd, now almost seventeen, could read and write at about fourth-grade level. Faustina Monet was as prepared for her college entrance exams as he could get her, and every other pupil had made at least some progress.

The village council voted to ask him to return in September. Since in his weekly poker games Jamie had now accumulated a stake of two thousand dollars, the fifty-dollar-a-month salary wasn't much inducement. He had enjoyed teaching, though. He said he would think about it and write the mayor his decision by July fifteenth.

When Armand Monet picked up Faustina after school the last day, he asked Jamie to come spend a couple of days at the ranch.

"Thanks," Jamie said, "but that's twenty miles in the opposite direction from where I'm going."

"Just what I told my daughter, monsieur. Bon voyage."

203

Faustina said, "Don't be so inhospitable, Father. Can't you urge him a little?"

Jamie had suspected she was behind the invitation. Since Christmas he had received Sunday dinner invitations from Faustina weekly, and had accepted a few. He liked both the food and the company at the ranch, and he enjoyed conversation with Faustina's father, but her obvious crush on him was a minor embarrassment, only minor because Armand was fully aware of it and seemed to think it was funny.

Jamie said, "I really can't, Faustina."

"I wanted you there at the birthday party," she said.

"You're having a birthday?"

"Sunday."

"Just a minute," Jamie said.

He went back into the schoolhouse, was gone for a couple of minutes, and returned carrying a book.

"Happy Birthday," he said, handing it to Faustina.

"Shakespeare's *Sonnets*," she said, opening the cover to read aloud the inscription he had written. "For Faustina Monet, with fond regards, on her fourteenth birthday, James McKay." She looked up at him adoringly. "Oh, Mr. McKay, thank you."

"You're welcome," Jamie said. "I'll see you next fall."

"No, you won't. I'll be away at the Bessie Tift Women's College."

"Then I'll write you a letter."

Her face became luminous. "Will you do that?"

"It's a promise."

It was Jamie's plan to make a short visit to his mother, then spend the rest of the summer traveling from town to town, looking for poker games. Little Doe had written that it was now safe to come home. Don Miguel hadn't for-

given him, but with Consuela now living in Mexico, his
rage had cooled. Little Doe said she had talked to him
frankly, and while the rancher would never rehire him, he
would do nothing to harm him if he returned. The one-
hundred-dollar bounty on Jamie had long since been
withdrawn.

School ended on Friday. Saturday Jamie crated his books
and everything else he couldn't carry in his saddlebags and
shipped it all home to Little Doe. He said his good-byes,
skipped the Saturday night poker game at the Palace Saloon and went to bed early. At half past seven on Sunday
morning he had just saddled his horse in the livery stable
and was preparing to mount when Cricket Denton appeared.

"I came to kiss you good-bye," she said.

He had already kissed her good-bye on her front porch
the evening before, but he wasn't stingy. After glancing
around and seeing that Izzy, the elderly hostler, was shov-
eling manure in a stall with his back turned, he held out
his arms.

"Not here," she said. "At the store."

Dropping his arms to his sides, Jamie considered. Why
not? he thought. They had been unable to get together last
night, except for the surreptitious good-bye kiss on her
porch, because, with the town full of drunken cowboys on
Saturday night, her father never let her leave the house.

Unhitching his gun belt, he hung it and his hat from his
saddle horn and said, "Let's go."

That early on Sunday morning there was no one on the
street to see them walk around behind the hardware store.
In the storeroom Jamie rolled the lime barrel over against
the door; both undressed, and she jumped up to seat
herself on the barrel with her thighs spread.

Fifteen minutes later both were writhing in the throes of
orgasm when the door Cricket was leaning back against

suddenly opened; she tumbled backward off the barrel, did a backward somersault on the ground outside, and agilely bounced to her feet facing the door. Standing to the right of the door, looking at his naked daughter, was Abraham Denton. Standing to its left was the Reverend Wilson Stentor, his eyes glittering at Cricket with outrage. It wasn't moral outrage, but at the moment Jamie was too horrified by the situation to analyze just what kind it was.

Cricket took a running start and dived over the barrel into Jamie's arms. Setting her on her feet, he reached across the barrel to grab the doorknob and pull the door closed.

"Get your key," he said.

Cricket ran to where her dress lay over a box and pulled the key from its pocket. Still gripping the knob, Jamie could feel one of the men outdoors trying to turn it from the other side. When Cricket handed him her key, he pushed out the key in the slot on the other side and locked the door from inside.

Then both of them began to dress furiously.

They were fully dressed when they heard footsteps heading their way within the store. Jamie unlocked and threw open the back door and was helping Cricket up onto the barrel when the door from the store was flung open and her father started to bring up the twin muzzles of a doubled-barreled shotgun.

Cricket jumped down outside and to the left of the door; Jamie dived headfirst over the barrel an instant before the shotgun roared, landed on his hands, rolled and bounced to his feet. Cricket slammed the door and ran around the corner of the store.

Jamie caught up with her as she reached the street, and together they sprinted along the deserted street toward the livery stable.

"I've ruined you," he said between breaths.

"No, Daddy will never tell."

At the livery stable they halted, panting, and looked back. Denton and the Reverend Stentor were just emerging from the hardware store a hundred yards away, Cricket's father still carrying the shotgun. Jamie ran into the stable, buckled on his gun belt, put on his hat, mounted and rode out into the street. Cricket's father and the preacher were approaching at a fast walk, but there was plenty of time.

"I'm sorry," Jamie said. "Maybe your father won't tell, but Stentor will probably preach a sermon about you."

"He can't," she said. "I would get to my feet in the middle of it and announce how many times the hypocrite has been in the storeroom with me."

Jamie then realized what kind of outrage he had seen on the preacher's face. It had been jealous outrage. Along with an odd, momentary twist of jealousy on his own part, he felt relief that he hadn't ruined another girl after all.

"Good-bye, Cricket," he said. "I guess I won't be back in the fall. I'll write Mr. Appleton to let him know."

Denton and the preacher were now only fifty yards away. Jamie headed north out of town at a gallop.

He wondered if he were destined to go through life being chased out of town by angry fathers with shotguns.

He rode hard for ten miles, in case Denton decided to come after him. When he finally reined in atop a rise from where he could see back nearly to town, he saw no sign of pursuit.

Up until now he had been interested only in putting space between himself and the hardware merchant's shotgun, and that had taken him in the opposite direction from where he wanted to go. He was considering whether to turn east or west in order to circle Rimfire when it oc-

curred to him it was only another ten miles to Goose Flats.
From there he could cut west to the Desert Springs Trading
Post, then south across the desert to bypass Rimfire by
twenty miles.

He reached Goose Flats at noon. The Hotel Parisian had
a closed sign on it when he rode by, and the whiskered
sweep-up man, Lolly, was seated on the front porch. He
smiled at Jamie and said, "Hey, mister, got the price of a
drink?"

Halting, Jamie said, "Isn't the bar closed?"

"The blacksmith keeps some handy. I kin get a bottle
from him for a dollar."

Jamie flipped him a silver dollar and rode on.

When he rode up to the ranch house, Faustina came
running out. "Jamie!" she said, "You came after all."

Dismounting, he said, "Jamie?"

"I am finished with school, so you are no longer my
schoolmaster, and you are only four years older."

"Five," he said.

"Four. Did you forget it's my birthday?"

"No, I'm just poor at subtraction. Happy Birthday,
again."

"Thank you. Do I get a birthday kiss?"

"Sure."

When he bent to kiss her cheek, she threw her arms
about his neck and kissed him solidly on the mouth. He
stepped back in astonishment.

There was a laugh from the doorway. Looking that way,
Jamie saw Armand Monet stepping out onto the porch.

"You must take care, Mr. McKay. My daughter has set
her cap for you."

Faustina gave him an indignant look. "Father, I told
you to stop teasing. You will scare off the poor man."

"Poor man is right, if he succumbs to such a firebrand.

Put your horse in the barn, Mr. McKay, and come in. We are just sitting down to the birthday repast."

Lunch, fried chicken and biscuits with honey, had been prepared, as usual, by Mortimer Brown. The two Indian hands were there, too, and in honor of the occasion they ate in the dining room instead of the kitchen. For dessert the black foreman-cook brought in a white cake with fourteen blazing candles.

As Faustina cut the cake, Armand asked Jamie how long he could stay, and he said just overnight. He wanted to be on his way early in the morning.

After lunch Faustina asked if Jamie would like to go fishing.

"Are they biting?" he asked.

"Who cares? The fun is loafing under a tree."

She got poles from the barn and he dug some worms. It was a hot day, but there was a slight breeze and it was comfortable in the shade of the tree next to the pool.

After they had been watching their floats for some time with nothing happening, Faustina said, "Do you know Juliet was only fourteen, Jamie?"

He looked at her. She still was in the gawky-yet-graceful stage of puberty, but she was beginning to develop into a beautiful girl. She didn't have much of a bustline, but what she had was definite.

He said, "I know."

"And Romeo was seventeen, just a year younger than you."

"I'll be nineteen in four months."

"You're only eighteen now. You're not in love with Cricket Denton, are you?"

"No."

"I figured that was only a carnal affair."

Jamie looked at her again, amused. "You're an odd one, Faustina."

"Do you find me repulsive?"

"I find you quite attractive. In another two years you'll probably be beautiful. But right now you're only a child and I'm a man."

"Will you come back in two years, and if I am beautiful, will you marry me?"

He laughed. "Girls aren't supposed to be that forward, Faustina. You're supposed to wait for the man to ask."

"You never would. I've been throwing hints at you all year, and figuratively you just pat me on the head and hand me lollipops. This is my last chance to get your attention. I'm madly in love with you, Jamie."

He was at a loss for what to say.

"What do you feel for me, if anything?"

That gave him something to say. "I like you a lot, Faustina, as much as any other girl I've ever know. Maybe even more. *But you are a child.*"

"We already went through that. I'm Juliet's age."

"I know, and I'm only a year older than Romeo. You're still a child. Your father may think your schoolgirl crush is funny, but he would come after me with a shotgun if I made love to you."

"I am not suggesting that we have intercourse before marriage, Jamie."

"Jesus," he said.

"Don't be blasphemous. Do you have a girl back in El Paso?"

After momentary hesitation, he said, "Not really. She married someone else."

She looked at him in astonishment. "Is she crazy?"

"It was an arranged marriage. She's from an old Spanish family which still believes in that."

"Oh. They sometimes arrange things quite young, don't they? Like betrothals at twelve or fourteen."

"Sometimes."

"If I spoke to my father, maybe he would arrange our betrothal."

He said, "Faustina, will you stop it?"

"No, you're going away and this has to be settled. Will you come back in two years and at least look me over?"

He burst out laughing. "I wouldn't miss it. I want to see if the Bessie Tift Women's College can convert you into a lady."

"You have a bite," she said.

He looked for his float, saw it was submerged and pulled in a small sunfish.

Since he no longer had a hundred-dollar bounty on him, this time Jamie came home in mid-afternoon. Little Doe wasn't there, of course, because she didn't get home from the chuck house until seven p.m. He wandered around the cabin and deduced that the boxes he had shipped had arrived, because the books were back in the central room library and all his extra clothing had been stowed away.

While waiting for Little Doe, he had a bath, washed his dirty laundry and hung it on a line, and about five o'clock fixed himself some supper. When he heard Little Doe's wagon coming at seven, he went outside to wait for her at the barn.

Little Doe jumped down from the wagon and gave him a hug. "I knew it was you when I saw the hanging laundry," she said.

He said, "I'll unhitch the horse."

"All right. I'll fix you supper while you're doing it."

"I did that myself two hours ago. Make some coffee and we'll just talk."

When they were across from each other at the table with coffee cups before them, she said, "Tell me everything you've been doing."

"I wrote it," he said. "Except for this." He took out a thick wad of currency and separated it into two stacks.

"You've been playing poker," she said.

He grinned. "I had a mental bet that you would accuse me of robbing banks."

"I know you would never do that. It must be inherited. Your father had great skill with cards, but he never had enough money to play."

He pushed one stack across to her. "A thousand for me and a thousand for you."

She pushed it back. "I have almost no expenses, Jamie, and draw fifty dollars a month. I have more than that in the bank."

"You're sure?"

"I'm sure. Put it away. You may need it if your luck turns."

He put the two stacks together and pocketed the money. "What's been happening around here?"

"I wrote you everything, too."

"Do you hear anything of Consuela?"

"She seems happy. She and her husband are visiting at the ranch right now."

The expression that put on his face put a worried one on hers. "Stay away, Jamie. You caused her enough trouble."

"I wasn't planning to make a formal call, Little Doe. Has Raoul given you any more trouble?"

She hesitated so long before saying, "I hardly see him anymore," that he knew Raoul had.

"What did he do?"

"Nothing, really."

His face darkened. "If you tell me, I might decide it

wasn't serious enough to kill him over. If you don't, I'll assume it was and go do it right now."

Little Doe emitted a resigned sigh. "Three months ago Raoul and Jake Fox came here drunk and tried the same thing Raoul did before. I put a rifle bullet in Jake's leg and they ran off. Next day I told Don Miguel about it, and also about the previous time Raoul was here, when you caught him and beat him. I don't know what Don Miguel said or did to the two of them, but neither has been near here since, and they look like they would like to run whenever they see me. Jake even keeps his eyes on the floor in the chuck hall when I'm dishing out grub."

"The bastards. I'll kill both."

"Please, Jamie, it's over and done with and won't happen again."

"It sure as hell won't if they're dead."

Little Doe sighed again. "Are you determined to break my heart by getting yourself hanged?"

Jamie sighed too. "All right, Little Doe, I won't break your heart. Next time do me a favor?"

"What?"

"Shoot both in the crotch."

"I'm not that good a shot. Where do you think I was aiming when I bored Jake's leg?"

That put Jamie in a better humor. He laughed.

At midnight Jamie left his horse behind the Derango barn, walked around to its west side and gave the owl-hoot signal. Tonight it was much darker than on his last visit a year ago, and he couldn't see Consuela's window from there. It occurred to him that he didn't even know if she and her husband used her old room when they visited, and she might be at the opposite end of the house.

Ten minutes passed. He was on the verge of trying the other side of the house when she suddenly appeared from the darkness. It was so dark that he couldn't see her clearly, but he made out that she wore a robe over her nightgown.

When he tried to take her into his arms, she sidestepped.

"What's the matter?" he asked, dropping his hands to his sides.

"I'm married, Jamie."

"I thought we swore love forever."

"I didn't say I no longer loved you. I just said I'm married."

He was silent for nearly a minute. Finally he said, "Do you also love your husband?"

"I'm very fond of him. I would do nothing to hurt him."

"I guess that means you wouldn't be interested in running off with me, even though I could support you now. Last time I had twenty dollars to my name. Tonight I have two thousand."

In the darkness he could just make out a soft smile on her lips. "There isn't a day I don't think of you. I will always love you. That's no harm to Juan, because in a different way I love him, too. He knows of you and how much you mean to me."

"You told him about us?"

"Yes, and he understands. After all, it was an arranged marriage and he knew I didn't love him at the time. He is very good to me, Jamie. He is a wonderful man. I could never cause him even the slightest hurt, and if I went with you, he would understand, but it would kill him."

Another long time passed before he spoke. "Then I guess this is our final good-bye."

"Yes."

He held out his hand. "May I wish you every happiness?"

Clasping it, she said, "And I, you. I hope someday you find a more worthy girl than me."

"There aren't any," he said.

He turned and rounded the barn to his horse.

CHAPTER XX

The agreement was that if the baby was a girl, Nate got to name her, and if a boy, it was Denise's option. Nate's choice was Abigail, after his mother. Denise picked Nathan first, which Nate vetoed, despite having no such right under the terms of the agreement, then Georges, after her father, which he also vetoed, and finally Ashley, after her maternal grandfather. Nate approved that.

Nate was clear off in southern Missouri when Ashley Cook made his debut on November 6, 1875. The baby's father had turned nineteen less than a month before.

Nate got back just before Christmas with a bounty check for four thousand dollars and with his left arm in a sling because of a bullet wound in his shoulder. Denise accepted a kiss and let him admire and play with the baby for a time before steering him from the added-on nursery into the bedroom. There she sat on the bed and began to cry.

Nate sat next to her and put his good arm about her. He knew why she was crying.

"It was a freak," he said. "I knew he had a back-up and had the back-up's description, but another fellow of the same description was in the saloon. I was watching the wrong man."

Denise cried harder.

"I won't be going away again until this heals," he said.

She got up, dried her eyes, put a valise on the bed and began to pack.

"Where are you going?" he asked.

"Home, with my baby."

"Hey, he's my baby, too."

"You may visit him, if you're ever in town long enough."

He got up and pulled her around against him into his good arm. "Let's talk," he said.

She stood stiff in the circle of his arm. "We've talked. And talked. And talked. Then you go off and risk your life again."

"We live well and have thirty thousand dollars in the bank."

"I would rather be a poor wife than a rich widow. This is not just a bluff to get my way, Nate. Either you stop or Ashley and I leave."

He dropped his arm from about her. "You knew I was a bounty hunter when you married me."

"I wasn't so close to it. I never knew what you were doing when I was at school. I worried about you, but just generally. Now I know who each horrible man is that you go after and what horrible deeds he had done to make him wanted, and I never sleep from the moment you walk out the door until you return. We almost lost the baby."

"What?"

"I wasn't in proper shape. The doctor said it was emotional stress."

"I'm sorry," he said. "I didn't realize it was so bad for you."

"Would I leave a man I absolutely adore if it hadn't become intolerable?"

He put his arm about her. "Do you absolutely adore me?"

"Yes." Her body was still stiff.

"I adore you, too, but what do you expect me to do? Go back to school and become a professor?"

"With thirty thousand dollars you could go into business."

"As what?"

"You love gambling. The casino owners in this town are all rich."

Again he dropped his arm from about her. "A major casino can take a loss of thirty thousand in one night. Even in one hour."

"Start small, with low-limit games. There must be hundreds of working people who like to gamble but are awed of the big casinos."

He pulled at his good ear while he thought about it. She said, "Daddy would probably come to the rescue if you need more backing."

The look he gave her put a defensive expression on her face. She said, "He's trying to repair things between you, Nate. You could meet him halfway."

"I'm willing to be friendly with him. I just couldn't stand him looking over my shoulder the way he does with your Aunt Lois. Will you compromise?"

"How?"

"Give me one more year of traveling."

"No, not one more day."

"Not bounty hunting," he said. "Poker. I make as much from that as from rewards."

"There are games right here in town."

He looked mildly irritated. "Have you forgotten everything I've told you about poker?"

"No, I know how good you are. That's why I suggested a casino."

"What did I tell you my tutor's first rule was?"

"Hank Pizzaro? I don't remember that."

"Never sit in a game where you aren't the best player, or at least one of the best. The games in this town seat some of the best players in the country. In small town games the players are mostly drunken cowboys who draw to inside straights."

She put her arms about his neck. "No bounty hunting at all?"

"None."

She kissed him. "Can you do it with your arm in a sling?"

"I haven't been having any trouble with dance-hall girls."

She gave him a light slap.

"I think it will work if I lie on my back," he said.

CHAPTER XXI

When Jamie McKay went home for a visit in July of 1876, the first thing he asked Little Doe was if Raoul Derango or Jake Fox had given her any more trouble.

"They still never speak to me, or even look at me," she said.

Second he asked about Consuela. Little Doe said she hadn't been home since Christmas; at that time she had been pregnant, and since then word had come that she had a little girl she had named Maria after her deceased mother.

The news put a momentary ache in Jamie's heart, but it was only momentary. Time lessened pain.

"You have some mail," Little Doe said, and handed him thirty letters from Faustina Monet.

Jamie had been mailing an occasional letter to Faustina at her school in Georgia, but had received no answers because he had moved too often to have a mailing address other than El Paso. Although he had written Little Doe regularly, she had been unable to answer either, or to forward Faustina's letters.

The first few letters were long and full of passionate declarations of love. Gradually they became shorter and cooler, until the last few, which were couched in suddenly ladylike terms and merely friendly. She was growing up, he thought, both charmed and amused. Bessie Tift must teach a course in decorum.

Then it struck him that the later letters had been just as frequent as the earlier ones and that she made no apology for her early emotionalism. Perhaps it was only her manners, not her feelings that had changed.

Her most recent letter said she would be at Goose Flats for the summer, and she invited him to visit. Jamie immediately wrote her there, explaining that he had never answered any of the questions asked in her letters because he had just gotten them in a bunch. He thanked her for the invitation, but said he wasn't yet sure of his summer plans and would have to let her know later.

During his past year of itinerant poker playing Jamie had accumulated twenty thousand dollars. He tried to give his mother part of it, but again she refused. But knowing he had all that money, she began a campaign of talking him into going to college. It didn't take much campaigning because he had been considering it anyway, and he had even picked a university if he decided to go. He wrote Washington University in St. Louis, first explaining that he had no formal education but was self-educated and had taught school for a year, and then asking what entrance requirements were.

A reply came at the end of July. He would have to take entrance examinations, and should report for those at least two weeks before school opened, which would be the fourth of September.

Jamie wrote Faustina that he would be unable to visit

her because he had to go to St. Louis, and explained why. He packed a heavy suitcase, including some of his favorite books, told Little Doe she could either keep his horse for her own use or sell it, and had her drive him into El Paso in the wagon to catch the stage.

CHAPTER XXII

During the four years Jamie attended Washington University, he and Faustina Monet never saw each other, although they regularly exchanged letters. The first two summers he spent banking a poker game on a riverboat out of St. Louis and managed to increase his stake by three thousand dollars each summer. He didn't even get back to see Little Doe either.

His third summer he decided it was time to visit his mother. He intended to stop to see Faustina on his way back to St. Louis, but had to drop that plan when, just before the school year ended, he got a letter from her saying that her college graduation present for her father was a summer in Europe and that she wouldn't return until mid-September.

His initial reaction was astonishment that Armand Monet would let a child travel across Europe on her own. Then he realized he was still thinking of her as he had last seen her, and she was almost eighteen. He wondered if she had developed into as beautiful a woman as she had shown promise of becoming at fourteen. If she had, it was possible she would come back from Europe with a husband.

Little Doe met him with the wagon when he arrived in El Paso and brought him up to date on local happenings during the ten-mile drive home. Consuela had just borne a son, whom she had named Miguel after her father. Raoul Derango and Jake Fox still carefully avoided her. Raoul, now twenty-six, was still unmarried, and he and Jake Fox still regularly got drunk in El Paso on weekends. A year ago Raoul had been accused by the peon father of a fifteen-year-old El Paso girl of getting his daughter pregnant, and the rumor was that it had been rape. The father had dropped charges, reportedly after a big payoff by Don Miguel. Marriage had been out of the question, of course, because the girl was from a poor family. She had borne a boy who looked just like Raoul.

"He hasn't changed his spots," Jamie said.

With his riverboat earnings, plus a substantial poker take from games on campus and in various St. Louis saloons, Jamie had more money now than when he'd started school, close to thirty thousand dollars. He had decided that this time he would insist that his mother accept some of it.

When she again rejected his offer, he said, "You make me feel like an ingrate. I'm practically rich, and my mother still cooks for a bunch of cowhands."

"I like working," she said. "What would I do if I retired? Sit at home and read all day?"

"You could buy a little house in El Paso and have some social life."

"The cabin has been my home for eighteen years."

"You don't even own it," he said.

"It's rent free."

"So would your house in El Paso be. I'll buy you one for cash."

"Your father built the cabin, Jamie."

He had no answer to that. He said, "I'm going into El Paso tomorrow and deposit ten thousand dollars in your account. It's up to you whether you just leave it there or use it to start having some fun."

When he got to the cabin, Jamie discovered he would have transportation during his visit because Little Doe had never sold his horse. He rode it back to El Paso the next day and deposited ten thousand dollars in her bank account.

During his two-week visit, Jamie spent his days in El Paso, usually playing poker at the new Acme Saloon on San Antonio Street, and his evenings with Little Doe. He didn't go into town at all at night, having no desire to see old friends—and even less desire to run into Raoul Derango and Jake Fox.

El Paso had grown during the years Jamie had been away, but it was still a small town. When it was incorporated in 1873, only a year before Jamie's hurried departure from the area, its population had been twenty-three Anglo-Americans and one hundred and fifty Mexicans, and it had one saloon, owned by its first mayor, Benjamin Dowell. When Jamie fled Don Miguel's wrath a year later, it was still less than one thousand and still had but one saloon. Now it was a bustling town of a couple of thousand with three saloons, a number of businesses, a sheriff and a county jail.

When the sheriff came into the Acme one day, Jamie was surprised to discover he was Nick Bowdry, a long, spare, mustached man of thirty with whom he had ridden at the Double-D ranch. Bowdry greeted him cordially and asked after his mother.

"She's fine," Jamie said. "'How'd you get appointed sheriff?"

Bowdry grinned. "It's elective, and Don Miguel backed me."

That explained that. No public office in El Paso County could be won without Don Miguel's backing, nor lost with it.

Just before Jamie climbed aboard the stagecoach in El Paso to start back for St. Louis, Little Doe said, "Are you going to stay away three years again?"

"I'll be back next year with a diploma to hang on your wall," he said.

She gave him a hug and a kiss. "That will be the proudest day of my life, papoose."

"Mine, too, Mother," he said, hugging and kissing her back.

Apparently Little Doe opted to let the ten thousand dollars Jamie had deposited just sit in her bank account, because letters from her, when he got back to school, indicated she was still working for Don Miguel as his chuck house cook.

In June of 1880 Jamie graduated with honors, taking a Bachelor of Arts degree in literature. Despite his usual careful play, a six-month run of second-best hands had depleted his stake to three thousand dollars. When he was offered back his old riverboat job, which involved no risk of his own money and gave him twenty-five percent of the winnings, he took it and wrote Little Doe that his return would be delayed. His bad run of cards broke, and by December 1st he had run his stake up to ten thousand dollars. He decided it was time to go home.

He wrote both Little Doe and Faustina, telling his mother he would spend Christmas with her and telling Faustina, who had returned from Europe single and now had his old job of teaching school in Rimfire, to expect him for New Year's Eve.

Little Doe had written that his horse had died. In his letter to her he told her she didn't have to meet him at the stage depot. Since he would need a horse, he would buy one in El Paso and ride it to the cabin.

On the stage he met a horse trader who told him prices in Las Cruces were half those in El Paso and advised him to buy his horse there. That would require a thirty-five-mile horseback ride instead of only ten, but actually wouldn't involve much more time because he would spend three hours less on the stage. He let his luggage go on to El Paso and got off at Las Cruces. It was half past eight a.m., the day before Christmas, and Little Doe was expecting him in mid-afternoon. By the time he bought a horse and saddle, a canteen and some range clothing, he figured it would be eleven, but he still should be able to make the cabin before dark.

"Which way you heading?" the hostler from whom he bought his horse and saddle asked.

"South toward El Paso."

"Better keep a sharp eye out. A band of Comanche is rampaging all over southwest Texas, rapin' white women and murderin' and scalpin' whole families."

By the 1867 Treaty of Medicine Lodge the federal government had established a reservation in southwest Oklahoma for the Comanche and had moved the entire nation there. Jamie said, "There aren't any Comanche in Texas anymore."

"There's been for the past week. A dozen renegades ran off from the reservation under a sub-chief named Stalking Horse, and they're trying to take back their old hunting grounds."

The only weapon Jamie had with him was his .41 Navy Colt. He decided it would be wise to carry something with more range. He found a gunsmith and bought a .30 caliber rifle and a saddle scabbard.

It took longer than he had anticipated to reach the cabin because periodically he went out of his way to ride atop hills in order to check the surrounding country for the renegade Indians. It was dusk when he reached the rise above the cabin.

No light showed from the cabin, which surprised him. While it was only six o'clock and Little Doe usually didn't get home until seven, she had written that she would be off both Christmas Eve and Christmas Day.

He rode down the hill to the barn, found the lantern hanging in its usual place on a nail and lighted it. Little Doe's horse and wagon were both there. She must be taking a nap, he thought. He unsaddled his horse, put it in a stall, gave it some oats and got the little box containing the cameo brooch he had bought Little Doe for Christmas from one of the saddlebags. He carried it and the lantern to the cabin.

The door was standing ajar. Pushing it open, he went in, set the lantern and the gift on the table and looked around. When a little mew of pain came from Little Doe's bedroom, he grabbed up the lantern and strode to her open door.

Little Doe, naked, sprawled on the bed with her thighs spread wide. Blood seeped from a stab wound between her breasts and a trickle ran from a corner of her mouth. She had been scalped.

Atop his grief and rage there was a sense of outrage that the renegade Comanche had done this to one of their own. Setting the lantern on the dresser, he fell to his knees beside the bed and took his dying mother into his arms.

"Mother," he said, weeping.

"It was not the Comanche, papoose," she whispered.

"Who then?"

"Raoul Derango, Jake Fox and a man I did not know."

Then she died in his arms.

When he was able to stop crying, Jamie returned to the barn, hitched up the wagon and drove it in front of the cabin door. Wrapping Little Doe's body in a blanket, he laid it in the wagon and drove to the Double-D ranch house, where he halted by the porch. When he knocked on the door, Consuela answered.

Her face turned white, thinking he was there to see her.

"Is Raoul here?" he asked.

The question relieved her, but she remained pale. "No, he went to town."

"When?"

"Hours ago—Jamie, there is blood all over your shirt."

"Who went with him?"

"Jake Fox," she said, still staring at his shirt.

"Who was the third man?"

"What third man? Jamie, what happened?"

"There was a third man with them."

"No, just Jake. Jamie, tell me what's the matter?"

From inside the house Don Miguel's voice said, "Who is it, Consuela?"

Jamie turned, descended the steps and climbed onto the wagon seat. He heard Don Miguel come out on the porch, but didn't look back. It was too dark for Consuela and her father to see what was in the wagon.

It was ten o'clock p.m. when the wagon pulled into El Paso. Jamie drove to a house on San Francisco Street where a sign attached to the porch rail read: LYMAN WEEPER— UNDERTAKER. The house was dark. Pounding on the front door brought a tall, thin man in a nightshirt and nightcap to the door with a candle.

Peering at Jamie, he said, "My gawd, is that Jamie McKay?"

"Yes, sir. I have my mother's body outside, Mr. Weeper."

"Oh, I'm sorry, boy. Come in while I get dressed."

An hour later funeral arrangements had been made and paid for. Jamie drove the wagon over to San Antonio Street and halted in front of the Acme Saloon.

Although the place was crowded, Raoul Derango and Jake Fox were the only ones at the far end of the bar. They were shaking the dice box for drinks.

As Jamie neared, both sensed his presence and simultaneously looked up. The expression on his face and the dried blood on his shirt told them why he was there. Both grabbed for their guns.

They never touched the butts. Two .41 slugs in the centers of their chests blasted them into oblivion.

As Jamie holstered his gun, a voice to his left said, "Drop your gun belt, Jamie."

Looking that way, Jamie saw Sheriff Nick Bowdry pointing a cocked pistol at him.

"It was self-defense, Nick."

"I don't see guns in their hands."

"They raped and murdered and scalped my mother."

The sheriff blinked. "They killed Little Doe?"

"If you would like to see what they did to her, she's over at Weeper's."

After a long pause, Bowdry said, "I'm sorry, Jamie. You still have to drop your gun belt. Better do it quick. This is a hair trigger."

Jamie unbuckled his gun belt and let it drop to the floor. The sheriff motioned for him to step away from it, picked it up and holstered his own gun.

"Anybody see what happened?" he asked generally.

A Double-D hand named Laramie Ferguson said, "Jamie just walked in and started shooting."

"They were reaching," Jamie said. "They knew why I was here when they saw the dried blood on my shirt, and both went for their guns."

The sheriff and everyone else nearby looked at the dark brown stain on the front of his shirt. "Their guns are still holstered," Bowdry said.

"Only because I was faster."

The sheriff looked around. "Anyone see them reach?"

No one immediately answered, then a dance-hall girl seated at the nearest table to the bar and faced that way said, "It happened too fast, Sheriff. I was looking right that way, and all I saw was the gun go off and those two hit the floor."

A Double-D rider named Pedro Ramirez said, "If they did what Jamie said, what difference does it make who reached first, Nick? He had a right to kill the bastards."

Jamie said, "There was a third man with them. Who'd they come in with?"

"Nobody," the sheriff said. "I walked in right behind them and talked to Jake for a minute. He looked drunk and I warned him not to start any fights. You say Little Doe was scalped?"

"Yes."

"What makes you think Stalking Horse didn't do it?"

"Because she was still alive when I found her. She told me."

"Who'd she say the third man was?"

"She didn't know him."

"I have to take you over to the jail," Bowdry said. "I'll decide whether to hold you for trial or turn you loose after I make an investigation."

"You mean after you ask Don Miguel?"

Bowdry gave him a cold look. "I said after I make an investigation. Come along."

After locking Jamie in the single cell behind the sheriff's office, Bowdry said, "This happened at the cabin, Jamie?"

"Yes. I got there at six, and my guess is it happened maybe an hour before."

"They came into the saloon at four, and that's at least an hour ride."

"Then she was lying there dying for three hours. Consuela knows when they left the Double-D. Ask her."

"She's home?"

"You think I'd tell you that if she was in Laredo?"

"Don't get touchy, Jamie. I have to ask these questions. Little Doe's over at Weeper's?"

"Yes. I brought her in the wagon. Incidentally, that's in front of the Acme. You'll have to put the horse in the livery stable."

"I'll take care of it."

"I also have a suitcase at the stage depot you could pick up."

"All right. See you in the morning."

Christmas morning Lorenzo Tubbs, the town drunk, brought Jamie breakfast. Lorenzo, about fifty, was short and tubby and not very clean. He supported himself by sweeping out the town's three saloons, doing odd jobs and cadging coins.

"You the sheriff's deputy?" Jamie asked as Lorenzo passed a bowl of porridge, a slice of bread and a tin cup of coffee through the service opening in the barred door.

"Just when the sheriff's off somewhere, Jamie. It ain't full time. Merry Christmas."

At nine a.m. Don Miguel appeared long enough to glare at Jamie through the bars, then went away without saying anything. At noon the sheriff appeared with Jamie's suitcase. He unlocked the cell door and stood by with a drawn gun while Lorenzo carried out the slop jar to empty it and brought in a fresh pitcher of water for the wash basin. Then he locked the cell door and sent Lorenzo to get lunch at the next-door cafe for both Jamie and himself.

"I'm going home for Christmas dinner now," the sheriff said. "Lorenzo will keep you company."

"You make your investigation?" Jamie asked.

"Yes, I just came from the cabin."

"What did you decide?"

"You'll hear at the coroner's inquest Monday afternoon."

"Don Miguel told you to hold me, eh?"

The sheriff made no answer. When Lorenzo returned with lunch, he left.

Monday morning all three funerals were held at the mission, Raoul Derango and Jake Fox's as a double funeral at nine o'clock, Little Doe's at ten. Jamie was allowed to attend the latter, handcuffed and in leg irons, but freshly shaven and wearing clean clothes. Out of respect for Little Doe, who had been his chuck house cook for fifteen years, Don Miguel stayed over from the earlier funerals for hers, too. Consuela was also there, seated between her father and a tall, handsome, gray-haired man Jamie assumed was her husband. She was pale and did not look at Jamie. Neither did Don Miguel.

The inquest was that afternoon, held in the warehouse of the Schultz Store on San Francisco Street because that was the largest building in town. Dr. Manfred Fowler, a stout, whiskered man in his mid-forties, was county coroner. When Jamie was led in by the sheriff, again handcuffed and wearing leg irons, there was a crowd of about fifty on wooden chairs, facing a table behind which the coroner sat. To the coroner's right a six-man jury, all Double-D riders, sat in a row. To his left were two vacant chairs. The sheriff had Jamie sit in one and took the other.

Beneath his chair Bowdry set a small burlap bag he was carrying.

Jamie looked over the crowd. In the front row Consuela sat between her father and her gray-haired husband. Her face was still pale and she looked ill. About half the rest of the spectators were Double-D riders. With the jury entirely Double-D riders, and with both the coroner and the sheriff beholden to Don Miguel because everyone holding local political office was beholden to him, it didn't look to Jamie as though this was going to be an entirely unbiased hearing.

Dr. Fowler said, "This is an inquest into the related deaths of three persons, one Little Doe McKay, a cook for the Double-D ranch, one Raoul Derango and one Jonathan Fox, locally known as Jake Fox. Although the first-mentioned died first, I have decided that the presentation of evidence will make more sense if the latter two deaths are considered first. This is not a trial, and the jury's sole duty is to determine causes of death. Procedures at an inquest are less formal than at a trial, and the usual rules of evidence do not apply. I will open matters by explaining to the jury my findings when I examined the bodies of the two men." He turned to the jury. "I won't bore you with fancy medical terminology. In lay terms, they died instantly from bullets through the hearts."

He then called on the sheriff to describe events at the Acme Saloon on Christmas Eve.

Bowdry said, "The decedants arrived together at four p.m., Doc. I know the exact time because I had just left my office up the street and looked at my watch as I walked out. We met at the door of the saloon and I stepped aside to let them go in first."

"Didn't the shooting occur much later than that?" the coroner asked.

"Yes, about eleven at night. Meantime, the decedants had not stirred from the end of the bar, where they were shooting dice for drinks. I was playing poker when the prisoner came in, and I didn't see him enter. I looked over when I heard the shots and saw the prisoner here, Jamie McKay, with a gun in his hand and the two deceased on the floor. I immediately went over, covered the prisoner, and ordered him to surrender his weapon. The guns of both dead men were still in their holsters."

"Did any witnesses see the shooting?"

The sheriff said, "It happened too fast, Doc. The place was packed, but nobody really saw it."

"How could that be, Sheriff?"

"The deceased were at the end of the bar together, and nobody was on either side. Generally they were left alone by the other patrons—" The sheriff broke off to glance at Don Miguel, turned red and hurried on. "Jake Fox picked fights when he was drunk, and he was a little drunk. A couple of men at the bar saw the prisoner draw his gun and fire, but their backs were to the decedants. A woman named Pamela Cross was at the nearest table to the bar and sat faced that way, but she says even she didn't see what happened as it happened so fast. I could run over to the Acme and get her, if you'd like."

"It doesn't seem necessary if she didn't see anything, Sheriff. Did the prisoner state why he shot the victims?"

"He said they and another unidentified man raped, murdered and scalped his mother."

There were gasps from a couple of women among the spectators. Dr. Fowler gave them an admonishing look before saying to Jamie, "James McKay, do you wish to make a statement?"

"Yes, sir. Both reached for their guns before I did. I just got mine out faster."

"The sheriff says both guns were still holstered when they died. Did their hands touch the butts before they drew?"

"No, sir, they were still reaching for them."

The coroner said, "I find it incredible that anyone could draw and shoot that fast, young man, if they made the first move."

"I will be glad to demonstrate if you give me my belt and gun, sir. Unloaded, of course."

One of the two women who previously had gasped now tittered. Dr. Fowler scowled at her, and no one else laughed.

Returning his attention to Jamie, the coroner said, "That won't be necessary. Even if I stipulated that you are the fastest gun in the world, it seems apparent that you could have simply covered the decedants and ordered them to raise their hands, instead of killing them."

"Why would I do that, sir?"

"To hold them for the sheriff to arrest. My understanding is that your motive for shooting them was your belief that they had murdered your mother."

"Not just belief, sir. Certainty."

"We will go into that later. Whether or not they were guilty of that crime, you believed they were, and you entered the Acme Saloon with the intent of killing them, right?"

Jamie considered this before saying, "It was certainly my intention to confront them. They made the decision to get killed by reaching for their guns."

"Did you say anything to them?"

"No, they just reached the instant they saw me."

"Why, if you made no accusation?"

"They knew why I was there. My mother's dried blood was all over my shirt."

The same two women as before again gasped. This time

the coroner didn't even look their way. He said, "Since you had them covered, couldn't you simply have ordered them to raise their hands?"

"When a man goes for his gun with the intention of shooting me, I don't stop to talk, Doctor."

The coroner said to the jury, "As you heard from Sheriff Bowdry, the prisoner's stated motive for these killings was his belief that the decedants had raped, murdered and then scalped his mother, a cook for the Double-D ranch known as Little Doe McKay. The crime took place at her cabin, which is on the Double-D ranch. My examination of the body disclosed that indeed she had been raped, probably repeatedly, that she had been scalped, and that she died of a knife thrust which penetrated the left lung and also damaged the left side of the heart." He turned back to Jamie. "Describe how you found your mother."

"I arrived at the cabin about six p.m. She was dying, and lived no more than a minute after I got there. My first thought was that Stalking Horse's renegades had done it, but she said it wasn't the Comanche. She said it was Raoul Derango, Jake Fox and a third man she didn't know."

"She said this distinctly?"

"As distinctly as I just did. It didn't surprise me. Raoul tried to rape her twice before, and the second time Jake Fox was with him. The first time, six years ago, I caught him in the act and beat the hell out of him. The second time I was away when the two of them tried it. Little Doe shot Jake in the leg and the next day told Don Miguel. What action he took, I don't know, but thereafter both stayed away from her until the other night when they murdered her."

Don Miguel interrupted to say, "My son was out of line with your mother twice, I admit, but they were attempted seductions, not attempted rapes."

Raoul had managed to sell his father a bill of goods. The coroner's loaded questions had been increasingly making Jamie hot, and now Don Miguel's attempt to gloss over his son's crime caused him to boil over. He said, "Seductions, hell. Your son was an habitual rapist. You've got a bastard grandson from another of his rapes."

There was stunned silence in the room. Don Miguel, his expression furious, jumped up to rush at Jamie. The sheriff rose and placed both hands against his chest.

"Simmer down, Don Miguel," he said.

The coroner slapped his hand against the table three times. "This is a court of law, and I will have order. Please sit down, Mr. Derango."

Don Miguel, his face pale with rage, resumed his seat. The sheriff reseated himself also. Dr. Fowler said, "If there are any more outbursts from you, Mr. McKay, I will postpone this hearing and let you rot in jail until you decide to behave yourself."

So much for even-handed justice, Jamie thought. Don Miguel was politely asked to sit down, while he was threatened with jail.

The coroner said, "To return to the subject at hand, is it possible, Mr. McKay, that your anger at Raoul Derango and Jake Fox for their alleged previous attempts to seduce or rape your mother, whichever it was, made you hear something that wasn't actually said?"

"No."

"Sheriff Bowdry has testified that the decedents entered the Acme Saloon at four p.m. If they did murder your mother, they would have had to have done it no later than three p.m., three full hours before you found her. The wound I examined was of such severity that it is my medical opinion that she could not possibly have lived three hours after it was inflicted. I submit that she was dead when you found her.''

Jamie said, ''If you checked your medical books, Doctor, you would learn that bleeding stops at the instant of death. My shirt was soaked with blood from holding my mother in my arms.''

The coroner flushed. ''I don't require a lecture on anatomy from you, young man. If she was still bleeding, she had to be stabbed no more than a half hour before you found her, not three hours previously.'' He turned to Nick Bowdry. ''Sheriff, tell the jury the result of your investigation into Little Doe's murder.''

The sheriff said, ''I visited her cabin Christmas morning. Her bed was covered with dried blood and a dress, and some women's underclothes lay on the floor of her bedroom, torn apart like they'd been ripped off her. In front of the cabin was the hoof marks of several horses. I found no other clues.''

''How many horses would you say, Sheriff?''

''It's been too dry to leave much sign. At least four, maybe a dozen.''

''Four,'' Jamie said. ''The three killers and me.''

The coroner said, ''Mr. McKay, you must not interrupt. Did you find the scalp, Sheriff?''

''No, sir. I thoroughly searched the cabin and the surrounding area. Later I searched the bodies of Raoul Derango and Jake Fox, and also their saddlebags.''

''The third man must have it,'' Jamie said.

The coroner glared at him. ''Mr. McKay, I told you not to interrupt.''

''I think this is it here,'' the sheriff said, reaching beneath his chair for the burlap bag.

From the bag he drew a scalp of long, black, wavy hair.

The two women in the audience gasped again, and the one who had tittered fainted. A couple of men carried her out.

"Where did you find that?" the coroner asked.

"I didn't. Lieutenant Howard Jefferson of the United States Calvary found it hanging from the belt of one of Stalking Horse's braves. The calvary trapped the renegades in a box canyon only fifteen miles from Little Doe's cabin yesterday afternoon and killed all of them."

A buzz of conversation rose throughout the room. Dr. Fowler brought order by slapping his palm on the table several times.

Jamie said, "That isn't Little Doe's hair. Hers had no curl to it. It's the scalp of a white woman."

"Mr. McKay, you will remain silent!"

"You said this procedure was supposed to be informal," Jamie said. "That seems to mean anyone but me can speak. You're not interested in the truth. All you want is a verdict that will please your political sponsor, Don Miguel."

The coroner said, "Sheriff, return the prisoner to his cell. We'll finish this inquest without him."

As Jamie hobbled from the room, dragging his leg irons and pulled along by the sheriff, he said over his shoulder, "You'll probably get your son avenged, Don Miguel, but live with it that he was a rapist and a woman killer."

An hour after locking him in his cell, the sheriff returned to report that the jury had found Little Doe to have been murdered by Stalking Horse and his renegades, and Raoul and Jake to have been murdered by Jamie.

"There was some sympathy for you," Bowdry said. "The jurors stated they thought you honestly believed Raoul and Jake killed your mom."

"When do I hang?" Jamie asked.

"This wasn't a trial, Jamie," the sheriff said. "Didn't you hear Doc explain it was just to determine causes of death? The circuit judge won't be around this way for another two weeks.''

"So it will be at least two weeks and one day before I hang, eh?''

"I'd guess about that,'' Sheriff Bowdry said.

CHAPTER XXIII

Because there was nothing else to do, Jamie slept a good part of what remained of Monday afternoon, with the result that he was unable to sleep that night. At midnight he still lay wide-awake on his bunk, staring upward into darkness and listening to the night noises made by Lorenzo Tubbs, asleep on a cot in the sheriff's office. The little man didn't snore, but periodically he snorted in his sleep like a hog rooting in garbage.

An owl gave three hoots and, after an interval, hooted twice, then waited and hooted once more. That signal belonged to so many years in the past that for a moment Jamie thought it really was an owl. Then he bounced erect and ran to the window.

When Consuela's pale face appeared from the darkness, for a long time they merely stood looking at each other through the bars. When she finally spoke, her voice was low.

"I believe you, Jamie."

"Thank you."

"Father won't listen to me. He can't accept that Raoul

would rape and murder. He keeps saying he only made a couple of drunken advances to Little Doe, that he was just sowing wild oats.''

Jamie gave a short laugh. "Sure, she was only an Indian.''

"That's not fair," she said. "Father liked her. It's just that he's blind about Raoul. My brother had him convinced that the young girl that bore his bastard was also only seduced, but people say it was forced rape.''

Jamie said nothing. After a time Consuela said, "What will they do to you, Jamie?''

"Hang me.''

In the darkness he could see her stricken expression. "No, I won't let it happen.''

"What can you do?''

"Something. I'll have to think.''

A series of snorts from the office put an alarmed look on her face.

"My guard," Jamie said. "Lorenzo Tubbs.''

"The town drunk?''

"Ex-town-drunk. He's been promoted to part-time deputy.''

Consuela looked thoughtful. "Will he be on duty tomorrow night?''

"I imagine.''

"Where is your horse?" she asked.

"In the barn at the cabin. I left him plenty of oats and water, but I'd appreciate your checking him.''

"I'll do better. Is there a saddle there?''

"Two. One has ten thousand dollars in a saddlebag.''

"That's the one I'll put on him," she said. "What time does Nick Bowdry leave you alone with Lorenzo?''

"At five today.''

"I'll be here at six to pass your key to freedom through the window."

"A gun?"

"I don't want anyone killed," she said. "A bottle of whiskey."

Turning, she disappeared into the darkness.

The next day dragged. Sheriff Bowdry was in and out, each time he came in peering through the bars and making small conversation.

After lunch, while Lorenzo was returning the dishes to the cafe next door, Bowdry said, "Lorenzo treating you all right?"

"Fine," Jamie said.

"Your horse and wagon are still at the livery stable. What you want done with them?"

"You mean after I'm hanged?"

"I mean now. They're running up a dollar-a-week bill."

"Sell them and give the money to Lorenzo."

"He'd get drunk. I'll have him drive out to the cabin with a riding horse tied to the back of the wagon and leave them there."

Jamie had a mental picture of Lorenzo finding the money in the saddlebag. He said, "Don't bother. I hereby deed them to Lorenzo."

"A deputy can't accept a gift from a prisoner," Bowdry said.

"He's only a part-time deputy. Hold the money until he's a floor sweeper again, then give it to him."

"I guess you can leave your money anyway you want," the sheriff said.

At 5:00 p.m. Sheriff Bowdry left for the day and Lorenzo went next door to get supper for Jamie and himself. At 6:00, just as it was getting dark, he returned the dishes.

While he was gone, Consuela appeared at the barred window and passed in a quart of whiskey.

"I'll be back at ten." she said, and faded away again.

Lorenzo lit a lantern when he returned, then sat at the sheriff's desk reading the *El Paso News*.

Jamie said, "I need a cup, Lorenzo."

Laying down his paper, the little man said, "You want I should make some coffee?"

"No, I just want an empty cup."

Lorenzo rose, got a tin cup from a shelf and passed it through the service hole. He stood watching as Jamie took the quart bottle from beneath the pad of his bunk, uncorked it and poured some in the cup.

"Where'd you get that?" the little man asked.

"Brought it with me."

"How'd you get it past the sheriff?"

"Had it stuck down my pants leg."

"You're not supposed to have that in there."

Jamie set the bottle on the floor, sat on his bunk, took a sip and smacked his lips.

"You going to drink alone?" Lorenzo asked.

"You're on duty."

"Not after five. I gotta stay here all night, but technically I go off duty at five."

"I might give you a little one," Jamie said. "You got to promise not to ask for more than one. I don't want any trouble with the sheriff for getting you drunk."

"When'd you ever see me drunk?" Lorenzo said, running to get another tin cup.

By nine o'clock the bottle was empty. Jamie had sipped perhaps two ounces. Lorenzo reeled over to his cot and collapsed on it without taking off his shoes or turning out the lantern.

At ten the office door cracked open and Consuela peered

in. When she saw Lorenzo sprawled on the cot with his mouth agape, she came in, closed the door behind her, lifted the cell key from a nail in the wall and unlocked the cell door. Jamie went over to the drunken man, heaved him over his shoulder, carried him into the cell and dumped him on the bunk. After locking the cell door, he hung the key back in place.

Jamie's gun belt and hat and jacket hung from hooks on the wall. He strapped on his gun, put on his hat and jacket and turned out the lantern before following Consuela outside. Silently she led the way around behind the jail, where two saddled horses stood.

"Your money is in the saddlebag," she said, the first words she had spoken.

Jamie bent to kiss her forehead. Even though it was quite dark, he could see the glint of tears at the corners of her eyes.

"I will pray for you," she said.

He could think of nothing appropriate to say. Thanks was too little, any mention of his aching love too much. He mounted his horse and rode off.

By riding all night, Jamie made the forty-five miles to Las Cruces before dawn. Turning west, he kept right on going, and by dusk on Wednesday he had reached Deming. With a hundred miles between himself and El Paso, he felt safe enough to catch a night's sleep there before continuing west. He was off again at dawn and by dusk on Thursday was crossing the border into the Territory of Arizona, another ninety miles farther.

Faustina Monet, knowing nothing of events in El Paso, expecting him for New Year's Eve. As there was no way he could make the additional two hundred and fifty miles in one day, there was no point in continuing his breakneck pace. With a safe two hundred miles and two territorial borders now between himself and El Paso, he stopped punishing his horse and rode north at a walk.

He circled twenty miles west of Rimfire by cutting across the desert to Desert Springs Trading Post, then turning east to Goose Flats. It took him eight days. At noon on Friday, January 7, 1881, he tied up to the hitching rail in front of the Hotel Parisian.

A half-dozen cowboys were at the bar, and the whiskered sweep-up man, Lolly, was seated at a table eating a sandwich. Armand Monet, unchanged since Jamie had last seen him five years before except for some gray in his hair and his waxed mustache, was tending bar. He rushed from behind it to give Jamie a Gallic hug.

"Faustina has worried herself into a decline of weight," he said. "I, too, my friend. See how skinny you have made me? It is good to see you alive."

"I couldn't get away," Jamie said. "My mother died."

The little man struck his forehead with his palm. "And I chide you for your delay. Forgive me. I grieve for you."

"Thank you. Is Faustina at the ranch?"

"She stay in Rimfire during the week, in your old room at the Appletons, and come home only on weekends. She will arrive perhaps six p.m."

Jamie had lunch at the saloon, then rode out to the ranch, where he was cordially received by Mortimer Brown and the two Indian hands. He stowed his gear in his assigned room, took a bath and put on fresh clothes.

When he heard hoofbeats pounding toward the house at six p.m., he stepped out on the porch in time to see Faustina rein up in a cloud of dust, leap from her horse and come running up the steps to throw herself into his arms. A full bust pressed against his chest and he was kissed fiercely.

When she finally leaned back to look up into his face, she said, "Father told me about your mother. I'm sorry."

He was so astonished by her changed appearance that he hardly heard her. While he knew she was now nineteen, and had expected change, he hadn't expected such an enormous one. She was a fully developed woman, tall, probably five-feet-seven, still slim but now rounded at the hips, and stunningly beautiful. She was dressed in denims, boots, a flannel shirt and a sombrero.

She said, "You haven't changed."

"You have," he said, and kissed her again.

She clung to him, opening her lips wide and pressing her body tightly against his. When this had a predictable physical effect, she jumped slightly, then leaned back again and laughed with delight.

"Ah, you love me," she said.

"That's just lust, girl. Didn't they teach you at Bessie Tift not to mention such phenomena in polite conversation?"

"This isn't polite; it's love talk. Do you love me?"

He was, of course, in love with Consuela and always would be. He had still felt the ache of it when he had parted with her behind the jail only ten days before. To his wonderment she suddenly became only an old and cherished friend, and he was blindingly in love with another woman.

"Yes," he said.

"I knew you would if you ever came back."

"Why did you wait for me?" he asked. "You must have been courted by a hundred men."

"Thousands." Then she giggled. "Actually eight. Three hand-kissing fortune hunters in Europe who thought I was rich because my father owned a hotel, and five around here. Three of the locals were illiterate cowboys, the other two basically educated but ugly. The pickings around here are zero. Don't feel flattered. You are my last hope."

Mortimer Brown stuck his head out the door and said, "You two want supper, or you going to spoon all evening?"

Breaking away from Jamie, Faustina said, "Oh my, do I have time to change into a dress?"

"You never change for the rest of us," the black man said. "How come you're getting uppity?"

"I'll be five minutes," Faustina said, running into the house.

Actually she was ten, but the transformation was worth it. Jamie had thought her beautiful in range clothes. When she reappeared in an off-the-shoulder gown, she made his head reel. He mentally kicked himself for waiting so long to return.

Faustina's father was not at supper because he kept the saloon open until midnight on Fridays. After supper Faustina and Jamie sat on the porch and talked until Armand came home. He told her about events in El Paso, and she was indignant at the treatment he had received. When he described how Consuela had helped him escape, she said, "I hated her when you first told me of her years ago, but now I could kiss her. I won't be jealous if you still love her some."

"I'll always be fond of her, but I can love only one woman at a time."

"That's me? Or rather, as they say at Bessie Tift, that is I?"

"Uh-huh."

"Are you planning to marry me?" she asked. "Or just use my body for a while, then cast me aside?"

"Would you marry a wanted man?"

"Are you wanted anywhere except Texas?"

"No."

"Then we'll just stay away from Texas. Was that a

proposal, or just an inquiry about my attitude toward marriage?''

"I meant it as a proposal."

"At Bessie Tift we were taught to say, 'I am deeply honored, but I need time to think.' I am thinking. I have thought. You're engaged."

They kissed to seal the bargain.

"When?" he asked when they finally broke.

"How about the Saturday after next?"

"You mean a week from tomorrow?"

"Two weeks from tomorrow. I need time to sew a wedding gown, and I'll have to arrange for a substitute teacher while I'm honeymooning. We'll have a honeymoon, won't we?"

"Of course."

"I'll have to finish out the school year after the honeymoon. I couldn't leave my pupils in the lurch. Cricket is all right as a substitute, but she isn't qualified as a full-time school teacher."

"Cricket?" he said, startled.

"Your old girl friend, Cricket Denton. Only it's Cricket Browning now."

"She's married?"

"Yes, and has a baby boy. We'll have to be married in Rimfire. It's the only church in fifty miles."

"Absolutely not. We'll travel a hundred and fifty miles before the Reverend Stentor marries me."

"Strentor's been gone two years. The Reverend Cartwright Browning is the preacher now. Young fellow about your age."

The name rang a bell. "Didn't you say Cricket's married name was Browning?"

"Yes, she's the preacher's wife."

Jamie successfully suppressed a laugh. His objection to

being married in Rimfire had been only partly because of
the Reverend Wilson Stentor, but mainly because of reluc-
tance to face Cricket's shotgun-wielding father. With her
now married to the town preacher, however, it hardly
seemed likely that Abraham Denton would still feel like
going after Jamie with a shotgun.

He said, "I'll ride in with you Monday to plan the
wedding."

When Armand got home about twenty minutes after
midnight, Faustina poked Jamie as her father came up the
porch steps and said, "Ask him."

"Ask him what?"

"For my hand."

Jamie had been unaware that this was still done, but he
had no objection to the convention. He got as far as, "Sir,
may I have the honor of—" when Armand grabbed his
hand and pumped it.

"You have my blessing, my son. The girl has talk of
nothing else for years. I will welcome a change of subject
after the event."

Faustina sighed.

Jamie said, "I appreciate your approval, Mr. Monet,
but I think you should know I'm a wanted man in Texas."

"You are wanted here, too. Listening to my daughter, I
have never hear of a man more wanted."

"Seriously," Jamie said. "I really feel you have to
know this."

When he described what had taken place in El Paso,
Armand Monet's reaction was identical to that of his
daughter: indignation at the treatment Jamie had received.

He said, "Is unfortunate that you can never visit your
home state, but the loss is to Texas more than to you."

Saturday morning Faustina appeared at breakfast wearing denim pants, a flannel shirt and her cowgirl boots.

"Going riding?" her father asked.

"Fishing, if I can talk my betrothed into it."

"I'm willing," Jamie said.

After breakfast Armand headed for the hotel. He would be gone until three a.m., as Saturday was the saloon's big day. Mortimer Brown, Bigfoot Harry and Bucking Horse rode off to mend some fence. Jamie dug some worms and he and Faustina headed for the swimming and fishing hole.

Breakfast had been early, and it was only eight a.m. when they threw in their lines. By ten o'clock they had a string of good-sized sunfish tied to a sapling and flopping in the water next to the bank. By then it had become pleasantly warm and the fish had stopped biting.

"Let's go skinny-dipping," Faustina said.

Jamie looked at her.

"In another two weeks we'll be seeing each other nude regularly," she said, "unless you're one of those inhibited people who only make love in the dark."

"I have no inhibitions," he said.

"Good, because I plan to be a raunchy wife." She pulled off one of her boots.

"If we get in that water naked, I can't guarantee nothing will happen," he said.

"I rather imagine something will." She pulled off her other boot.

"The last time we were here, you said something that has stuck in my mind ever since. You said, 'I am not suggesting that we have intercourse before marriage, Jamie.' "

Faustina laughed. "I remember. I was fourteen. This is five years later, and I've lusted for you the whole five years."

She unbuttoned and took off her shirt. Her bare breasts,

firm and round and with pink nipples, gave him an erection. He started to undress.

She beat him and dived into the water while he still had on his pants. Moments later he had shed them and his underdrawers and had dived in too, with a full erection. She was treading water in the center of the pool, facing him with an anticipatory expression on her face, when he dived. The water was cool, but not frigid enough to make him lose his erection.

As he surfaced in front of her, she said, "I'm glad you didn't bellyflop. You might break the bone."

He reached for her and she swam backward toward the far bank. After a couple of strokes she stood up in chest deep water. He swam to her and took her into his arms.

After a long kiss, she said, "I never did it underwater."

"Where have you done it?"

"Everywhere in fantasy. In bed, on the grass, in a tree, standing up in a hammock. But only with you. I'm otherwise a virgin even in my make-believes."

With her left arm clasped about his neck, she threw her legs about his waist, reached underwater with her right hand and positioned his erect penis against her vulva. "Be easy," she said. "You really are getting a virgin."

Cupping her buttocks with both hands, he pulled her against him with gradually increasing pressure until he felt her hymen pop and she said, "Ow!"

"Sorry," he said.

"Don't be. It's the nicest pain I ever had. Is it all the way in?"

"No."

She felt downward and her eyes widened. "It's barely started, yet it feels like lots. How are you going to get all the rest of that in?"

"Like this," he said, pulling forward on her buttocks.

Her eyes grew even wider. "Ow!" she said again. "I mean, wow!" She felt downward again. "Good grief, there's even more."

He pulled her closer. "That has to be it," she said. "I can feel those round things against me."

He drew nearly out, then shoved back in. "Oops," she said. "You can do that all you want."

Ten minutes later she was writhing in orgasm. When her jerks subsided, she said, "I'm a lousy fantasizer. They were never like this."

"We have only just begun," he said, almost withdrawing and driving himself back into her.

Later they lay on the bank and dried in the sun and then made love again on the grass. A while after that she said, "Want to try it in a tree?"

"I think not," he said. "Let's go find a hammock."

"The house is empty. What's wrong with a bed?"

"Nothing," he said, getting to his feet and starting to dress.

Except for Abraham Denton, Jamie's reception in Rimfire on Monday was exceedingly cordial, and even the dour hardware merchant wasn't uncivil, although he was a trifle curt. Faustina asked Missy Appleton, who was still unmarried at twenty-four, to be her bridesmaid, and Jamie asked Marshal Jess Pinter to be his best man. Martha Appleton offered to bake the wedding cake, and Cricket Browning, who greeted Jamie with unself-conscious friendliness and introduced him to her preacher husband as an old friend, volunteered to organize a potluck for the reception following the wedding.

Faustina insisted that Jamie have a bachelor party the Saturday night before their wedding. Although Jamie would have preferred to spend the evening with her, he didn't want to fly in the face of tradition. He let her arrange it.

She arranged it thoroughly. Big Foot Harry and Bucking Horse decorated the barroom of the Hotel Parisian with paper streamers and joke signs such as GOOD-BYE, JAMIE—REST IN PEACE and LAST NIGHT TO HOWL, and Mortimer Brown put on a meal of barbecued ribs and baked beans for the entire Saturday night clientele. Always heavy on Saturday nights, custom doubled when word of the free meal spread to nearby ranches. Every table was packed and men were three deep at the bar. Armand always hired blacksmith Caleb Thorpe as an extra barkeep on Saturday nights, but tonight he also drafted a cowboy named Alec Small. Bigfoot Harry and Bucking Horse assisted Mortimer Brown in dishing out the spread.

The celebration lasted until two in the morning. By then the crowd had thinned to a single poker table of eight players; the cook and his two helpers had long since packed up and gone home, and the cowboy who'd helped tend bar had left. Jamie was banking the poker game, which was only for nickel chips with a fifteen-cent limit. Ordinarily he wouldn't have sat in such a small game, let alone bank it, but as the guest of honor he felt obligated to when he was asked. Some of the players had suggested raising the stakes when they started to get drunk, but Jamie had vetoed all such suggestions because he didn't want to take advantage of the guests at his party. As usual in all games where he played, he was the only completely sober player, for he never had more than two drinks when playing poker.

Lolly was sweeping near the door and Armand and Caleb Thorpe were washing glasses when a tall, thin man came in. He looked striking. About forty, he had a gaunt, sharp-nosed face, eyes like blue ice, a drooping blond mustache and a goatee. His shirt was fringed leather and his flat-crowned black hat had a snakeskin band. He wore two guns waist-high on a wide belt—the left one holstered, the right hanging free and permanently fixed to the belt by a metal stud welded to the frame, so that it could be tilted upward and fired in a single motion.

As the man paused just inside to glance around the room, Caleb Thorpe said, "That's Niles Redshank."

"The bounty hunter?" Armand said, staring at the man.

"Right. I saw him kill an outlaw in Rimfire two years ago."

Redshank said something to Lolly, who pointed to the card table. The bounty hunter walked over and halted on the opposite side of the table from Jamie, who was dealing.

"Jamie McKay?" Redshank said.

His tone alerted Jamie even before he looked at the man, and his reaction was instantaneous. Dropping the deck, he tilted his chair over backward and drew before it hit the floor. Redshank's naked gun swung level and fired a split second before Jamie's went off. The bounty hunter's slug drilled air where Jamie's chest had been an instant earlier, and Jamie's slug caught the thin man squarely in the center of the chest.

Bouncing to his feet, Jamie ran around the table to look down at the dead man. Armand, the blacksmith and Lolly all ran over.

Holstering his gun, Jamie said, "Who the hell is he?"

Caleb Thorpe said, "Niles Redshank, the bounty hunter."

Lolly said, "He asked for you, Mr. McKay. I didn't know who he was."

The tip of a folded sheet of paper protruded from the breast pocket of the fringed leather shirt. Bending, Jamie plucked it out, gave it a brief glance, refolded it and put it in his own breast pocket. He took out a roll of bills and tossed a twenty on the table.

"That should cover everybody's chips," he said. "Give the change to Lolly. Good night, gentlemen."

He strode outdoors, and a moment later they heard him ride away.

At the ranch house Jamie left his horse in front of the porch, felt his way to his room and lit a candle. Quickly he packed his saddlebags, made up his blanket roll and carried both outdoors. After filling his canteen at the pump and hanging it from his saddle horn, he went back inside and carried the candle to Faustina's room. She was asleep with her hair spread in a dark cloud across the pillow. Setting the candle on her bedside stand, he shook her awake.

"What is it?" she said, sitting up and staring at him.

For a few moments he just looked at her, savoring what would probably be his last look for a long time. She wore a flannel nightgown, but even in that unromantic wrap, and with her dark hair falling about her shoulders in disarray, she was beautiful.

He said, "A bounty hunter named Niles Redshank just tried to kill me. I killed him instead."

He unfolded the sheet of paper he had taken from Redshank's body and handed it to her. She tilted it so that the candlelight fell on it and read:

$5000 REWARD
DEAD OR ALIVE FOR
JAMES (JAMIE) McKAY
Murderer and Jail Escapee
Subject Escaped from El Paso County Jail
December 28, 1880

DESCRIPTION
Age 24, height 6 feet, weight 190 pounds, black
hair combed back, dark brown eyes, smooth, dark
complexion. Subject is half Comanche Indian.
Reward offered by Don Miguel Derango
Contact Sheriff of El Paso County, El Paso, Texas

When Faustina looked up with frightened eyes, Jamie
said, "I guess the wedding is off."

"Oh, Jamie!"

"If we went ahead, I'd probably have to kill my best
man."

Faustina started to cry. Sitting on the edge of the bed,
he took her into his arms. When her tears finally stopped,
he gave her his handkerchief to dry her eyes. She laid her
head on his shoulder.

"Where will you go?" she asked, accepting that he was
going to have to run.

"I don't know, except it will be far. I'll change my
name, and when it seems safe, I'll send for you."

"It isn't fair that a man can legally buy another's
murder," she said. "That's what this Don Miguel is trying
to do. The state of Texas has offered no reward, has it?"

"None I've heard of."

"Then no one would come after you if he hadn't. It
isn't fair."

"An advantage of wealth." he said. "You can buy your
revenge. I had better get going."

"So soon?" she said, clinging to him.

"If one bounty hunter found me four-hundred-and-fifty
miles from home, others are bound to be along.

Taking her arms from about him, she pushed against his
chest. "Yes, I am selfish. Go quickly."

He gave her a final soft, quick kiss, rose and went out without looking back.

Jamie headed northeast, for no reason except that it led toward territory where he had never been. In the morning he stopped at an isolated trading post and stocked up with enough canned goods to last him a week and a bag of oats for his horse, as he planned to camp out and avoid towns for a while so as to leave no trail for bounty hunters to follow.

Three days later he came to the edge of the Painted Desert. He marveled at its harsh beauty. A wondrous wasteland, with buttes, mesas and valleys painted in bright reds and yellows, in pastel blues and lilacs, stretching fo two hundred miles along the Little Colorado River, it fascinated him so much that he decided to risk crossing it despite its barrenness and lack of water or forage for his horse beyond the Little Colorado.

Fifty miles later he wished he hadn't. A sandstorm rose and drove him into a narrow gorge between sheer cliffs. He had to go deep into the gorge to escape the cutting sand shipping through its opening. He was two miles within it before he found still air around him. He couldn't see his surroundings because overhead a black cloud of sand, screaming above the canyon walls, turned what had been a bright afternoon an hour before into night.

Dismounting, he was startled to discover he was standing in grass. His horse began to graze.

The storm ended as suddenly as it had begun—one moment sand whistling overhead and blotting out the sun; the next dead silence, with sunlight pouring into the canyon.

It was a box canyon, he saw, fifty yards across, with its far wall only fifty yards ahead, carpeted with lush grass from fifty yards behind him to the wall. A narrow stream flowed across it from the mouth of a cave to the left, then disappeared into a hole in the wall on the right.

Leaving his horse grazing, he walked to the cave and peered in. Its head-high opening let in enough light for him to see that it was a single round room about twenty feet in diameter, with a number of ancient Indian pots lined along the walls. The little stream, no more than two feet wide, came from a spring high in the rear wall of the cave, flowed across the center of the floor and on across thecanyon. There was no sign that anyone had ever been in the cave since the Indians had left, perhaps hundreds of years ago, and no sign that animals would have to cross fifty miles of barren waste without food or water to get there.

He tasted the water, found it was good and filled his canteen. What an ideal hieout it would make, he thought, if it weren't so isolated. A man would go batty there after a time.

When he got back to the mouth of the canyon, he looked around in all directions. To the north there was a flat-topped purple butte, to the south a needlelike spire of brilliant red, to the east a pinnacle of bright yellow. He wasn't quite sure why he was noting landmarks, because he had no intention of ever returning here.

CHAPTER XXIV

Don Miguel's hate for Jamie McKay for killing his son was compounded by Jamie's still unforgiven sin of ravishing his daughter. When news came that Jamie had killed famed bounty hunter Niles Redshank, his death became Don Miguel's obsession. He ordered Sheriff Nick Bowdry to issue another bulletin, raising the bounty to ten thousand dollars.

In mid-February there was a newspaper report that Jamie, under the name of Jackson Hunt, had killed a bounty hunter team of brothers named Jose and Manuel Esperanzo in a gunfight at the Indian village of Tulsey Town, in Okalahoma Territory. The item referred to Jamie as one of the deadliest gunfighters in the Southwest, now with a score of five men killed in three gunfights.

Don Miguel came roaring into Sheriff Bowdry's office with the newspaper in his hand. Throwing it on the sheriff's desk, he said, "I want Jamie McKay dead. Raise the bounty to one-hundred thousand dollars."

"No one has ever offered a bounty like that, Don Miguel," Bowdry said. "You're already posting double the bounty on each of the two James brothers."

"I want a bounty of one-hundred thousand on him," the rancher said.

In Austin, City Marshal Ben Thompson, generally regarded as the fastest gun in Texas, now that Wes Hardin was in prison, read the new flier when it came into his office, promptly named his deputy as acting marshal and went home to change clothes and pack. He had to change clothes because he never went manhunting without looking his best. His killing uniform was a black suit, cane, gloves and a stovepipe hat. He caught the afternoon stage out of Austin for El Paso.

John Barclay Armstrong's reason for being at the Willacy County Courthouse in Raymondville, Texas, was to pay his property tax. But after doing that, he dropped in to see his friend, Sheriff Willie Macon, who had once served under him in the Texas Rangers. Armstrong, who at the height of his career as a Ranger had been known as "McNelly's Bulldog," after the famed chief of the Rangers, was now retired and operated a fifty-thousand-acre ranch he had purchased with the four-thousand-dollar bounty he received in 1877 for the capture of John Wesley Hardin.

Sheriff Macon greeted his former captain cordially, took a bottle from his desk and poured two drinks. The two toasted each other and tossed them off.

"Too bad you're retired," Macon said. "There's a bulletin in this morning right up your alley." He pointed to a "Wanted" poster on the wall.

Ex-Captain Armstrong went over to look at it. It offered $100,000 reward, dead or alive, for an escaped murderer named James McKay. Armstrong recalled reading of the man killing a couple of bounty hunters.

"Who's retired?" he said, heading for the door.

In Uvaldo, Texas, handsome, mustached Deputy Sheriff

John Fisher King read the new flier and announced to the sheriff that he was taking a leave of absence. The sheriff didn't argue with the reformed rustler, thief and acquitted murderer of a half-dozen men. People seldom did. Two hours later Deputy King, wearing his customary fringed shirt, crimson sash and belled spurs, caught the stage to El Paso.

William Matthew Tilghman, Jr., was in Dodge City to purchase supplies for his nearby ranch. In 1881 his future as the most famous lawman in the history of the West was hardly apparent. Except for a brief stint as a deputy sheriff in Ford County, Kansas, his only fame to date was as a buffalo hunter, army scout and accused rustler. Tall, handsome and powerfully built, at twenty-six he had left such adventures behind him and seemed to have settled down with his wife and a couple of children.

Outside the general store he stopped to read a reward poster. He continued inside, made his purchases, loaded them on the wagon and drove back to his ranch. After unloading the supplies, he cleaned and oiled his gun and told his wife to pack him a suitcase.

In Tombstone, Arizona, gaunt, hollow-cheeked John Henry (Doc) Holliday was reading the new poster tacked to the outer wall of Marshal Wyatt Earp's office when he became conscious of someone standing beside him. Looking around, he saw it was John Ringo, a man as handsome, dour-natured and alcoholic as Holliday. Ringo was reading the same flier. As the pair disliked each other so much that on two occasions only intervention by lawmen had averted gunfights, neither spoke. Ringo walked away and Doc entered the marshal's office.

U.S. Marshal Earp was seated at his desk. Holliday said, "I'll be out of town for a while, Wyatt."

Since, on the day before, Doc Holliday had wounded

saloon keeper Mike Joyce and another man in a gunfight, Earp assumed his reason for leaving was to let tempers die. "All right, Doc," he said. "Don't stay away too long."

Shortly afterward, in different parts of town, Doc and Ringo were both packing.

On April 16, 1881, William B. (Bat) Masterson arrived in Dodge City on the 11:30 a.m. train in response to an urgent wire from his brother Jim requesting help in his feud with two former business associates. As he got off the train, Bat found his brother's two enemies waiting for him. All three drew guns and began firing. Bat wounded one of the men before the fight was stopped by Mayor Webster and Sheriff Ford Singer, who appeared with shotguns and arrested all three.

After paying a small fine and being ordered out of town, Bat returned to the depot to take the evening train back north. A posted flier changed his mind, and instead he took the southbound Sante Fe. That only went as far as Deming, in New Mexico Territory, and from there he had to take the stage to El Paso.

Crosby Fox and Rebel Joe Sommers made an odd pair. Fox was a rawboned six-feet-three, Rebel Joe a slimly built five-feet-five. At thirty Fox was ten years older, but Rebel Joe was the dominant one because the older man was awed by the pale young killer. Rebel Joe had killed four men before they became partners, and three since, all outlaws with bounties on their heads.

Fox had committed one murder and had killed one man in a gunfight before he and Rebel Joe teamed up as bounty hunters, but to impress his young partner, he claimed five. He felt such constant compulsion to impress Rebel Joe that not only had he made up crimes, but he had also confessed all the details of his actual crimes.

Fox was seated alone at a table in the Pecos Saloon in Las Cruces when Rebel Joe came in, dropped a flier in front of him and said, "Let's go."

After reading it, the bigger man tossed off the whiskey before him and got to his feet. He and Rebel Joe had traveled to Goose Flats, in Arizona Territory, when the bounty on Jamie McKay had grown to ten thousand dollars, but the trail from there had let nowhere, and Rebel Joe had decided they were wasting their time.

Crosby Fox was glad they were going after him again, for a reason aside from the money. One of the two men for whose murders McKay was wanted had been Crosby's brother.

CHAPTER XXV

Two days after Nate and Denise Cook learned that their bank had failed and wiped out every cent of their savings, a second disaster struck. At six o'clock in the morning they were awakened by pounding at the door of their cottage, and both went to answer. It was Emory Gates, the Negro chef at the Club Denise; he was panting from running eight blocks, and his hair and eyebrows were singed.

"The club's burning, Mr. Cook," he said. "I done it. That new gas oven blew right in my face."

"You're burned," Denise said. "Come in and let me rub lard on you."

"No, I'm all right, just singed a little. The firemen are there, Mr. Cook, but it looks bad."

"Anybody but you hurt?" Nate asked.

"No, wasn't no one there but me, lighting the oven to bake today's bread."

"Go out back and hitch up the carriage while we dress," Nate said.

"Yes, sir," the black man said, and ran around behind the cottage to the carriage house.

Five-year-old Ashley awoke while Nate and Denise were dressing, and so they took him along. Emory, Denise and Ash sat in the back of the victoria while Nate drove the eight blocks to the club.

The crowd watching the building go up in flames prevented them from getting any nearer than half a block. Alighting, they pushed through the crowd, Denise and Nate holding Ash between them by both hands and Emory trailing, until they reached the rope the fire-fighters had strung to hold back the crowd. Flames were spurting fifty feet in the air, unfazed by the water being played on them from a half-dozen hoses.

The fire captain recognized Nate and came over. "Looks like a total loss, Mr. Cook. It's too hot to send anyone in there. Know if anyone's inside?"

Indicating Emory with a nod of his head, Nate said, "Our chef here was the only one in the building when it started. He was lighting the oven to bake bread when it blew."

"I figured it was gas, the way it burned. We shut it off at the main, but it already had a good start."

He walked away, and Nate and Denise and Ash and Emory watched the Club Denise burn to the ground.

Denise said, "I shouldn't have nagged you to add the restaurant. The casino was doing fine."

Nate smiled at her. "We had a kitchen and a gas stove before we built the restaurant wing, honey. We always served food at the bar."

"Daddy would advance us the money to rebuild."

Nate stopped smiling. That suggestion had been a mistake, Denise thought. Nate would never accept financial help from her father.

When the building was reduced to embers and it was possible to get close enough to see if anything was salvagable, the fire captain let Nate under the rope and walked over to the wreckage with him. The only thing Nate could see worth recovering was the iron safe. The fire captain had it hosed off until it was cool enough to handle and had it dragged from the wreckage.

The fire hadn't welded the door closed. It opened without difficulty. Inside was the last two thousand dollars Nate and Denise had in the world.

During the drive home, Nate said to Denise, "At least we still own the land, and with no building on it the taxes should go down."

It was noon when Nate and Denise and Ash got back to the cottage. Nate carried in the newspaper, dropped it on the kitchen table and went to his and Denise's bedroom to wash up while Denise prepared lunch. Ash went into his added-on room to play until he was called.

After lunch, when Ash had been excused to run outdoors and Denise had poured coffee, Nate opened the newspaper.

"I don't suppose the fire's in the *Chronicle* yet," Denise said.

Nate gave her a quizzical glance. "The paper was lying in the yard when we got home, honey."

Coloring, she said, "Don't you have a smart wife?"

"I married you for your beauty and passion."

He returned to his paper. Denise said, "What are we going to do, darling?"

Nate had become too engrossed to hear. When she repeated the question, he still made no answer. Finally he laid aside the paper and stared into his coffee cup.

"What were you reading that was so interesting?" Denise asked.

He opened the paper to an inner page, folded it to the

item and passed it across to her. It was a reprinted news story from the *El Paso News*, with a byline.

MANHUNT OF THE CENTURY
by Alan Cutler

Don Miguel Derango, southwest Texas' wealthiest rancher, has instigated the greatest manhunt of the century by offering the incredible reward of $100,000, dead or alive, for the murderer of his son and one of his ranch employees. The murders were committed by twenty-four-year-old James (Jamie) McKay, who, according to witnesses, gunned down Raoul Derango and Jonathon Fox without warning or provocation in El Paso's Acme Saloon last Christmas Eve. Arrested for the murders, McKay escaped from the county jail three days after Christmas.

Don Miguel first offered a reward of $5000. When famed bounty hunter Niles Redshank was killed by McKay in Goose Flats, Arizona Territory, attempting to collect that reward, the bounty was raised to $10,000. The bounty-hunting brothers, Joe and Manuel Esperenzo, died in the Indian village of Tulsey Town, in Oklahoma Territory, trying for that bounty.

On April first Don Miguel raised the ante to $100,000, which not only attracted the nation's most noted bounty hunters to El Paso, but has drawn a number of famous gunfighters who have never previously gone bounty hunting. The list to date includes Austin City Marshal Ben Thompson, ex-Ranger Captain John Armstrong, most noted for his capture of John Wesley Hardin, John King of Uvaldo, William Tilghman, Doc Holliday, John Ringo, Bat Masterson, Crosby Fox and Rebel Joe Sommers.

Since the gunfight at Tulsey Town, Jamie McKay

has been reported seen all over the Southwest, sometimes simultaneously in several places hundreds of miles apart. Unfortunately the outlaw has never been photographed, so that his reward posters carry only his description, which is as follows: Age 24, height 6 feet, weight 190 pounds, black hair combed back, dark brown eyes, smooth, dark complexion. He is half Comanche Indian.

Looking up, Denise said, "Except for your scar and the way you wear your hair, this could be your description."

"I noticed that." He got to his feet. "I have to shave and pack."

Denise got up too. "Nate, you're not going after this killer?"

"It would put us back in business."

He went into their bedroom and she ran after him. "You promised you would never go bounty hunting again."

Pouring water in the wash basin, he began to lather his face.

"Nate, you promised."

He started to strop his razor.

"Will you answer me?"

"Sure," he said. "I'm going. You can nag, you can threaten to leave me, and I'm still going. Shall we part still in love or not speaking?"

Emitting a sigh, she stood watching him shave. When he finished and put away his razor, he took her into his arms.

"I used only to love you, but now I adore you," he said.

"I adore you, too," she said, clinging to him. "I won't nag, and I would never leave you, but don't expect me not to worry every minute you're gone."

Giving her a kiss on the nose, he released her and took their last two thousand dollars from his pocket. Dividing it into two stacks, he handed her one and said, "Here's expense money until I get back."

"Do you have enough?"

"Plenty. If I start to run short, I'll find a poker game."

The Southern Pacific now ran all the way from San Francisco to San Diego, and from there east to within twenty miles of El Paso. It was scheduled to reach El Paso in mid-May, but for now it was still necessary to ride the stage on the last lap.

Nate arrived in El Paso in mid-afternoon on Monday, May second. A teen-age baggage handler came from the stage depot to catch the baggage thrown down from the stagecoach roof by the driver. Nate's suitcase was the last piece thrown down.

Pointing to it, Nate said to the teen-ager, "Can I check this in the depot for a while?"

The boy looked at him; his eyes widened and he backed a step. "Yes, sir," he said in a frightened voice.

Nate glanced over his shoulder to see what had frightened the lad, saw nothing but the other three passengers entering the depot and turned back. "You'll take care of it?"

"Yes, sir." The boy was studying his face with fascination, now seeming less frightened than astonished.

"Something about my appearance bother you?" Nate asked.

"No, sir, not a thing."

Maybe it was the scar on his cheek, Nate thought, although he had never had such a reaction to it before. He said, "Where's the sheriff's office?"

"Block-and-a-half up," the boy said, pointing.

As Nate walked toward the sheriff's office, several people gave him startled looks. He thought he had better find a mirror and check to see if his face was dirty.

In the sheriff's office a tall, spare, mustached man wearing a vest with a star pinned to it sat behind a desk. When Nate came in, he pushed back his chair, came to his feet and stood bent forward with both hands supporting him on the desk as he stared in disbelief.

Nate said, "Why the hell does everyone in this town look at me like I'm from Mars?"

The sheriff blinked, fixed his gaze on Nate's scar, emitted a relieved sigh and straightened up. "You gave me a turn, mister. Who are you?"

"Nathan Cook."

The sheriff looked surprised. "The famous Nate Cook from California?"

"I'm from California," Nate said. "I don't know about the famous."

"You are." The sheriff extended his hand. "Nick Bowdry."

Clasping the hand, Nate said, "Why'd I give you a turn?"

"Except for that scar and the way you comb your hair, you're the spitting image of Jamie McKay. You could be his twin. You're even wearing the same kind of gun and carrying it the same way."

Nate raised his eyebrows. "Then he ought to be easy for me to recognize."

A chubby man of about thirty, wearing a suit, a necktie and an excited expression, came in and said, "Nick, guess who's in town?" Then he looked at Nate and turned pale.

"Meet Nate Cook," Bowdry said. "Alan Cutler of the *El Paso News*, Mr. Cook."

The reporter gazed into Nate's face for some moments

before cautiously extending his hand. "Excuse my reaction, Mr. Cook. I thought you were someone else."

Gripping the offered hand, Nate said, "I know, Jamie McKay. Sheriff Bowdry's already told me."

Alan Cutler's face suddenly lighted with inspiration. "Would you stick around for a few minutes, Mr. Cook, while I run get our photographer?"

"For what?"

"To take your picture. If you would comb your hair straight back and we covered that scar with a little grease paint, the *News* would scoop the country with the first photograph of Jamie McKay."

"Forget it."

Alan Cutler looked surprised. "You won't do it?"

"For two reasons, Mr. Cutler. You know why I'm here?"

"I assume you're after the hundred-thousand-dollar bounty."

"Uh-huh. Since I'm McKay's image, I know what he looks like, which gives me an advantage over the other bounty hunters. If you publish what's supposed to be his picture, I'd lose the advantage. My other reason is that if you print my picture as Jamie McKay, the first one of the other bounty hunters I run into will shoot me on sight."

The reporter looked disappointed. "I guess there's no point in trying to talk you into it."

"None." Nate turned to Nick Bowdry. "Sheriff, do you know where McKay was last sighted?"

"Everywhere from here to Kansas City, except it's never really been him. Authentic sightings are zero. My guess is that he's somewhere like Chicago or New York City under a changed name."

"Do you know where the other bounty hunters are now?"

"Most. They keep wiring their locations so I can wire back any information I have."

"Can I get a list?"

Bowdry shrugged. "This is a contest only from you bounty hunters' point of view. Don Miguel doesn't give a hoot in hell who wins. He just wants McKay's hide."

He reseated himself at his desk and lifted a stack of telegrams from the center drawer.

Since Jamie McKay had left no clues as to his whereabouts, Nate decided his best bet was to track down the other bounty hunters to find out what clues, if any, they had uncovered. If they had no leads, at least he could narrow his search by eliminating the ground they had covered.

Judging from Sheriff Bowdry's stack of telegrams, they were spread all over the territories of Arizona, New Mexico, Oklahoma and Utah, plus the states of Colorado and Nevada. As the nearest to El Paso were Doc Holliday and Bat Masterson, who had sent a jointly signed telegram from Deming, Nate took the stage there. The two, who were old friends and apparently had decided to hunt as a team, had bought horses in Deming and had headed west toward Arizona Territory. As nearly as Nate could determine from questioning some of the people they had talked to, they had picked up no useful information in Deming. Nevertheless, he bought a horse and followed them because they were going in the same direction he wanted to go anyway. Ben Thompson had sent a wire from Tucson and John Ringo from Phoenix, and Nate wanted to run them down as well.

During the next two months Nate caught up with all nine of the other bounty hunters in various places. All but one had paired up. Crosby Fox and young Rebel Joe Sommers had been a team all along. As Nate had guessed,

Doc Holliday and Bat Masterson were working together. Ben Thompson had paired with his old friend John King. Ex-Ranger Captain John Armstrong and Billy Tilghman had decided to work togehter. Only Nate and the misanthropic John Ringo were still working alone.

None had uncovered any reliable information about Jamie McKay's whereabouts.

Fortunately Nate ran down all the other bounty hunters and got to know them before another story by Alan Cutler in the *El Paso News* was widely reprinted. It read:

DOUBLE OF OUTLAW ON HIS TRAIL
by Alan Cutler

On May 2nd a tenth bounty hunter in search of the fabulous $100,000 reward on the head of outlaw Jamie McKay appeared in El Paso, startling those townspeople who saw him, including Sheriff Nick Bowdry and this reporter, by his uncanny resemblance to the hunted man. California's most famous gunfighter, Nathan (Nate) Cook, so closely resembles Jamie McKay, except for a scar on his left cheek and the way he combs his hair, that he could be a twin. Sheriff Bowdry noted to this reporter that he even carried the same type of gun, a Navy .41 Colt, wore it high on his right side in the same manner as the outlaw, and had the same habit of pushing his flat-crowned hat off the back of his head when indoors, to let it ride on the back of his neck by its chin strap.

Cook refused to let the *News* photographer take his picture, citing two reasons. Since Jamie McKay had never been photographed, none of the other bounty hunters knew exactly how he looked, Cook said, whereas he had the advantage of knowing that

his prey resembled him. His other reason was that
if his photograph appeared in the *News* as Jamie
McKay, the other bounty hunters might shoot him
on sight.

The story destroyed Nate's advantage over the other
hunters, but since he had met all of them before it was
printed, he was safe from being shot on sight.

During the courses of their searches all the bounty hunters,
including Nate, visited the scenes of the two gunfights
between McKay and bounty hunters. The Indian village of
Tulsey Town seemed to have been a chance location,
merely the spot where the Esperenzo brothers caught up
with the outlaw after trailing him all over the Territory of
Oklahoma. None of the Indian residents had ever seen any
of the three before. The crossroads in Arizona Territory
calling itself Goose Flats was no more productive. The
proprietor of the saloon-hotel there, a funny little Frenchman
named Armand Monet, told Nate he hadn't known who
McKay was until the outlaw had ridden out of town after
the shooting, and Monet had found a "Wanted" circular in
the dead bounty hunter's shirt pocket.

"Saturday nights I am too rush to notice who is here,"
the little man had said. "There are a hundred, perhaps a
hundred-fifty thirsty cowboys, all yell for drinks at once."

That must be the only time there was any business, Nate
thought. When he was there, on a Monday afternoon, the
only other person in the place was a whiskered old man
sweeping the floor.

While he learned nothing from Armand Monet about
Jamie McKay, there had been an intriguing sidelight to the
conversation. When Nate tried the little bit of French he
had learned in college on the man, Monet said he never
conversed in French because it spoiled his English. Nate

had gotten the curious impression that actually, except for a smattering of words, the man didn't know French, and his accent was assumed.

With no leads of any kind, by July first all the bounty hunters had suspended search until some kind of lead developed. Leaving their addresses with Sheriff Bowdry, along with requests to be wired if any leads developed, all except Nate returned home.

Nate had a feeling, based on no more than a hunch, that when McKay surfaced, it would be somewhere in the Territory of Arizona. Instead of going clear back to San Francisco, he checked into a hotel in Tucson, wired his address to Sheriff Bowdry and asked him to wire him there if he heard anything about McKay.

CHAPTER XXVI

After the gunfight in Tulsey Town, Jamie McKay had headed south into Texas, figuring that was the one place bounty hunters wouldn't be looking for him. He wandered west, along the northern border of Texas, never staying in any town more than twenty-four hours, always sitting in poker games with his back to the wall, and never completely relaxing. With half his attention on the door and only the other half on his cards, his game suffered. By mid-March his stake was down to three thousand dollars.

When he reached the Panhandle without being recognized anywhere, he began to regain confidence. As he worked his way across into New Mexico Territory, and then across it into the northern end of Arizona Territory, he managed to pick back up one thousand dollars in addition to expenses.

In a small town in northern Arizona he saw a reprint of the story from the *El Paso News* reporting the increase in bounty to a hundred thousand dollars and listing the small army of famous gunfighters searching for him.

His confidence evaporated. Buying a pack horse, he

stocked up with enough food to last two months, bought a stack of the only available books, dime novels, and rode south into the Painted Desert.

Despite having made every effort to fix in his mind the location of the three landmarks he had chosen on his previous visit to the oasis in the narrow canyon, he had to search for some time before he finally suddenly came upon them. He rode down the canyon and holed up in the cave until mid-July. He saw no newspapers during that time, of course, and therefore never read the story of the look-alike bounty hunter, Nate Cook, joining the chase.

When his food got low, Jamie decided to emerge long enough to find out how persistently he was still being hunted. Figuring it might be some time before he had another opportunity, he laundered all his clothes, bathed and shaved and trimmed his hair before starting out. As Goose Flats was only a hundred miles away, he headed for it.

Traveling by night and sleeping by day, Jamie reached Goose Flats at midnight on Wednesday, the twentieth of July. It was a dark, moonless night and not a light showed in town. As he rode past the Hotel Parisian, a voice from the porch called, "Hey, mister, got the price of a drink?"

Peering that way, Jamie could barely make out the dim form of the sweep-up man, Lolly, seated on the porch. Without slowing, he tossed him a coin.

It was past midnight when he arrived at the Monet ranch, and both the house and bunkhouse were dark. Not wanting to awaken anyone, he put his saddle horse and pack horse in stalls in the barn and spread his blanket on a pile of straw.

He was awakened by the sound of conversation outdoors. Looking at his watch, he saw it was six a.m. After pulling on his boots, he cracked open the barn door to peer out.

When he saw Bigfoot Harry and Bucking Horse washing up at the pump, he opened the door far enough to slip outside.

"Morning," he said when he was within six feet of them.

The two Indians looked around. With no evidence of surprise lanky Bigfoot Harry said, "Morning." Moon-faced Bucking Horse summoned a slight smile. "Welcome home, Paleface. You're just in time for breakfast."

"I'll wash up first," Jamie said.

The two Indians headed for the back door of the house. Jamie had washed and was drying on the towel hanging from a nail on the washstand next to the pump when Faustina came flying out the back door to throw herself into his arms. Both lost themselves in a long kiss.

When they came out of it, they found themselves surrounded by admiring spectators. The two Apaches had come outdoors again, and so had Faustina's father and Mortimer Brown.

Armand said, "I knew you were alive or the papers would have called you dead, *non*?" The big black man said, "How you want your eggs?"

During breakfast Jamie explained where he had been, and Armand and Faustina brought him up to date on the news. Two weeks ago a reprinted story by Alan Cutler from the El Paso News had reported that the ten bounty hunters had temporarily given up their search because Jamie seemed to have vanished. The reporter speculated that he had either fled to Mexico or was living somewhere such as Chicago or New York City under a changed name.

Jamie said, "Ten bounty hunters? Last I read, there were only nine."

"The California gunfighter, Nate Cook, has been added," Armand said. "He is like your twin, *ami*. What a start he gave me when he came to the hotel."

"He's been here?" Jamie said.

"There is no worry. It was back in May. I have read in the paper how he look like you, or I would have called him Jamie. There is no difference except he have a scar on his cheek and part his hair to comb over his ears."

"You will be safe here," Faustina said. "After a few weeks, when the bounty hunters give up for good, we'll do what that reporter guessed you have already done—move east and change your name."

"You would go with me?" Jamie asked.

"Try leaving without me."

Mortimer Brown said, "Did you pass through any towns between the Painted Desert and here?"

"Only Goose Flats, and that was at midnight last night. Lolly was sitting on the hotel porch, but he couldn't have recognized me because I could barely see him. There been any important events in the world while I was out of touch?"

Armand said, "One week ago Sheriff Pat Garrett shoot and kill Billy the Kid at Fort Sumpter."

"It was only a matter of time," Bigfoot Harry said. "All those outlaws die with their boots on."

When everybody looked at him, the lanky Apache's usually expressionless face turned sheepish. "Know why I'm called Bigfoot?" he asked.

"Because it's always in your mouth," Bucking Horse said.

It was five days since Jamie had left the Painted Desert, and he had been sleeping in the same clothes. After unpacking his gear in his room, he emerged carrying a towel and fresh clothing.

Armand had left for the hotel and the three hands had gone to work. Faustina had washed the breakfast dishes and was putting them away when Jamie entered the kitchen.

Eyeing the towel and fresh clothes, Faustina said, "Want me to heat you water for a bath?"

"Thought I'd just take a dip in the old swimming hole."

She smiled with delight. "What a wonderful idea. Wait until I get a towel."

Faustina wanted to make love in the water again, and then they repeated it on the grassy bank. Afterward they lay in each other's arms for a while, telling each other about their love and discussing where they would go to start a new life.

"Georgia is nice," Faustina said. "Probably both of us could get teaching jobs at Bessie Tift."

"They would want my academic records, honey, which would involve giving my real name. How about Florida?"

"I don't care where, so long as it's with you," she said, squeezing and kissing him.

They took a final dip, dried themselves and dressed. As Jamie transferred items from the pockets of his dirty denims, he said, "Hell."

"What's the matter?" Faustina said.

Jamie showed two silver dollars in his palm. "I had these yesterday and my good-luck twenty-dollar gold piece is gone. I tossed Lolly a coin last night."

"Oh my," Faustina said. "He'll get drunk."

They had hardly gotten back to the house when Armand rode up and ran inside.

"Lolly is missing," he said. "Caleb Thorpe says he caught a ride into Rimfire with a rancher driving a wagon there." He was so excited, he forgot his accent. "He recognized you and has gone to the marshal."

Faustina said, "There isn't any. Jess Pinter took a job in Phoenix just before school ended, and the new marshal they hired can't come until fall."

Jamie said, "Probably he just went to get drunk. I accidentally tossed him a twenty-dollar gold piece last night instead of a dollar."

"We had best discover," Armand said, recovering his accent. "My daughter, ride to see what he is doing."

"All right, Father."

"I must return to the hotel. Stop there when you have find out."

Faustina changed from her dress into range clothing for the twenty-mile ride to Rimfire. It was noon when she got there. After looking into the Palace Hotel and the McCarthy Hotel dining room without finding Lolly, she went to the general store. Missy Appleton was waiting on a customer and her father was behind the post office counter, which was also now the telegraph counter since Rimfire had gotten that service.

"Hi, Faustina," Amos said. "Good to see you."

"You, too, Mr. Appleton. Have you seen Lolly?"

"Yep, cashed a twenty-dollar gold piece for silver dollars and took the stage to Tucson."

"Was he sober?"

"Sure. Didn't have time to visit the Palace before the stage left. Barely had time to send his telegram."

"What telegram?"

Amos took a sheet of paper from the drawer and placed it before her. "Told him he was mistaken, that who he probably saw was that look-alike bounty hunter who came through here once before, but he sent it anyway."

The wire was to the sheriff of El Paso County, El Paso, Texas, and read:

OUTLAW JAMIE MCKAY SEEN VICINITY GOOSE FLATS STOP IF APPREHENDED I CLAIM $100,000 REWARD.
                    BERTRAM LOLLY

"I always thought Lolly was his first name," Appleton said.

So had Faustina, but the wire upset her too much to think about that. She said, "I want to send a wire too."

"Sure," he said, giving her a blank form and a pencil.

Addressing it to the sheriff at El Paso also, she wrote:

IGNORE WIRE FROM BERTRAM LOLLY STOP
MAN IS TOWN DRUNK STOP PERSON HE SAW
IS A TRAVELING PREACHER
ARMAND MONET
MAYOR OF GOOSE FLATS

After reading the message, Amos said, "Mayor of Goose Flats?"

"He's as close to the mayor as it has," Faustina said.

The mayor of Rimfire shrugged. "Fifty cents," he said.

Faustina had lunch in the hotel dining room before returning to Goose Flats. It was late afternoon when she reached the Hotel Parisian.

When she told her father of the wire Lolly had sent and of her canceling wire, he said, "We must take no chance. In case the first instead of the second wire is believed, tell Jamie to be packed and ready to ride if any bounty hunters show up."

CHAPTER XXVII

The wire a messenger delivered to Nate Cook at the hotel was long:

> TWO WIRES RECEIVED FROM RIMFIRE ARIZONA TERRITORY STOP BERTRAM LOLLY REPORTED JAMIE MCKAY SEEN IN VICINITY GOOSE FLATS STOP FOLLOWING WIRE FROM GOOSE FLATS MAYOR ARMAND MONET SAID IGNORE FIRST WIRE BECAUSE LOLLY TOWN DRUNK AND PERSON HE SAW WAS TRAVELING PREACHER STOP USE OWN JUDGMENT
> NICHOLAS BOWDRY
> SHERIFF EL PASO COUNTY

While it hardly sounded promising, it was the first lead since the hunt had begun, and Nate had no intention of passing it up. It was two hundred fifty miles from Tucson to Goose Flats, and no train ran there. As a matter of fact, the stage didn't even run there, its closest stop being the town of Rimfire. As the stage would be a lot faster than traveling horseback, Nate sold his horse and took the next stage to Rimfire. There he bought another horse and rode on to Goose Flats. He arrived in mid-afternoon on Monday, the twenty-fifth of July.

Again he found the Hotel Parisian nearly deserted. Armand Monet was behind the bar and two cowboys sat at it, drinking beer.

Monet said, "Ah, Monsieur Cook, it is good to see again your face, but if you are here for the reason I surmise, you have, alas, wasted time on the goose chase."

"Oh? Where do I find Bertram Lolly?"

"He is off to Tucson on a drunk. He will return only when his money is gone, perhaps a month."

Nate considered returning to Tucson to hunt for Lolly, then reconsidered. He said, "This traveling preacher you wired about, is he still around?"

"Alas, no, monsieur. He bore only the most superficial resemblance to you, whom I understand looks much like the man you pursue. For one thing, he was probably forty; for another, he wore no gun. Lolly was quite drunk when he saw him."

"What was the preacher's name?"

"Hiram Prescott," Monet said.

Nate said to the two cowboys, "You gentlemen know anything about Jamie McKay being in this area?"

One of the men said, "The outlaw with the big price on him? No, we're just passing through."

"I would like a room," Nate said to Monet.

"I would be delighted to have you as a guest, monsieur, but be assured you waste your time."

"I would still like one."

The little man spread his hands, palm up. "It has been weeks since we had a guest, monsieur, and the rooms are filthy."

"Don't you have someone to clean them?"

"*Oui*, Lolly, whom I explained, is off drunk. I cannot leave the bar to perform such chores."

"I'll clean it myself," Nate said. "How much?"

The proprietor sighed. "Fifty cent per night."

"I'll take it for six nights," Nate said, laying three dollars on the bar.

Picking up the money, Monet said, "Choose which one you wish, monsieur."

"Do I get a key?"

"There are no locks, monsieur."

Nate went upstairs to look. There were seven rooms off the balcony overlooking the barroom, all identically furnished with two single brass beds, two dressers, a washstand and a chamber pot. While there was a little dust, none of the rooms were filthy, and the sheets looked clean.

Nate went downstairs and outside for his saddlebags, deposited them in the central room, and went outside again to board his horse at the livery stable next door.

At five o'clock that afternoon Nate was reading a book in his room with the door open when he heard a woman's voice from the barroom. Walking over to the balcony railing, he looked down. The two cowboys were still at the bar and a plump, matronly looking woman was talking to Armand Monet.

Glancing up and seeing him, Monet said, "This is my next door neighbor, Madame Thorpe, our chef, Monsieur Cook."

"How do you do, Mrs. Thorpe," Nate said.

"Fine, thank you."

Monet said, "Ordinarily Madame Thorpe comes only on Saturday, for as you can see, we have little business during the week. I asked her this evening because I assume you wish dinner, *non*?"

"*Oui*," Nate said. "What time, Mrs. Thorpe?"

"Six all right?"

"Just fine."

"Beefsteak all right?"

"Also just fine."

The woman disappeared into the kitchen and Nate returned to his room.

A half hour later Nate heard men's voices below and again walked out on the balcony. The two cowboys were gone, and Doc Holliday, the derby-hatted Bat Masterson and John Ringo were standing at the bar. Ringo stood apart from the other two.

Nate knew that all three had given Sheriff Bowdry addresses in Tombstone, which was only a few miles beyond Tucson, and assumed they had come together to Rimfire on the stage, then had either bought or rented horses for the last twenty miles.

It must have been a pleasant trip, he thought, since neither Holliday nor Masterson could stand Ringo, and their dislike was heartily returned.

When Nate said, "Evening, gentlemen," all three looked up. Holliday and Masterson returned the greeting, but Ringo merely scowled. He didn't actively dislike Nate, but he really didn't like anyone.

Nate descended the steps.

Monet was saying, "Fifty cent a night, messieurs, or seventy-five cent if you wish to share a room. Two beds are in each room."

Masterson looked at Holliday and said, "Doc?"

The gaunt dentist said, "Suits me, Bat. Flip for four nights?"

"Bet." Taking out a silver dollar, Masterson said, "Call it," and spun the coin in the air.

"Heads," Holliday said.

The coin landed on the bar. "Your treat," Masterson said, and picked it up.

Doc Holliday gave Monet three dollars; then he and Masterson went outdoors for their saddlebags and to board their horses next door. John Ringo gave Monet two dollars for four nights in a single room, then also went outside.

"Thanks for not suggesting he sleep in with me," Nate said.

"A rather sour man, *non*? Do you imagine we will get more guests, Monsieur Cook?"

"I wouldn't be surprised if by tomorrow you had ten."

"I had better have my daughter come in to assist tomorrow." Going to the kitchen door, the hotel proprietor said, "Are you prepared to feed three more, Madame Thorpe?"

"I can feed up to ten," she said.

Holliday and Masterson invited Nate to dine with them. If Ringo had issued the same invitation, Nate probably would have accepted his rather than leaving the man to eat alone, but when he pointedly took a corner table by himself, Nate decided he wasn't going to go out of his way to be friendly with a man who obviously preferred to be left alone. He sat with Holiday and Masterson.

Both Doc Holliday and Ringo ordered bottles of whiskey, and each had several drinks before dinner, without showing any effect. Masterson had a single glass of red wine with dinner and Nate, wanting to keep a clear head, had only coffee.

During dinner Masterson said to Nate, "I assume you questioned Monet about those wires."

"Uh-huh. Did you?"

"First thing we got in. What do you think?"

"I'm wondering if he stashed Bertram Lolly somewhere."

Doc Holliday said, "No, we talked to the blacksmith,

who incidentally is our chef's husband. Lolly really is off
on a drunk. Apparently drinks up every cent he gets,
which can't be much. His job is sweep-up man here at the
hotel.''

''I know,'' Nate said. ''I saw him when I was here in
May. Little old man with a two-week beard.''

''Think we're wasting our time here?'' Masterson asked.

Nate was sure they weren't. Monet's attempt to discour-
age him from staying, which apparently he had decided
was useless to try on the others, had convinced him
that Jamie McKay was somewhere in the area. The
only reason he could think of for the hotel proprietor wanting to keep that secret was that he hoped to collect the bounty
himself. Nate had no intention of passing on his theory,
though. It would suit him fine of all the other bounty
hunters decided it was a false alarm and returned home. In
fact, he had no intention of searching the surrounding
countryside, and thereby perhaps inspiring the others to do
the same, until they had left the area.

Shrugging, Nate said, ''Probably, but it's our first lead,
and I'm going to stick around awhile and wait for Lolly to
come back.''

Jamie and Faustina were seated on the front porch when
Armand came home after midnight.

He said, ''Four of the bounty hunters are stay at the
hotel, waiting for Lolly to return.''

Jamie got to his feet. ''I'd better get going.''

''No, I have half convince them Lolly had but a drunken
hallucination. I think they will go if Lolly do not soon
return. One has engage a room for six night, but the others
for only four. You are safer here than to run in the open.''

''What if Lolly returns before they leave?'' Faustina
asked.

"In morning I will give Bigfoot Harry twenty dollar and send him to Rimfire to meet each stage. If Lolly get off, Harry will give him the money and send him back to Tucson."

"Who are the bounty hunters?" Jamie asked.

"Nate Cook the one who rented a room for six night. The other are Doc Holliday, Bat Masterson and John Ringo."

Faustina looked distressed. "I think you better get away from here, Jamie."

Armand said, "No, we will instead establish warning for any who head this direction. Faustina, you must go with me in the morning to help anyway, as tomorrow we may have six more guest. If any decide to search the countryside, you must ride here fast to alert Jamie. I will instruct Caleb to keep saddled your horse and run quick to tell the instant any hunter come for his horse."

Faustina said, "I'll put a gun in my saddlebag, Jamie. If any head this way and it looks like they'll get here before me, I'll fire three shots."

In the morning Nate was the first down for breakfast. A beautiful dark-haired girl of about nineteen, dressed in denims, boots and a flannel shirt, was setting three places at the table where Nate, Doc Holliday and Bat Masterson had eaten the evening before. A single place was already set at Ringo's corner table. Monet introduced the girl as his daughter, Faustina.

"She has come to assist me and Madame Thorpe, Monsieur Cook," Armand said. "Be seated and she will take your order."

Nate was half through a breakfast of salt pork and eggs when the other three came down. Holliday and Masterson seemed pleasantly surprised to find such a lovely waitress.

Nate was bemused at the way Ringo treated the girl. Apparently it was only men the dour gunfighter disliked, because he treated Faustina with the gallantry of a knight of the Round Table. It was not an attempt to make time with her. It was merely surprisingly gentlemanly respect bordering on reverence.

Watching, Doc Holliday said, "Ringo has a thing about women."

"So do I," Masterson said.

"You're just horny. He puts them on pedestals. He even doffs his hat and bows to whores."

"But never screws them, I hear. The man is daft."

Shortly after lunch tall, rawboned Crosby Fox and his slim, pale partner, Rebel Joe Sommers, arrived from Las Cruces and rented a room together. In mid-afternoon the dandified Ben Thompson, wearing his black suit and a stovepipe hat and carrying a cane and gloves, came in with his friend John Fisher King. As usual, the handsome King wore a fancy fringed shirt along with the crimson sash, and jingled when he walked because of his belled spurs. Ex-Ranger Captain John Armstrong got there in mid-afternoon. The three, all coming from Texas, had made the trip so fast because the Southern Pacific had reached El Paso the month before, and they had been able to ride the train clear to Tucson before switching to stagecoach.

Uncle Billy Tilghman was the last to arrive, getting in from Dodge City that evening. He moved in with Bulldog Armstrong, and as Thompson and King were together, that left six of the seven rooms occupied. Nate and Ringo were still in single rooms. As Armand decided to stay over nights as long as the guests were there, he moved into the seventh. From an overheard conversation between Mrs. Thorpe and Faustina, Nate learned that the girl planned to stay in town, too, and sleep at the Thorpe house. Where she and her father stayed ordinarily, Nate didn't know, but apparently it was somewhere out of town.

Tuesday night, after Tilghman arrived, Doc Holliday organized a poker game. Ringo wasn't asked to play, and probably wouldn't have anyway, as he spent all his time seated at his corner table drinking. Holliday asked Nate, but his rule never to play with experts kept him out of the game. If he had sat in, someone else would have been frozen out anyway, since there was room only for eight players.

After watching the game for a while, Nate decided he had been wise. While he could hold his own with anyone, he would have had no percentage advantage in this game, because there were no amateurs in it and no heavy drinkers except for Doc Holliday, on whom whiskey seemed to have no effect whatever.

Aside from the bounty hunters, not more than a halfdozen customers dropped into the saloon Tuesday night or during the day on Wednesday. Nate gathered that Monet's main profit was made on Saturday nights, when the place drew from one hundred to one hundred fifty customers from nearby ranches.

Time dragged for Nate. The poker game lasted until late Tuesday night, resumed Wednesday morning and was still going that night. Ringo drank alone at his corner table, and Nate spent most of his time either reading or writing to Denise. After one wander around the village, which took about fifteen minutes, there was nothing left to see.

Late Wednesday afternoon Nate decided to sneak off and make a tour of nearby ranches to see if anyone had spotted Jamie McKay. Slipping over to the livery stable next door, he threw the saddle on his mare. The blacksmith who also ran the stable, went into the saloon. As

Nate rode from the stable, Faustina stepped out on the front porch of the hotel.

"Going for a ride, Mr. Cook?" she asked.

"Need a little exercise. Like to show me the byways?"

"Sorry, but I have to work."

The other nine bounty hunters filed outside onto the porch and stood looking at Nate. The silent message was that if he was going to start searching the surrounding area for Jamie McKay, they would all saddle up and go along.

Nate rode his horse back into the stable and unsaddled it.

That evening there was a larger crowd in the saloon than on Tuesday. Cowboys kept streaming in until there must have been fifty. They surrounded the poker table or else gawked at Nate and Ringo, and Nate realized that word of the bounty hunters had spread and the cowboys had come to rubberneck.

About ten o'clock a couple of poker games started, one with eight players and the other with seven. When Nate wandered over to check them out, he discovered both were for nickel chips, with a fifteen-cent limit.

A cowboy at the table with a player short said, "Want to sit in, Mr. Cook?"

The stakes were too low to interest Nate, but he was bored. Taking a seat, he said, "Mr. Cook was my father. I'm Nate."

That brought first-name-only introductions from the other players, who were variously Tex, Shorty, Buck, Charlie and three Bobs. Tex, a rawboned man somewhat older than the rest, who were all in their twenties, was the banker. Nate bought two dollars worth of chips from him.

"You sure do look like Jamie McKay, Nate," Tex said as he counted out chips. "What makes you fellows think he's around here?"

"Bertram Lolly wired El Paso that he'd been seen in the vicinity."

Everyone at the table laughed. Shorty said, "Was he riding a pink elephant?"

"You fellows think Lolly was just drunk?"

"He's always drunk," one of the Bobs said.

Tes said, "I think Jamie's either in Mexico or back east, like that reporter fellow in El Paso says. This is the last place he'd try to hang out, where everybody knows him."

"Shut up and deal," Charlie said.

It was Buck's deal. Everyone anted a nickel while he shuffled the cards.

Nate said, "How do you mean, everybody knows him? I thought the night he shot Redshank was the only time he was ever here."

Buck offered a cut to Tex on his right and dealt the cards. Tex said, "Hell, that was his bachelor party. Now that I think of it, he was sitting right where you are when Redshank walked up. Damnedest fastest draw I ever saw. Redshank had that swivel gun he just had to tip up and fire, and Jamie still beat him out."

"No, he didn't," Shorty said. "Redshank fired first. Only he missed because Jamie tipped his chair over backward."

"It's your open," Buck said to Shorty.

Shorty looked at his cards and passed. Nate, who was next, passed a pair of jacks. It went around to Tex, who opened for a nickel. Everyone but Nate stayed. Tex drew three cards and no one else drew less. Two players drew four cards.

Nate said to Tex, "What did you mean, his bachelor party?"

"He was supposed to get married in Rimfire the next Saturday. Bet a dime."

Everyone folded.

"He was marrying a girl from Rimfire?"

Tex raked in the chips. "No, Faustina over there."

Armand Monet's reason for trying to convince the bounty hunters they were wasting their time became blindingly clear. Nate said, "McKay's folks live around here?"

"No, he met Faustina when he used to teach school in Rimfire years back. She was one of his pupils as a kid. I guess they hadn't seen each other for years when he come back to visit. Then bang, they got engaged. Ol' Redshank spiked the marriage plans."

Everyone anted again and Shorty shuffled the cards. Nate said, "Faustina live with her father?"

Shorty said, "Yeah, he's got a little ranch a couple of miles north of town." After dealing, he said, "Your open, Nate."

Nate had lost all interest in the game, but he couldn't drop out in the middle of a hand. He looked at his cards, saw three kings and passed. Charlie, to his left, opened and everyone stayed around to Nate.

Tossing in his cards, he said, "I can't draw anything. I'm going to bed."

He pushed his chips over to Tex, collected $1.90 and got up from the table. "Night," he said, walked over to the back door and outside. As soon as he closed the door behind him, it opened again and Ringo looked out.

"Where you going?" Ringo asked.

"The outhouse."

"Oh."

Ringo stood watching as he made his way to the outhouse and stepped inside. Through the half-moon carved in the door he watched Ringo standing on the back stoop. After a couple of minutes the man went back inside. Nate

emerged from the outhouse and headed for the back door
of the livery stable.

It was a bright moonlit night, but inside the stable it was
pitch black. Nate lit a match to locate his horse and saddle,
then saddled her in the dark by feel. Quietly he led her
from the stable's front door and to the north. By now it
was about eleven o'clock, and the only light in town came
from the hotel. He led the horse by the reins a good hundred yards before mounting.

A mile from town he came to a lane marked by a
wooden sign on a post. Dismounting, he peered at it in the
moonlight. It said LAZY S RANCH—DEL MONTE. He
rode on until he came to another lane a mile beyond, also
marked by a sign. This one read IDF RANCH—MONET.

Instead of remounting, Nate led the mare up the lane by
the reins. When he spotted a lighted window fifty yards
ahead, he dropped the reins and walked toward the light. It
came from a window to the left of the front porch. Quietly
mounting the steps, Nate peered in the window.

He was looking into a parlor. The light came from a
porcelain lamp on an end table next to a high-backed easy
chair to the left of the window. It was turned so that Nate
was unable to see if anyone sat in it.

He moved to the front door, tested the latch and found it
open. Cautiously he pushed the door ajar just enough to
slip inside, then gently closed it behind him. He was in a
hallway leading to the rear of the house. The parlor was to
his left and light also came from an open doorway halfway
along the hall on the opposite side from the parlor.

Nate peeked into the parlor. The easy chair's back was
to him from this angle also. He tiptoed in and up to the
right side of the chair. It was empty.

He was turning to reenter the hall when a man carrying
a book came through the door. Nate swept out his gun at

the same instant the man dropped the book and swept out his. There was a single loud click as the hammers were simultaneously cocked. Then both turned rigid with their fingers on the triggers, prevented from squeezing them by some powerful extrasensory force neither could fight.

Nate stared at his mirror image and the image stared back. Jamie McKay lowered the hammer and sheathed his gun. Nate lowered the hammer of his and sheathed it also.

Nate said, "I knew you looked like me, but this is ridiculous."

"Was your name once Ashley?" McKay asked.

"No, but my son's is."

The outlaw looked startled. "After who?"

"My wife's grandfather, Ashley Fenner."

"Coincidence," McKay said. "What was your mother's maiden name?"

"Abigail Harmon."

Jamie McKay ran fingers through his long black hair. "I guess it's all coincidence."

"She isn't my real mother," Nate said. "That was somebody named Little Doe."

Jamie McKay's face paled until Nate thought he was having a seizure. After a long time he said, "So was mine."

Nate felt his own face paling. He could think of nothing to say.

Jamie said, "You're not Nate Cook; you're Ashley McKay, my older brother by five minutes."

Nate thought of something to say. "Do you have any coffee?"

"I'll make some," Jamie said, turning and going into the hall.

Nate followed him to a kitchen at the rear of the house, where Jamie lit a lantern and built a small fire in the stove.

They sat at the table and looked at each other while waiting for the coffee to brew.

"My father was a doctor named Ephraim Cook," Nate said. "He found me in the arms of a dying Comanche after the massacre at Prairie Dog Town Fork."

"That was probably your grandfather, Fighting Wolf."

"Just before he died, the Indian said to return me to my mother, Little Doe. Dad had no idea who she was."

"She was the most beautiful woman in Texas."

"Was?"

"She was raped and murdered and scalped by Raoul Derango, Jake Fox and some unknown third man."

There was a long silence before Nate said, "The men you're wanted for killing?"

"Yes."

"I wish I had known her. Tell me about my father."

"Ashley McKay, which is your real name, too. He died on the Confederate side of the war."

"What was he like?"

"Most of what I know came from Little Doe, because I was only six when I last saw him. She loved him very much. He taught me to read and write. He taught her, too. He loved books and left me a library of five hundred."

"My father—my adoptive father—loved books, too, but he left me only three hundred."

The coffee pot began to steam. Jamie rose to get two cups from a cupboard and poured them full. "You take it black," he said. It was a statement, not a question.

"Yes."

Reseating himself, Jamie said, "Isn't is strange how we're so alike after a separation of twenty-four years? Your hat is riding on your neck like mine does when I wear one. You wear the same kind of gun the same way, and you're just as fast but no faster. Without that scar you'd be me.''

Nate said, ''I understand you're engaged to Faustina Monet.''

Jamie looked puzzled at what seemed a switch of subject. ''Yes.''

''We even both picked French women. My wife Denise's maiden name was Delavigne.''

Jamie said, ''You wear your hair different than me.''

Nate pushed the hair back from the right side of his head. ''The same man who gave me the scar,'' he said. ''Cole Gannon.''

''The man who murdered your father?'' Jamie said. ''I remember reading when you killed him years ago. At the time I thought you were an older man.''

''I was sixteen. Is my birthday October fifteenth?''

''October tenth.''

''He missed it by five days,'' Nate said. ''My birthday had to be guessed, of course.'' Then he laughed.

''What's funny?'' Jamie asked.

''I was thinking of my seventeenth birthday present. I had really been seventeen for five days.''

Jamie sipped his coffee. ''Something I forgot to ask. Are the other bounty hunters en route here?''

''They're all in a poker game except Ringo, and he's drunk.''

''You think they'll stick around long?''

Nate sipped his coffee and thought for a time before saying, ''I think they'll be out here eventually. Maybe by tomorrow.''

''Why?''

''I figured out where you were after only a few minutes conversation with some local cowboys. So far eight of them have been talking only among themselves, and Ringo never talks to anybody, but eventually they're bound to hear about your engagement to Faustina, and that will be it."

"Then I'd better start running."

"Let me go back to the hotel and check the lay of the land. If they start this way, I'll either send Faustina or get here myself."

They finished their coffee and both rose to their feet. They stood looking at each other.

Jamie held out his hand. "Hi, Ash."

Gripping his hand, Nate pulled him against him and threw his left arm about his shoulder.

"Hi, Jamie."

CHAPTER XXVIII

A hundred yards from the livery stable Nate dismounted and led the mare the rest of the way on foot. He got her back in her stall and unsaddled her without lighting a match, then slipped out the livery stable's back door. Easing open the back door of the saloon, he peered in.

It was now past midnight and the crowd had diminished considerably. Nate saw a group of the bounty hunters ringed about a couple of cowboys, and Ringo was still seated at his corner table with a bottle before him. He slipped inside and over to the edge of the crowd around the two cowboys. No one seemed to notice that he had just joined them.

The bar hadn't been within his view from the back door, but as he merged with the group about the cowboys, he saw that Armand, behind the bar, and Faustina, before it, were both pale and that they were under the watchful eye of young Rebel Joe Sommers. The two cowboys, whom he now saw were Tex and Shorty, were the only customers left in the place aside from the bounty hunters.

Tex was saying, "The ranch is two miles north, Mr.

Holliday. There's a wooden sign says *IDF Ranch*, dash, *MONET*. But if all you got to go on is Lolly's word, you're not gonna find nothing there. Like Mr. Monet says, he's a drunk.''

"We'll chance it," Doc Holliday said. "Who lives there aside from Mr. Monet and his daughter?"

"Nobody in the house. There's a black foreman and two Indian hands sleep in the bunkhouse."

Holliday looked around at the other bounty hunters. "The problem arises as to which of us collects the bounty."

Dandified Ben Thompson said, "How about dealing five face-up cards? Eight of us are already divided into two-man teams, and Nate and Ringo can form a fifth. High card wins."

From his corner table Ringo said, "How about a general shootout, with the survivor going after him?"

Bat Masterson said to Doc Holliday, "I told you the man is daft."

Uncle Billy Tilghman said, "Seems to me we're going to have to settle for ten thousand each."

Bulldog Armstrong said, "That's the first sensible suggestion. I'll vote for it."

Ben Thompson glanced at his partner, John Fisher King, and the handsome King said, "All right with me."

There was a general murmur of assent from everyone else except Nate and Ringo. Doc Holliday said, "I didn't hear you, Nate."

Because there would have been no point in objecting, Nate said, "I'll go along."

Holliday looked at Ringo. "Well?"

"With a stipulation," Ringo said. "The agreement applies only for now. If it turns out he's not there, we're all on our own again."

There was a general agreement to that.

Doc Holliday turned to look at Faustina and Armand. "There is the problem of these two. We don't want them runing home to give warning."

"That's simple," young Rebel Joe Sommers said. "We tie them up."

John Ringo rose from his corner table and walked over to face the pale young gunfighter. Although the quart whiskey bottle on his table was three-fourths empty, both his movement and speech were those of a man dead sober.

He said, "Nobody ties up the lady."

Crosby Fox said, "Hang on," walked behind the bar and opened a door behind it. After peering in, he said, "There's no windows in this storeroom, and it locks from outside."

"Any objection to that, Ringo?" Holliday asked.

After giving Doc a glance of dislike, Ringo bowed to Faustina. "I regret the inconvenience, Miss Monet, but there seems to be no alternative."

Before anyone else could do it, Nate went over to take Faustina's arm and steer her around behind the bar. So as not to rile Ringo, he did it gently, almost solicitously. Fox came from behind the bar to leave room for the two of them. Nate gestured for Armand to enter the storeroom first, then ushered Faustina through the door.

Stopping in the doorway himself, he said, "We don't want to leave you in the dark. Is there a lantern in here?"

Monet lifted a coal-oil lantern from a shelf and set it on a box. Nate moved into the room to strike a match. As he bent over the lantern, he said in a low tone, "I'm Jamie's twin brother. Got any ideas?"

Faustina's eyes grew wide in her pale face. She seemed unable to speak. Without moving his lips, Armand said, "The warning signal is three shots."

Nate shook out the match, dropped it on the floor,

adjusted the lantern wick and left the storeroom. Locking the door, he laid the key on the bar.

Pointing to a grandfather clock against the wall, Doc Holliday said to Tex and Shorty, "Note the time, gentlemen. I am going to give you a chore. In exactly one half-hour, unlock that door."

The two cowboys looked at the clock, which showed 12:25. Tex said, "Yes, sir."

Holliday said, "We would all take it unkindly if you unlocked it sooner."

"Yes, sir, we won't."

The gaunt gunfighter laid a ten-dollar bill on the bar. "You may drink this up to pass the time. You'll have to serve yourselves, and it would displease me if you didn't keep exact track of what you owe."

"We won't cheat, Mr. Holliday."

"Good." Holliday glanced around at the other bounty hunters. "Shall we ride, gentlemen?"

They rode north, walking their horses, two abreast—Doc Holliday and Bat Masterson in the lead, Nate and Crosby Fox next, Ringo and Rebel Joe behind them, then Ben Thompson and John Fisher King, and Bulldog Armstrong and Bill Tilghman bringing up the rear. The moon was bright enough to give clear visibility. Nate looked at the saddle decoration hanging from Fox's saddle horn.

"What the hell is that, a scalp?" he asked Fox.

"Indian squaw. Collected it myself."

Up to now, while he hadn't found either Fox or his young partner particularly charming, he had not disliked them. Now he developed instant active dislike for the lanky bounty hunter.

"My mother was an Indian," he said.

That effectively ended conversation for the rest of the trip.

Nate's plan was to fire the three warning shots when they reached the lane at the Lazy-S ranch. His excuse was going to be that he had spotted a puma lurking in the shadows. It was less than a brilliant plan, but he couldn't think of a better one.

A better excuse developed by pure accident just before they reached the Lazy-S lane. Fifty feet ahead of them a coyote ran across the road in the moonlight. Nate's gun came out and he fired three closely spaced but distinct shots.

The coyote leaped into the air and fell dead. Horses reared and were brought under control. Nate ejected the spent casings and reloaded.

"What the hell's the matter with you?" Doc Holliday said over his shoulder after he had quieted his horse.

"One less chicken killer," Nate said.

"And maybe one less outlaw when we get there."

"Hell, we're still a mile away, Doc."

They continued on.

When they reached the lane leading to the Monet ranch house, Holliday dismounted and the rest followed suit.

"From here on we walk," Holliday said.

They had barely started up the lane when Holliday halted everyone with a raised hand. "Take those damn bells off your spurs," he said to John Fisher King.

Looking sheepish, King knelt to remove the bells and drop them into a pocket. They moved on.

Light no longer showed from the parlor window, Nate saw when they got to within fifty yards. He hoped Jamie was not asleep so as to miss hearing the warning shots. Briefly he considered firing three more, then instantly rejected the idea. Not only was there no way he could explain such firing, but it was too late for a warning to do anything but get Jamie killed. If he was asleep in bed, he would be captured, but there would be no reason to kill him.

Holliday held up his hand to halt everyone. "First we'll take care of the hands," he said. "Fox, you and Rebel Joe get over to the bunkhouse and tie them up. Don't harm them. Understand?"

"All right," Fox said. "We won't hurt them."

"The rest of you, except for Bat, spread out and surround the house. Fox and Joe, after you tie up the hands, position yourselves near the bunkhouse. I'll give you fifteen minutes to take care of the hands and get yourselves in place. Then Bat and I will go inside after McKay. Anyone have questions?"

When no one did, Holliday said, "All right, Fox, you and Joe get going, and the rest of you spread out."

Everyone but Holliday and Bat Masterson moved off. Nate circled around to the barn, saw Tilghman drop prone along the near side of it, circled behind to see Armstrong situate himself on its other side, and continued on behind the bunkhouse. When a light went on in the bunkhouse, he peered in a rear window. A lantern had been lighted and Fox and Sommers were wakening the three sleeping occupants by poking them with gun muzzles. Nate watched as Fox hogtied the three on their bunks while his partner kept them covered.

Rebel Joe turned out the lantern, and Nate heard him and Fox leave the bunkhouse by its front door. A moment later he heard Fox say from the side of the bunkhouse which faced the house, "This is as good a spot as any."

Stepping softly, Nate moved to the corner and saw the pair, lying behind a stump with their backs to him and their guns in their hands. Nate estimated there was still five minutes before Doc and Bat went in.

Crosby Fox laughed.

"What's funny?" his partner asked.

"I was just thinking that dumb half-breed in there would shit if he knew his mother's scalp was a saddle decoration."

Nate felt his stomach muscles tense.

Rebel Joe said, "Did you really do that? I always thought you were bullshitting."

"When did I ever bullshit?"

"All the time. How come McKay never hunted you down like he done the others?"

"He didn't know about me. I told you about it."

"I wasn't listening. Tell me again."

Fox said, "This time keep your ears open. I was riding from El Paso to Las Cruces when I ran into Jake and Raoul riding for El Paso. The weekend before they had got me drunk, so I repaid the favor. I had a gallon jug with me, and we split it three ways. We got so fucking drunk, we could hardly sit our horses. Then Raoul said let's have a little fun with the Indian squaw."

Nate had to restrain himself from drawing his gun and drilling a hole through Fox's head. He also had to restrain himself from vomiting.

"Was she good?" Rebel Joe asked.

"That was one good-looking redskin, kid, even though she was around forty. We all had her twice. Sobered the hell out of us. Raoul got worried about the squaw telling his father, but that was no problem. Them renegade Comanches was raping and killing and scalping all over the place, so we shut the squaw up good and let the Comanches take the blame—Hey, a light went on in the house."

Nate couldn't decide whether to blow out Crosby Fox's brains or beat him to death with his bare hands. He decided to do neither when a better plan struck him. His burning rage subsided to icy, but controlled hate.

Doc Holliday's voice called from the front porch, "Nobody's here."

Fox and Sommers got up, holstered their guns and headed toward the house. In the moonlight Nate could see Tilghman and Armstrong going that way, too. He went around to the front of the bunkhouse and inside.

The black man and the two Indians hogtied on their bunks gazed at him when he lit the lantern.

Nate said, "Some men will be in here to ask questions in a few minutes. I haven't time to explain, but if you want to save Jamie McKay's hide, you'll give the answers I tell you. Don't pretend you've never seen him, because they know he and Faustina were scheduled to get married, they know he was once her teacher in Rimfire, and they know he was having a bachelor party when he shot Redshank. Admit everything you know about him except one thing. Since the night he shot Redshank, he's never been back here and you haven't the slightest idea where he is. Understand?"

"We understand," the black man said.

The bunkhouse door opened and Doc Holliday came in, followed by the rest of the bounty hunters. "What's going on here?" Holliday asked.

"I've been asking questions," Nate said. "They claim McKay's never been here, but I think they're lying."

"I'll ask a few," Holliday said. "I might have a more convincing manner."

It was 1:30 in the morning when they all got back to the hotel. Tex and Shorty were gone, and Armand and Faustina were drinking coffee at a table. Faustina was still pale, and her face was drawn.

Doc Holliday said to both of them, "We apologize for the inconvenience we caused you. We will be leaving in the morning."

Faustina looked at Nate in silent inquiry.

He said, "As you already know, he wasn't there and hasn't been. May I add my apology?"

"We all apologize," Ben Thompson said. "I'm going to bed."

Nate sat in his room in the dark, fully dressed, until he heard Faustina tell her father good night and the light downstairs went out. He continued to wait as he heard Armand climb the stairs and his room door close. Then he looked out onto the balcony. When he saw no light coming from any room, he lit a candle and went next door to Fox and Sommers' room. He didn't knock, just opened the door and walked in. When both sat up in their beds, he closed the door behind him.

"I think I know where McKay is," Nate said.

The two looked at him, waiting.

"I'll need help, but not nine other guns. Interested in a fifty-fifty split, half for me and half divided between you two?"

"Why not three ways?" Fox said.

"I'll ask Doc and Bat." Nate headed for the door.

"Hold it," Fox said.

When Nate stopped and turned, Fox said to Sommers, "Okay with you?"

"Twenty-five thousand is better than nothing."

"Deal," Fox said to Nate. "Where is he?"

"When I said I thought I knew where he is, I wasn't quite accurate. What I meant is, I think I can find out in the morning. I just wanted to make sure you didn't take off tomorrow before I could line you up. Sleep late in the morning, so that the others are all gone before we go down. I'll knock on your door when it's all clear."

"All right," Fox said.

"Sleep tight," Nate said, and went out.

CHAPTER XXVIII

During the ride out to the ranch Nate stayed to Crosby Fox's right because the scalp hung from the left side of the pommel and Nate was afraid he would kill the man if he looked at it again.

"What do you expect to get out here?" Fox asked.

"Information."

"That black foreman and the two Apaches didn't seem to know anything."

"Faustina does."

Rebel Joe, riding behind them, said, "Why would she know any more than them?"

"I overheard her talking to her father," Nate said over his shoulder. "She just got a letter from McKay. The post office stamps the point of origin on letters. We'll ask her for it kindly."

"Hey," Fox said. "Maybe we can have a little fun with her, too, her old man still being at the hotel."

There was a limit to how much sugar Nate was willing to spread to draw Fox into his trap. He let his eyes glitter at the man. "We won't touch her. If you'd like to be dead, try it."

"Hey, I was only joking," Fox said.

When they reached the ranch, they rode right up to the front porch. Faustina stepped out on it.

"You two wait here until I call for you," Nate said, dismounting. "Miss Monet, may I see you inside for a moment?"

Silently she turned and reentered the house. He followed her in and closed the door.

"Why did you bring those men here?" she asked.

"I want my brother to meet them. He here?"

"In the kitchen."

He followed her along the hallway to the kitchen at the rear of the house. Jamie stood there, looking as though he was run by a coiled steel spring. Nate stopped in the doorway.

"Who are those men?" Jamie asked.

"Two of the bounty hunters, Crosby Fox and Rebel Joe Sommers. The other seven have left town."

"Why did you bring them here?"

"Crosby is Jake Fox's brother."

When his twin gazed at him in astonishment, Nate said, "His saddle ornament is the scalp of our mother."

Jamie's nostrils flared. "Get out of my way."

"Hold your horses."

"Get out of my way, Ash."

"I'm your older brother," Nate said. "Shut up and listen."

Jamie continued to look at him, still coiled.

Nate said, "I overheard him bragging to Rebel Joe about that day. You have me and Rebel Joe as witnesses. With our combined testimony, Sheriff Bowdry ought to be able to get a confession out of Fox. Then you go free and he hangs."

Jamie relaxed ever so slightly. "How do we get them to Nick Bowdry?"

"We start by going outside and taking their guns away. But first, I have a business proposition. How would you like to be my partner in a San Francisco casino?"

"You want to talk business at a time like this?"

"Fox and Sommers aren't going anywhere. They think they're in for twenty-five thousand dollars apiece. I had a thriving supper club and casino in San Fransico, but first my bank failed and then the club burned down. A hundred thousand dollars would put us back in business."

"The reward money? How do you both collect that and prove me innocent?"

"Proving your innocence will be no problem. I'll collect the reward first, and we'll split fifty-fifty. You in?"

Jamie said to Faustina, "You want to live in San Francisco?"

"Almost anywhere would be better than Goose Flats," she said.

Jamie said to Nate, "Let's go out on the porch."

Three weeks later Faustina drove a small covered wagon drawn by two horses up in front of the cabin where Jamie had spent his youth. As Faustina jumped down from the seat and Nate, following on horseback, dismounted, Jamie and Mortimer Brown climbed out of the back of the wagon. Jamie led the way into the cabin.

Except for a layer of dust, it was unchanged. Books still lined the far wall of the central room. Little Doe's wrapped Christmas gift still lay on the table. The bloodstained spread was still on her bed and her torn garments still lay on the floor. After a glance into the bedroom, Jamie turned away.

"Bring them in," he said to Mortimer.

Outside, the black man helped the prisoners out of the wagon. They needed assistance because they wore both handcuffs and leg irons. "Inside," he said.

When Mortimer herded the prisoners into the cabin, Nate said to him, "If they make a break, try to shoot them in the legs. We need their testimony."

Jamie said, "Let them sleep in Little Doe's room. Don't bother to change the spread."

"I'll take good care of them," the black man said, patting the gun at his hip. "When you plan to be back?"

"The sheriff will probably be out tomorrow," Jamie said. "If everything goes right, I should be out the next day."

Holding out his hand to the black man, Nate said, "I probably won't see you again, Mortimer."

Clasping his hand, Mortimer said, "It's been good knowing you, Nate."

"My horse and saddle are yours to ride back home."

"Why, thank you."

"Only practical," Nate said. "How the hell would you get there otherwise?"

Nate found Sheriff Nick Bowdry talking to a chunky man with a round face, a mass of curling gray hair and a small gray mustache. The man gazed at Nate with a mixture of hate and astonishment.

Bowdry said, "It isn't Jamie McKay, Don Miguel. It's Nate Cook, the bounty hunter."

The rancher looked abashed. "You gave me a start, Mr. Cook." He offered his hand.

Clasping it, Nate said, "I'm glad you're here, sir, because I have a question. Is the reward on Jamie McKay payable on delivery, or only after conviction?"

"On delivery, dead or alive."

"In cash?"

"That or a bank draft, whichever you prefer."

"How long will it take you to raise the cash?"

"I have it in a bank vault. Do you have McKay?"

"Yes, sir."

"Alive?"

"Yes, sir."

"Where?"

"Right outside."

Don Miguel strode outdoors, followed by Nate and the sheriff. In front of the sheriff's office Faustina sat on the driver's seat of the covered wagon. Nate led Don Miguel and the sheriff around behind the wagon. Jamie sat in the back in handcuffs and leg irons.

A gloating expression formed on Don Miguel's face. "You'll hang this time, you murderer," he said.

After Jamie, still in chains, was safely locked in the cell behind the sheriff's office, Nate and Don Miguel walked to the bank. When they returned, Nate was carrying a small leather valise. He and Don Miguel entered the sheriff's office. They emerged a few minutes later, and Don Miguel mounted a horse tied to the hitching rail in front of the office and rode off. Nate tossed the valise in the back of the wagon and climbed up on the seat next to Faustina.

Looking at his watch, he said, "I have twenty minutes to catch the train."

As she turned the wagon around to drive back in the opposite direction, Faustina said, "Too bad you can't wait so we can all ride to San Francisco together."

"Don Miguel might want his money back. He'd have no legal right to it, but Jamie says he makes his own laws. It will be safer in California."

At the railroad depot Nate lifted his suitcase and the

valise from the back of the wagon. As they stood on the platform, he said, "Soon as the train pulls out, hand the sheriff my sworn deposition and break the news that you have two witnesses to corroborate it. It probably won't be necessary, but tell him I'll return to give my personal testimony if he needs it. Are you and Jamie going to wait until you get to San Francisco to get married?"

"I hope not."

"I thought you wanted a big wedding. Denise and I will give you a bang-up one. I'll be best man and she can be matron of honor."

"You talked me into it," she said. "Jamie and I can live in sin a while longer. We'll be a while in any event. Jamie wants to pack and ship his books, and then we'll have to sell the team and wagon and everything at the cabin he doesn't want to ship. Father will probably get there before us."

"If he can sell the hotel and the ranch."

"Caleb Thorpe wants to buy the hotel, and Father is going to let Mortimer, Bigfoot Harry and Bucking Horse buy the ranch on a long-term mortgage, which he'll hold himself, and with nothing down."

The train conductor called, "Bo-a-r-d!"

Faustina gave her future brother-in-law a kiss of goodbye. Nate climbed aboard carrying his suitcase and valise.

Faustina climbed up on the seat of the covered wagon and drove back to the sheriff's office.

THE GAMBLERS
Lee Davis Willoughby

NEW ORLEANS: 1856—dashing Jason Lowell, uncrowned king of the riverboat gamblers, seems to have fulfilled his dream. In his own boat, *Argos,* bought with gold he'd won in California, he prepares for a series of trips up and down the mighty Mississippi that will bring him untold riches.

At first glance, the passenger list looks promising. There is the distinguished—and extremely wealthy—Senator Stephenson, who cannot resist a game of chance, along with his lovely and mysterious young ward, Melissa Wainwright. There is the well-heeled Duncan Sargent, who claims to be researching a book. And there is the picture-pretty Elizabeth Brigham and her wild brother Charlie, an incurable gambler.

But Jason and his loyal young brother Gus don't realize that there's a cargo of death in the hold, and that the *Argos* is headed toward their biggest gamble—in Bloody Kansas.

THE ROBBER BARONS
Lee Davis Willoughby

Tall, intense Clay Monroe, long isolated from his family, a dynasty of lumber merchants, was suddenly called home from abroad. Why did multi-millionaire speculator Harvel Packer want him as his assistant? What did Packer's seductive daughter, Eugenia, really want from him? Why had his brother, Cyrus, vowed to destroy him? Was the husband of his secret love actually his natural father?

Everyone seemed to know more about Clay Monroe than he did himself, and as he moved brilliantly ahead in the world of Harvel Packer, Philip Armour, J. P. Morgan, John D. Rockefeller, Jay Gould and Jim Fisk, the mystery deepened.

Only in the midst of a bloody battle for control of America's railroads—pitting Clay against the power of Jim Fisk, biggest, boldest Robber Baron—does the daring young man discover the key to his past, and to his true destiny.

Don't miss *THE ROBBER BARONS*— forty-fifth in the series, *The Making of America*, on sale now from Dell/Bryans

THE ASSASSINS
Lee Davis Willoughby

On April 11, 1865, young Capt. Stephen Beford, late of the Confederate Army, meets and falls in love with a beautiful Unionist from Boston, Becky Winfield. On that same day, Capt. Bedford, a strong Secessionist but a man of honor, comes upon evidence of a plot to murder Secretary of State Seward, Vice President Johnson, General U.S. Grant and President Lincoln.

Becky is in Washington, D.C., to persuade the great actor, John Wilkes Booth, to perform for War Relief, and thus she is unknowingly drawn into the network of conspiracy. When Stephen Bedford's sword is stolen and used to murder his closest friend, he realizes that if he can find it in time, he can save the lives of America's leaders— and the life of Becky, who has been kidnapped by the conspirators.

Be Sure To Read *THE ASSASSINS*—
forty-sixth in the series, *The Making of America*,
on sale now from Dell/Bryans